BRIGHTER THAN FLAMES

Momentarily disoriented, Trace slumped heavily to the floor of the cabin. Groaning, he struggled to regain his senses as he blinked almost comically at the woman standing over him. Hair brighter than the flames behind her spilled in riotous curls onto her shoulders. Great, darkly fringed eyes matched the glittering strands as she stared at him from a face with features so fine as to appear almost unreal. Her bared shoulders were narrow and her breasts were rounded appealingly in the sheer chemise covering them. Long, slender legs were clearly outlined in the revealing underskirt that was her only other attire.

She was beautiful.

She could be no other than Meredith Moore.

And she was pointing his own gun directly at him.

Other books by Elaine Barbieri:

HAWK'S PRIZE *(Hawk Crest Saga)*
HAWK'S PASSION *(Hawk Crest Saga)*
TEXAS TRIUMPH
TEXAS GLORY
TEXAS STAR
HALF-MOON RANCH: RENEGADE MOON
TO MEET AGAIN
THE WILD ONE (SECRET FIRES)
LOVE'S FIERY JEWEL
NIGHT RAVEN
AMBER TREASURE
HAWK
WISHES ON THE WIND
WINGS OF A DOVE
EAGLE
AMBER FIRE
TARNISHED ANGEL
CAPTIVE ECSTASY
DANCE OF THE FLAME

The *Dangerous Virtues* series:

HONESTY
PURITY
CHASTITY

Sign of the Wolf

Elaine Barbieri

LEISURE BOOKS NEW YORK CITY

A LEISURE BOOK®

February 2007

Published by

Dorchester Publishing Co., Inc.
200 Madison Avenue
New York, NY 10016

ISBN 0-8439-5824-3

Visit us on the web at www.dorchesterpub.com.

Prologue

Letty

New York City, 1880

Letty awoke with a start and glanced around her silent bedroom. She turned toward the pillow beside hers and frowned at the fellow sleeping there. What was his name? Charles . . . Henry? No, it was James.

James didn't know it yet, but she was through with him.

The eerie howl of a wolf cut the nighttime silence and Letty froze, suddenly aware that the sound had awakened her. The lonely wail reverberated against the vaulted ceiling of her luxurious bedroom, and chills raced down her spine. Standing, she walked unsteadily to her window high above the city and stared out vainly into the darkness.

Letty gasped as a familiar, wizened figure appeared before her mind's eye. The howling continued as the image cleared, and she saw long hair streaked with gray lying against bony, naked shoulders; a

1

lined face baked by the sun; and small, dark, penetrating eyes that appeared to see much while disclosing little. She heard again a droning song and the throb of repetitive drumming on a reverent silence. She saw a fire burning brighter. Fascinated, she watched as if seeing for the first time the faceless silhouettes dancing around the flames. The cadence of the drumming increased, reawakening an intrinsic part of her that she had tried desperately to ignore.

The vision disappeared.

Fascination passed.

Only fear remained.

Letty turned her back on the window in an attempt to refute the continued, unnatural howling. She jumped with a start when her own shadowed image flashed in the baroque mirror nearby. In it, she saw a wide-eyed, ebony gaze staring back at her from a face framed by dark hair untouched by gray. She glimpsed light, pale skin still tight over chiseled cheekbones, and classic features that defied age. She caught her breath at the ghostly look of the filmy white nightdress that covered her naked, deceivingly youthful form.

Her appearance was startling, and ageless, but Letty dismissed it. Emerging more clearly in her mind was the thought that beyond the bedroom window of her opulent suite stretched New York City's Park Avenue, a symbol of civilized wealth and affluence distinctly dissimilar to the far West of her birth.

She realized that in this sophisticated city, the wild, feral cry of the wolf was unknown. Frightening her even more was her certainty that only *she* heard its plaintive, warning howl.

She knew why the wolf called her.

She knew what its howling meant.

Startled when James' arms closed around her from behind, pulling her against him, Letty struggled to resist. She felt his surprise when she demanded sharply, "Let me go!"

He was handsome and virile, but that was no longer enough; and, unlike him, she was no longer interested.

Letty repeated, "Let me go."

"What's wrong, Letty?"

What was wrong? Letty stared at him silently. Everything was wrong—and allowing him to spend another night had not been the answer.

"Letty?"

The steady howling continued, and Letty responded sharply. "I want you to leave."

"That isn't what you said last night."

"That was last night."

"It's three o'clock in the morning."

"Does that make a difference?"

"I think it does."

"I don't." Letty attempted a more placating tone at James' frown. "It was fine while it lasted, James, but it's over. I want you to leave."

"But—"

"Just . . . leave."

Letty stood unmoving as James assessed her silently. She watched as he finally dressed and walked toward the door. She took a breath when it closed behind him, then waited patiently for the apartment door to snap shut.

The howling continued and Letty closed her eyes. That sound had haunted her throughout her life. Her attempt to escape it had only caused her to realize that the effort was useless, despite her use of the temporarily distracting male presence with which she so easily filled her bed.

Where had it all gone wrong?

The wolf's howl sounded again, and Letty shuddered as she remembered:

"Don't go, Wes." Letty's plea emerged softly in the darkness before dawn as Wes dressed in the shadows of their small bedroom. Yet she knew as soon as she voiced her concern that it was a waste of time. Still, she tried again.

"Please, Wes. I . . . I have a bad feeling about this."

She had heard the howling throughout the past night, and had attempted to ignore it. She had tried to tell herself she had been dreaming, that it was merely a figment of her imagination . . . of her fears, but ultimately in the predawn shadows, she was unable to keep silent. She whispered, "I love you, Wes . . . and I'm afraid."

Wes's hands halted midmotion as he fastened his shirt. Frowning, he turned to catch her gaze, and love surged hot and deep inside her.

Weston Moore was so handsome, so passionate . . . and she had been so young. She was sixteen years old the first time she saw him, but the moment was as clear in her mind as if it were yesterday. With hair the color of shining copper and eyes the same burning shade, Wes was tall, muscular, and all man. She fell in love with him at first sight.

Wes was similarly stricken, enough to ignore the whispers that persisted about her origins, despite her mother's claim at the time of their rescue from the Kiowa camp that the same Indians who had killed Letty's father five years earlier had kidnapped both her *and* her infant, Letty.

As her mother and she resumed their life in a "civilized" society, Letty had attempted to obey her mother and disregard everything she had been taught during the first five years of her life spent with the Kiowas. Her mother's ridicule of Kiowa society was unrelenting—a derision that was especially malicious in reference to the ancient Kiowa shaman's supposed mystical powers. Calling the mysticism "a savage's hocus-pocus," her mother insisted that she had allowed Letty to address the shaman as Grandfather only to avoid confrontation in the camp. She warned Letty that she would face great difficulties in the white man's world if her bloodline was believed "tainted."

And when in her loneliness, Letty whispered the secret to her mother that she missed Gray Wolf's kindness and his softly voiced introduction to his mystical world, her mother had punished her severely.

It did not take Letty long, however, to realize that her mother's warnings were correct.

Letty started to believe that meeting Wes had stilled the haunting images of her previous life forever, but the howling returned unexpectedly one day when she was seventeen. Her mother vehemently discredited the sounds and images they had evoked in Letty's mind, and Letty forced herself to ignore them.

Her mother died unexpectedly the next morning.

Weston Moore and she were married a week after her mother was buried.

Letty stared at Wes in the semidarkness. The howling had returned again. The bed sagged as Wes sat down beside her and cupped her cheek with his callused hand. She saw the love in his eyes as he whispered, "You know I have to do this . . . I have to join our neighbors to fight for our rights in this range war. We can't let the big landowners win or our lives won't be worth a damn. You understand, don't you, darling?"

She understood, but understanding did not halt her fears. She repeated, "I love you, Wes. I don't want anything to happen to you."

"It won't." He pressed his hand gently against her bulging stomach. His voice grew hoarse with emotion when he said, "I want our son to have a free-and-clear birthright. I can't be satisfied with less. Tell me you believe what I'm doing is right, Letty."

Letty took a breath. She whispered, "Yes, I do, but please come back to me."

Her firstborn child was not a son. It was a daughter born to the sound of a wolf's howl the day Wes was killed.

Memories continued an unrelenting parade through Letty's mind, and a slow quaking enveloped her:

"I love you, Letty. I want to marry you."

A frightened, nineteen-year-old, destitute mother, Letty looked at blond, slim John Higgins as he spoke. Clean-cut, earnest, and gentle, he had been inordinately attentive to her from the first day she had met him in the restaurant where she worked. He held her hand earnestly as he continued, "I don't have much right now, but I can support you and the baby, and I have ambition. I'll make us all rich someday. I promise you that."

Letty hesitated. John was a good man. She earned barely enough to survive, she had no potential for the future, and rumors about her origins were becoming rife in the small Texas town where they lived. She could see that John was sincere . . . and she was so alone.

6

Too emotional to speak the words, Letty finally nodded her consent.

They were married, and they departed for Arizona a few days later.

They were happy in their rough Arizona cabin until the night when a savage howling awakened Letty abruptly from her sleep as she lay abed with John beside her. Terrified, she turned to face her sleeping husband.

No, it could not happen again! She would not surrender to this persistent nightmare.

Letty waved good-bye to John when he left to prospect on an isolated mountainside the following morning. Forcing herself to believe her fears were baseless, she went back to work in the cabin. She told herself afterward that it was merely a tragic coincidence that John was thrown from his horse and killed that afternoon, leaving her a pregnant, penniless widow, again, this time at the age of twenty-one.

Letty raised a trembling hand to her cheek in the shadows of her New York apartment, recalling her attempt to support her two young daughters in a hostile environment. Finally deciding to return to Texas, she was relieved to find work as a maid with an elderly, traveling couple that knew nothing of her background. She was determined to escape the persistent rumors of her heritage, and when Archibald and Elizabeth Fitzsimmons offered to take her back to New York with them, she snapped at the chance.

Letty's expression hardened as she recalled the traumatic day she left:

"Don't leave, Mama!"

Three-year-old Meredith clung to her possessively. Although too young to appreciate the circumstances, baby Johanna joined her sobs, yet Letty remained firm. She glanced up at Sophie Martin as the older woman prepared to take both her children into the orphanage dormitory. She then looked back at Meredith. "You don't understand now because you're only a little girl, but you will someday," she said. "I'll send for you and your sister as soon as I can. I promise."

Forcibly tearing her daughter's arm from around her waist, Letty left her children with the struggling matron of the Texas orphanage. An hour later, she boarded the train with Archibald and Elizabeth Fitzsimmons and was on her way.

Letty sat tearfully beside Elizabeth Fitzsimmons' deathbed a year later. She felt the dear lady squeeze her hand lovingly the moment before she breathed her last. Inconsolable and childless, Archibald leaned on Letty heavily during his grief. Letty was uncertain when mutual grief became more, but she was ecstatic when she bore Archibald a child—her third daughter.

It didn't matter to Letty that Justine was born out of wedlock. She trusted Archibald to do what was best for them both. He did not object when she finally sent for the two daughters she had left behind; yet they had all barely had time to become acquainted when a wolf's howl in the middle of the night again predicted disaster.

Letty wanted desperately to ignore it, to believe her world could not come apart again, but she was too frightened to remain silent. She kept her children close and begged Archibald not to leave her the following day. His reaction was a gentle laugh at her "superstitious nonsense" before he kissed her good-bye.

Archibald was killed in a carriage accident that afternoon. Even more devastating than his death, however, was Letty's discovery that Archibald had not yet signed his new will, and the bulk of his estate would go to a trust for orphaned children, with his only other bequest a sum awarded to his nephew, Mason Little.

Alone again, Letty was furious at the cruel twist of fate. She knew there was only one clear way to stop the downward spiral of her life. Accepting the obvious, she acknowledged that by denying the mysticism that was so much a part of her life, she had become a partner to her own fate.

Letty stared out her bedroom window, down onto the shadowed street below. With that acknowledgment, she had taken the first step toward her new life by *secretly* accepting her Kiowa heritage. Aware that she could not declare her Kiowa blood and succeed in a world that would disdain that part of her past, she was determined to honor it in the only way she knew—by changing her name to that of her Kiowa grandfather.

Then, while still young, beautiful, and desirable at the age of twenty-three, she took the second step by going forward as *Letty Wolf.*

Her third step was a deliberate campaign to use the contacts she had made with Archibald's wealthy peers to advance her future and guarantee that she would never be penniless again.

Letty unconsciously smiled at the ease with which she accomplished her goal. With a stylish salon and thrice-weekly parties that catered to the sophisticated pleasures of powerful men, she became wealthy and successful beyond her wildest dreams. She took enjoyment in the questionable celebrity that she had deliberately earned—as opposed to the hypocritical, whispered suspicions of her origins that had plagued her.

Letty's smile faded as other memories followed. She was so determined to retain her new freedom that she relegated her daughters' care to a series of nannies. She ignored the nannies' concerns and complaints about her daughters' attitudes as she took care of business, and solved the problems they voiced by going on to the next nanny "who would be more capable of handling her children." She disregarded her children's resentments as childish nonsense when they claimed she had made them and their fathers irrelevant by changing her name. She felt it was unnecessary to explain her reasoning to them because of their youth, and was offended by their behavior when they banded together to voice their complaints as they grew older. She finally settled the problem by placing them in different boarding schools so they could not present a united front against her. She believed her solution was sound as she busied herself accumulating the wealth that had formerly escaped her.

In short, she did not concern herself with her daughters' feelings of being abandoned until they came of an age to abandon her as well.

The warning howls trailed away as Letty continued staring out her window high above the city. She had neither seen nor heard from her daughters in almost a year.

The howling ceased, but she was aware that she could not afford to ignore its warning any longer. She knew what she must do.

She'd do it soon . . . tomorrow.

She could not afford to waste any time.

Letty paused in the doorway of Wallace, Pittman, and O'Brien, her expression sober as the morning sun held her image in momentarily dark relief. All sign of her previous night's uncertainty erased from her expression, she entered the elaborate law offices and closed the door behind her. She was a client of longstanding with this particular firm. Wallace, Pittman, and O'Brien was accustomed to handling her business affairs, and she knew she could count on the firm to accommodate her.

Letty smiled when Alexander Pittman emerged from his office to personally escort her inside. Slender, well built and light haired, Alexander was a full partner in the firm although he was not yet out of his twenties. Dressed as she was in a vibrant green dress that accented her petite figure and the deep color of her upswept hair and heavily fringed eyes, Letty was at her beguiling best, and she knew it. Alexander flushed at the power of her smile as he took her hand and ushered her into his office.

Letty liked doing business with the younger member of the firm. Her beauty impressed him, and he labored to impress her as well. She knew the business she had to discuss with Alexander that morning included tasks that would go beyond the norm, but she was also certain he would go out of his way to do whatever she asked of him.

Perspiration dotted Alexander's forehead revealingly as he closed the door behind them and watched her settle herself into the leather chair opposite his.

He was so young.

Briefly amused, Letty started to speak.

Chapter One

Meredith

Meredith Moore glanced with dismay at her fellow travelers as she walked through the decrepit train depot where the first leg of her journey had delivered her. The eldest of Letty Wolf's daughters, she had always considered herself the most confident and determined of her sisters, yet her step slowed uncharacteristically as she neared the Texas train that would deliver her to the state of her birth. She had disembarked from the luxurious, well-equipped rail car that she had boarded in New York City a short time earlier, only to be faced with a noisy hoard of male travelers in such direct contrast with the elegantly dressed, carefully groomed, and courteous gentlemen of the city that they seemed to have emerged from another time. Almost without exception, they were bearded and mustached, dressed in ragged garments with revolvers stuck in their belts. Doors slammed behind them, and—seemingly to a man—their luggage consisted of heavy, dirty bundles that they carried without visible sign of strain. Their talk was loud and stormy, and clouds of blue tobacco smoke seemed to follow them wherever they went.

Unable to miss their conversation as two of the men passed by, Meredith heard references to the Sioux and Pawnee Indians inhabiting Nebraska and the Dakotas, and to their anticipation at returning. She breathed a silent sigh of relief that those men were not headed her way.

Meredith entered the shabby Texas rail car, deliberately ignoring the glances she received from her fellow passengers as she settled herself in a seat. It did not miss her notice that for the most part, her fellow passengers were male, and were also hairy, unwashed, bearded, odoriferous, and armed to the teeth. It annoyed her that the few well-chaperoned women in the car appeared as shocked and as disapproving as the men to see her traveling alone.

Meredith raised her chin determinedly. She was accustomed to disapproval. She accepted without a trace of conceit that she was beautiful, and she was no novice to the speculative glances that fact alone so often stimulated. Aside from the conservative but fashionable gray traveling costume she wore, the attention she drew with her uncommon coloring was not unusual, either. Although she knew very little about her father, she knew she had inherited her vivid coloring from him—thick hair as bright as a copper penny, and eyes that glittered an amber gold. Her naturally brown brows and lashes were thick and dark, and she could only assume that her own delicate features were a feminine version of his because she did not resemble her mother in the least. Small as a child, she had matured to the unusual female height of almost seven inches past the mark of five feet, with a multitude of womanly curves in between.

Yes, she was beautiful, but Meredith knew how little being beautiful really meant. Her mother was beautiful. Her sisters and she bore little resemblance to either their mother or each other, but they were equally beautiful, which she feared would only add to their problems as they sought the paths of their futures.

Thoughts of her sisters brought momentary tears to Meredith's eyes. She missed them, but they had carefully planned the steps they were taking. She wished she could protect them from the difficulties they were bound to encounter, but protecting each other was not currently what their quests were all about.

Their quests were important to them—so important that she, at twenty-one the eldest of her sisters had waited patiently, teaching at the boarding school where her mother had placed her until her youngest sister reached the age of eighteen and was old enough to join the sisters in making a mature decision on the direction of her future. Her sisters and she had grown close when their mother placed them in the care of nannies, almost excluding contact with them while they were young. Perversely, they had grown even closer when their mother put them in different boarding schools in an attempt to separate them. Meredith had allowed their mother to believe the separation plan had worked, but, in reality, her mother's attempt to keep them apart had been the final straw. She and her sisters had stayed in contact secretly. They had visited each other over the years without their mother's knowledge, and the bond between them had flourished. Yet they had remained strong-willed enough to realize that the closeness between them could become a crutch. It had taken them several months after removing themselves from their mother's care to finally formulate their individual plans, and they were each resolved to follow through.

Meredith raised her chin in silent defense of the choices she and her sisters had made. She knew they were doing the right thing in trying to find their own paths—because *Grandfather* had told her so.

The plan was pretty simple, after all. They had decided to separate for a year to find their individual directions. They would keep in contact with each other by means of a general post office box at a central location where mail could be picked up or directed to them. They would then meet after the year came to an end to assess their paths from there.

Meredith could not help but frown at the thought of Johanna's intention to travel west to make a success of her father's dream of striking it rich. Justine's goal to become a world-renowned entertainer also seemed a bit unrealistic to her. Yet in both cases, her sisters had made their decisions and she accepted them.

To Meredith's mind, however, *she* was the only one of her sisters who was striving toward a truly reasonable goal. She would travel to Texas to discover her roots and learn more about the past that her mother had so steadfastly refused to discuss. She knew that was right for her—because *Grandfather* had approved.

Grandfather—who was a secret known only to herself.

Grandfather—who was an enigma she was determined to solve somewhere along the way.

Meredith's heart jumped an excited beat when the rail car jerked suddenly forward, interrupting her thoughts with a metallic groan and a cloud of grainy smoke as the train snapped into motion. A surge of breathlessness unexpectedly assailed her, as she became fully aware for the first time that all the years of careful planning that had brought her to this time and place were over.

Her quest had begun!

"You can't be serious!" Trace Stringer looked at Robert Pinkerton with disbelief. He had been summoned to the Pinkerton National Detective Agency's New York office for his new assignment, but couldn't now believe his ears. "You couldn't possibly have accepted a job like this."

"I wouldn't have asked you to come in if I hadn't. Alexander Pittman of Wallace, Pittman, and O'Brien came here personally a few hours ago to discuss this job. It's a legitimate case, and it will be a lucrative commission for our company."

"I'm not a babysitter, Robert."

"These women are adults, not babies."

"A rich, spoiled mother asking us to find her rich, runaway, and equally spoiled daughter? What else would you call it?"

"Listen for a few minutes, and I'll tell you." Robert's round face reddened as he continued directly. "Letty Wolf has three daughters."

"I've heard of Letty Wolf. That would be three daughters with three different fathers, of course."

"That's right, but whether they're legitimate or not is neither my concern nor yours."

Trace could feel his face cloud with annoyance. He didn't like the sound of this assignment. He had no patience for the petulance of rich children. He had seen too many men and women in the far West who worked hard every day with their children alongside them as they struggled to make a success of meager circumstances—laboring without complaint just to keep their dreams alive. His own parents had been one of those couples. He had been proud to share their dreams until fate took a deadly hand, and he had no respect for those who didn't have the sense to be grateful to be spared the heavy sacrifices that life often demanded.

"Are you listening, Trace?"

"I'm listening."

Robert continued. "It seems that Miss Wolf's daughters declared themselves legally free of her and disappeared from the boarding schools where she had placed them on the same day that her youngest daughter became of age. That was almost a year ago. In anger, Miss Wolf countered by writing her daughters out of her will—but she has recently come to regret her hasty action. It is her intention to reinstate her daughters to their rightful place in her will if they will agree to meet one stipulation."

Trace mumbled, "If I had a mother like Letty Wolf, I'd run off, too."

"Trace . . ." Squinting a deadening glance at him, Robert continued. "In the will that she wrote in anger a year ago, Miss Wolf left the bulk of her estate to Mason Little, the nephew of an . . . intimate friend who was also Justine's father. Evidently Mason resumed contact with her after his uncle died." Robert added almost in afterthought, "Aware of the fellow's reputation, I can only assume he made sure to get to know her again when his *aunt* started to become wealthy."

"Smart fellow, huh?"

Choosing not to respond, Robert continued, "In any case, Miss Wolf, who is still a beautiful woman, I might add, will have a fortieth birthday in a little less than a year. She proposes that if her daughters contact her before that time, she will reinstate them appropriately in her will. In that case, she will leave Mason Little a substantial sum instead of the bulk of her fortune as the will now states. If they do not contact her, the bulk of her estate will revert to Mr. Little."

"So she's extorting her own daughters."

"Miss Wolf wants her daughters back, Trace, and it's her money. What we need to find out now is whether her daughters will consider it worthwhile to return."

Trace raised his brows.

"Right . . . well, as Alexander Pittman explained it, the part that the Pinkerton National Detective Agency is to play concerns Miss Wolf's desire to dispatch three detectives to find her daughters—one detective assigned to each daughter—to make sure that each one of them is made aware of the provisions she has set up. I'll take care of the assignments for the other two daughters, but I'm assigning the eldest one to you."

"What am I supposed to do with her?"

Robert did not hide his annoyance. "You find her first, then inform her of the stipulations of her mother's will. If she agrees to see her mother, you will escort her to see Miss Wolf. If she doesn't agree, you will get a signed statement to the effect that she was made aware of the stipulation her mother made and declined it."

Trace was momentarily silent. "You said, 'You find her first.' Am I to assume that she's no longer in the city?"

"Assume whatever you want. Letty Wolf doesn't know where her daughters are. It's your job to find one of them."

"Great."

"You're a detective, Trace. You've done this kind of thing before. I want to add that I think you're particularly suited to this assignment because you were born in the West, as were Miss Wolf and two of her daughters." Picking up a slender folder on his desk, Robert handed it to him and said, "This is all the background information we have on Meredith Moore."

"Meredith *Moore?*"

"Letty's eldest daughter. None of the daughters carry her name. They changed their names back to that of each of their fathers."

"That figures."

Robert snapped, "You've handled this type of case before—children separated from their parents."

"Not exactly." Drawing himself up to his full, muscular height, Trace slipped the folder under his arm and said, "But despite my reservations, I'll find Meredith Moore for you, Robert. You can depend on it."

Trace did not bother to add that he'd do the job because he owed Robert that much—and more—but that he'd then wash his hands of the spoiled brat and bid a final farewell to the agency. Only then might he finally resume the life he now realized he was meant to lead.

Tipping his Stetson in a familiar gesture, Trace walked out of the office. He stopped just beyond the door and opened the folder. Surprised to see a picture of a frowning, freckle-faced, red-haired girl who was approximately ten years old staring back at him, he pushed the office door back open. When Robert looked up, he held up the photograph and said, "Is this the most recent photograph you have of Meredith Moore?"

"It's the picture her mother provided, so I can only assume it's the most current one she has. I admit that's strange, but . . ." Failing to complete his remark, Robert added more softly in afterthought, "Meredith doesn't look like a particularly happy child, does she?"

Inwardly groaning, Trace slid the photo back into the folder and left without responding.

A late morning sun shone brightly as Meredith Moore stepped down off a dusty stagecoach in Winsome, Texas. She had been a passenger in the uncomfortable, cumbersome vehicle since dawn when her train journey came to an end. Since that time, she had ridden for countless miles on bumpy, rutted, dust-ridden roads before finally arriving at her destination.

Incredulous at the driver's attempt to throw her carpetbag down to her from atop the stage, Meredith waved him off and started slowly down what appeared to be Winsome's main street. Her heels clicked hollowly on the board sidewalk as she scrutinized her surroundings, and she frowned at the sound. The false-fronted buildings and small stores, the majority of them only a single story high, were archaic; and the unpaved, deeply pocked street was a step back in time. In short, the small Texas town appeared barely civilized, so different from the elaborate edifices and cobbled streets of New York City that it boggled the mind.

In retrospect, she supposed she should have been prepared for the likes of Winsome after first transferring to the ancient Texas train; yet somehow, she had not expected to arrive at a place where even the women dressed plainly in homespun dresses and common bonnets that totally ignored fashion. Appearing just as lax in appearance, the men generally wore rough trousers, plain cotton shirts with bandanas in lieu of ties, boots that were obviously hand-tooled but were too shabby to be acceptable, and wide-brimmed Stetsons. Even more unacceptable to her eye were the heavy gun belts most of the men wore strapped around their hips, bearing nasty-looking revolvers and enough ammunition to support an army. Her thoughts returned to the rough individuals headed for Nebraska and the Dakotas that she had seen in the train station as she had prepared to board the Texas rail car. Those men had worn revolvers, too. She could not make herself believe all that armament was necessary.

Another assessing glance confirmed that transportation also seemed to suffer in this far corner of the country. It took her only a moment to see that rough wagons took the place of stylish buggies, and that horses of an indiscriminate breed were more common than the well-groomed steeds that traveled New York City streets. She couldn't help but chuckle, however, at her sudden realization that the average man apparently spent more money on his horse's saddle than he did on his own clothing.

"Howdy, ma'am. Nice day, ain't it?"

Meredith raised a haughty brow at the drawling fellows who doffed their hats courteously to her as she passed, revealing hair plastered to their scalps with sweat. She pretended she did not hear their laughter when she raised her chin and continued on without replying.

Fixing her gaze on the bank in the distance, Meredith walked faster. She and her sisters had cautiously saved over the years with an eye toward futures free of their mother's influence. After she withdrew sufficient funds from the draft she had forwarded there, she would be on her way—and she was anxious to begin. She knew that her mother had lived briefly in this general area. She was determined to learn more about the man who had fathered her, and about the family her mother so steadfastly refused to discuss.

Meredith's thoughts returned again to her beautiful mother. Except for the fact that her mother had rarely missed a payment in financing her boarding school education, Letty was a virtual stranger to her. Strangely, she wondered what her mother was doing now.

Distracted, Meredith was unaware of the bearded

fellow standing near the bank doorway until she attempted to step through and felt the unexpected stab of a revolver muzzle thrust against her ribs. Stunned, she looked up to hear the fellow whisper warningly, "I was waiting for someone like you, darlin'. Just do what I say and you won't get hurt, because we're going to walk into the bank together—like we was friends."

When Meredith was momentarily frozen to the spot, the fellow added with a menacing growl, "Let's go, darlin' . . . and remember. Do what I say if you expect to come out of this alive. *Comprende?*"

Incredulous, her heart pounding and her eyes wide, Meredith was struck speechless by the startling turn of events. Unable to do anything else with the gunman's revolver still pressed against her side, she walked shakily through the entrance of the small bank with him. She stared at the unfamiliar faces that turned toward them, hardly able to breathe when the gunman announced to the shocked customers in the cool interior, "All right, everybody, put your hands in the air! This is a holdup!"

Meredith's mind froze. This couldn't be happening!

"Get moving, sweetheart." Somehow unable to take a step, Meredith heard the gunman's voice drop a note lower as he ordered, "Start collecting the money from the tellers . . . now!"

Meredith snapped into motion. As she approached the teller's window she passed a thin, elderly woman in homespun who looked as if she was going to faint, and then a burly man in a wide-brimmed hat who was sweating profusely. The gunman moved up behind the fellow and removed the big man's gun from its holster. He threw it across the floor as she reached the first teller's cage. He instructed the teller curtly, "Give the money from your drawer to my girlfriend here, and do it quick!"

His hands shaking, the thin, bespectacled teller reached under his desk and produced a canvas bag. He filled it from his drawer and then looked up at Meredith and said in a trembling voice, "That's all there is, lady. Tell him not to kill me."

Confused by the fellow's frightened request, Meredith moved to the second teller's cage and put the canvas bag down with trembling hands. The teller there was a bigger man with a strangely determined look in his eye that caused her to warn hoarsely, "Just do what he says. Put the money in the bag or he'll shoot. The cash in that drawer isn't worth your life."

When the teller hesitated, she glanced back at the gunman nervously and said, "Hurry up, please."

The teller stared at her coldly for a few moments before he filled the bag from his drawer.

Relieved, Meredith took the bag and said, "Thank you," then flushed at the absurdity of her comment. She turned back toward the bearded bank robber. "That's all there is."

"No, it ain't." The robber approached the stocky man seated at a desk in the corner. He glanced at the sign on the desk and said, "You're Howard Larson, the head man here, ain't you?"

Pale, hardly able to respond, the fellow managed, "Yes, I am."

"Open the vault."

Perspiration ran down the fellow's temples as he responded, "I . . . I . . ."

"Don't give me no excuses!" His expression rabid, the bank robber commanded, "Just do it! Put the money in the bag for my girlfriend here, or you'll be a sorry man."

Meredith followed the bank manager to the vault. She stood rigidly as he turned the combination lock and the door sprang open. She followed him into the shallow interior and held the money bag wordlessly as he filled it from the shelf, then preceded him out of the vault, bag in hand.

"Bring that bag here."

Desperately wanting the debacle to end, Meredith hastened to comply with the bank robber's command. She waited breathlessly as the robber then turned toward the bank customers and said, "My girlfriend and me are going to leave now, so don't nobody move!"

"What?"

The gunman didn't bother to respond as he grabbed Meredith's arm and pushed her out the doorway in front of him. She stood unmoving as the robber mounted a surly-looking horse at the rail, his gun still fixed on her as he attached the money bag to the saddle horn. She gasped when he reached down unexpectedly and pulled her up onto the saddle in front of him. Her spontaneous struggle stopped abruptly when the gunman snapped, "Stay still! You're my insurance. Nobody's going to take a chance of shooting at me with a pretty lady like you sharing my saddle."

Incredulous at the sudden, bizarre turn of events, Meredith could do no more than grip the saddle horn as the gunman jammed his heels into his horse's side and the animal bolted forward.

True to the gunman's expectations, they had almost reached the edge of town before a sudden burst of gunfire erupted behind them. Gasping as bullets whizzed past them, Meredith heard the gunman swear under his breath as he kicked his horse to a faster pace and turned to fire back.

Fear tightened Meredith's throat as a rapid exchange of gunfire followed. Her mind went cold when she glanced back to see a fellow within the crowd behind them suddenly fall to the ground.

The bank robber clutched her instinctively closer as men within the assembled crowd began mounting up to pursue them. Suddenly aware that her life was at risk from the posse as well as from the bank robber, Meredith was overwhelmed by a disbelief that numbed her mind as the gunman turned his mount off the trail unexpectedly and began plowing through the high grass outside town.

Aware only of the sound of the belated posse's pounding hooves growing increasingly closer, Meredith gasped when the gunman headed his horse directly toward a deep crevasse in front of them. She held her breath as the animal plunged wildly over the edge, slipping and sliding endlessly down the rocky terrain. They were almost at the bottom of the depression when the gunman's horse stumbled and they lurched forward. Meredith heard the gunman's grunt of satisfaction when he managed to right the animal at the last moment, and then glanced back briefly to see that the posse refused to follow.

Suddenly laughing aloud, the gunman continued their furious escape. His laughter came to a jolting halt with a loud curse only moments later as he exclaimed, "It's gone, damn it! The money bag is gone!"

Looking down, Meredith felt a new fear assail her at the realization that the money bag had indeed fallen off the saddle horn during their wild ride.

Meredith ventured breathlessly into the silence that followed, "Nobody's chasing us now. Let me go. You can ride faster without me. No one will ever catch you."

"Shut up!"

"But—"

"I said, shut up!"

Her heart pounding, Meredith abruptly realized that it didn't matter what she said. She had become the hostage of a thief and a killer, and he had no intention of letting her go.

Trace stepped down from his mount as the sun began setting on the sleepy town of Winsome, Texas. He unfastened his saddlebags, stepped up onto the board sidewalk, started walking toward what appeared to be Winsome's only hotel, and realized that he felt completely at home in this small Texas town despite his long years in the city. Of course, he probably would never have left Texas if an epidemic had not taken his parents' lives, leaving him alone. Somewhere along the way during the lost years that followed, he discovered a talent that led him to the Pinkerton Agency, and work that introduced him to the city and provided him with a liberal education about life. Now mature at the age of twenty-five, he was healthy and strong, was tall and muscularly built, with heavy dark hair and strong features that often prompted female members of New York society to refer to him as "ruggedly handsome." He was not vain enough to accept that assessment, but he was grateful that his experiences had made him almost as comfortable in the conservative dark suit, trousers, and the large black Stetson that had become his trademark in the city, as he was in the western clothes he now wore.

It still bothered him that he had not informed Robert Pinkerton of his recent purchase of a Texas ranch or his decision to return to the state of his birth. He consoled himself as he continued walking toward the Red Willow Hotel that he would do that as soon as this job was finished—a job that appeared to be going more easily than expected.

Actually, he'd had no trouble locating Meredith Moore's direction after he went to the boarding school where she had taught when her schooling was finished. He had easily found the place where she had met up with her sisters before they had separated only a short time earlier. In speaking to the locals there, he had learned that Meredith Moore had made inquiries as to where she could take the fastest train to Winsome, Texas.

Trace inwardly snickered at that. As if there was more than one train she could take in the direction of this small town.

He had then gone to the train station where it was difficult to find a fellow there who did *not* remember the beautiful, redheaded Meredith Moore.

Strangely, considering how long it had been that the sisters had been estranged from their mother, it appeared they had only recently decided to go in different directions. He was not sure of the reason that the sisters had spent time with each other before going off on their own. He wondered whether the young women had argued and split up, or if they had simply allowed themselves time to form definite plans. He favored the latter, considering that Meredith Moore seemed to know exactly where she wanted to go.

In any case, he had made up considerable lost time by choosing to ride a saddle horse on the final leg of the journey, thereby eliminating the delay of public transportation schedules. For that reason, he expected that he had probably arrived in Winsome right behind the young woman he was looking for.

As for himself, Trace was glad to be back in Texas. He was especially adept at "getting his man" in these parts, and his record stood for itself. If he didn't miss his guess, he would find Miss Meredith Moore registered at the Red Willow Hotel. It would then be a simple matter to wrap up the case one way or another, and to finally tell Robert that although he was appreciative of all the agency had done for him, he was going back to the life he was meant to live.

His worn boots echoed hollowly against the boardwalk as he headed toward the hotel. With his faded shirt and pants, his Stetson sweat-stained, and the gun belt that he wore low on his hips holding a six-shooter that had the look of being well broken in, Trace did his best to contain the rangy, self-possessed stride that set him as far apart from the average cowpoke as did the powerful stretch of his shoulders, and the acute, light-eyed gaze with which he instinctively studied his surroundings. His muscles cramped by the long ride, he took a subtle breath, ignoring the interest of a young matron entering the mercantile, as well as in the smiles of the two saloon girls standing outside the Last Chance's swinging door as he reached the Red Willow Hotel. He was interested in one woman only—a spoiled, redheaded, rich girl with a questionable background, who had come back to the place of her birth for a reason he had no interest in ascertaining.

With that thought in mind, Trace entered the hotel lobby and said to the clerk behind the desk, "I'd like a room."

The small, balding fellow smiled pleasantly as he replied, "We've got plenty of vacancies. Just sign here."

Trace said casually, "I'm hoping to meet up with a woman who should have registered here earlier. Her name is Meredith Moore."

Surprising him, the clerk shook his head. "Sorry. Nobody by that name registered at this hotel."

"You're sure?" Trace was surprised. "She's an unusually attractive woman, an easterner with red hair. She should have arrived on the stage earlier and she—"

Trace halted abruptly when the clerk's eyes widened. He heard the gulping breath the fellow took before he said, "You know her?"

Trace replied with sudden caution, "I don't really *know* her. Why?"

"Are you the law?"

Immediately on his guard, Trace replied, "No, I'm not the law." He hedged, "I heard she's quite a looker, and that she was traveling this way alone. I figured I'd take a chance of hooking up with her somewhere along the line if I could."

"That would be a bad idea."

"Why?"

31

"Because she ain't as alone as she looked. As a matter of fact, that lady and her partner just robbed the bank this morning."

Trace went momentarily still. "We can't be talking about the same woman."

"You said she was an easterner—a right pretty young woman with red hair. You said she probably arrived on the stage a little earlier than you."

"That's right."

"Well, there ain't many like that around here, so I'd say that's her, all right. The whole town's talking about her. Everybody figures that her partner and her planned to meet at the bank, because she got off the stage this morning, met him at the door, and then strolled into the bank beside him as bold as you please. While her partner held his gun on everybody, she collected all the money from the tellers, and then from the vault. He kept calling her his girlfriend, and he used pet names like sweetheart and darlin'—as if she was somebody special. She did what he told her to do without saying a word, except to warn one of the tellers when he didn't move fast enough to suit her, and then to thank him for filling up the sack with the money from his drawer."

"That's hard to believe."

"She looked nervous, but that didn't stop her from riding off on the same horse with her fella in front of half the town. Not a man in town fired a shot at them for fear of hitting her—not even the deputy—until the sheriff ran up and started shooting. That's when her partner turned around, fired back, and hit Sheriff Keller in the chest."

"The sheriff . . . he's dead?"

"No, not yet, anyways."

Incredulous, Trace shook his head.

His eyes suddenly narrowing, the clerk said, "Wait a minute, you said the woman you was looking for was named Meredith Moore?"

Trace nodded.

"Well, the deputy is holding the carpetbag that woman left on the stage. You might find her name in there so you can be sure it's her."

Attempting an offhanded shrug, Trace responded, "I don't know if it's worth my while, considering that I never met the woman, but I'll think about it." He forced a smile, slapped down his coin on the counter, and said as casually as he could manage, "In the meantime, I'll take my key."

Barely restraining his haste, Trace started toward his room. Minutes later he slipped out the back door of the hotel and headed toward the sheriff's office.

His Pinkerton status was still a secret when Trace emerged from the sheriff's office a half hour later. While conversing with the extremely talkative deputy who did not hesitate to divulge the details of the robbery to a virtual stranger, he had sensed it was better that way—especially since he had discovered that the woman who had robbed the bank with her partner was indeed Meredith Moore. The name was neatly embroidered inside the carpetbag she had left on the stage.

Which left him with only one question.

Why?

Meredith stood shaken and silent under the eye of the furious bank robber. He had pulled her down from his mount when they reached an isolated cabin, and had then dragged her inside as she struggled fiercely against him. His menacing glance when he reached for his gun halted her protests abruptly.

Standing motionless as he glowered at her, Meredith was intensely aware that sometime during their frantic escape, her upswept hair had fallen into a fiery tangle against her shoulders, and that nervous perspiration marked the underarms of the conservative gray traveling dress that had become ripped and stained beyond repair. She was disheveled and sweaty, yet the bank robber continued his heated perusal, his offensive odor overwhelming.

A nervous twitter touched Meredith's senses as she returned the bank robber's stare. She took a breath and glanced around the shack. It was cold and dank, and unfit for human habitation, but she kept her opinion to herself. They had stopped only occasionally throughout the day to rest their mount. Twilight now made further travel impossible, and her captor was still railing at the bad fortune that had caused him to lose the money bag while escaping. Silently glad that he would not profit from the robbery that had ended in a shooting, she was still keenly aware that the wrong word spoken at that time could be disastrous.

Meredith jumped with a start when the bank robber questioned abruptly, "What are you lookin' at! You think it's funny that I lost that money bag, don't you?"

Meredith responded cautiously, "I wasn't even thinking about that. I was just wondering when you were going to let me go."

The bank robber stepped closer, intensifying the

tension of the moment. "Who says I'm going to let you go?"

Meredith took an instinctive backward step as she attempted to respond emotionlessly. "Why would you want to keep me here? Your supplies are limited and you certainly can travel faster without me. If you let me go, it'll be days before I can find my way back to civilization, so you'll have plenty of time to get away."

"What if I don't want to get away?"

"What do you mean? You can't stay around here. Everybody saw your face. You'll be recognized."

"Maybe, but nobody will find this place for a while. We've got plenty of time to have some fun together."

"Fun?" Meredith swallowed as the bank robber edged closer. "I don't know what you mean."

"Yes, you do." Smiling unexpectedly, revealing yellowed, uneven teeth, the bank robber continued. "It's real private here. We can take the time to enjoy ourselves."

"No." Meredith shook her head. "I don't think so."

The bank robber's sudden laughter was harsh. "You don't think so, huh? Well, I think you're wrong." Grabbing her shoulders unexpectedly, he pulled her close. His body hardened as he moved sinuously against her. "Come on, make love to me, darlin'. I figure that'll make up for my losses today, and I like it real good when a woman makes love to me."

"Let me go!" Gagging at the thought, Meredith struggled to avoid his searching kiss as she blurted, "You're disgusting . . . unwashed . . . filthy! No woman would enjoy making love to you, most especially me!"

"Is that so?" Abruptly discarding pretense, the bank robber gripped the collar of her dress and ripped it open to the waist as he said with a vicious growl, "I'll teach you what I can do . . . and I'll make you beg for more!"

Meredith twisted and turned in a frantic attempt to break free. Managing to loosen one arm, she pounded at his face, scratching and clawing, her breath coming in ragged gasps when the bank robber released one hand to wipe his cheek. Appearing infuriated at the sight of his own blood, he hit her hard—a sudden, stunning blow that would have sent her reeling had he not held her forcibly upright.

Momentarily disoriented, Meredith struggled to focus as her captor dragged her toward the cot in the corner. She heard the sound of his malevolent laughter when he ripped her dress from her body and flung it in the corner.

Meredith stumbled against a nearby table. The sight of her dress lying in shreds cleared her mind, and she grabbed a rusty fork lying on the table beside her. Turning back toward the bank robber, she stabbed it into his arm with all her might.

The bank robber's bloodcurdling scream sent Meredith dashing toward the door. Breathless and sobbing with fear at the sound of his footsteps behind her, she raced into the yard. She darted toward the shadows at the edge of the clearing—only to stop abruptly at the sight of small, yellow eyes staring at her from the semidarkness.

She heard a warning growl.

She saw the shape of a large, furry animal poised to attack.

The bank robber's running footsteps were suddenly close and Meredith glanced behind her. She needed to make a choice. She needed to—

Going still when the animal leapt out of the shadows, Meredith watched as it hurdled past her to attack the bank robber.

Frozen with fear, Meredith heard him scream as the animal clamped its powerful jaws on his arm. Blood streamed from the wound as the animal released his arm and lunged for his throat. She saw the bank robber's blood spurting in his vain attempt to protect himself, and she started to run. Racing past the gory struggle toward the robber's horse, she managed to mount after two unsuccessful, breathless tries, and then kicked the horse into motion. The sound of her captor's screams echoed in her ears, but she did not look back. She was unsure how long she had been riding in the lengthening shadows when she heard the howl of a wolf reverberate in the sudden silence behind her.

A chill ran down Meredith's spine as she pressed on.

Twilight shadows had lengthened into darkness when Meredith drew up beside another cabin. She slipped to the ground, her momentary elation fading at the realization that the cabin was dark, and that its dilapidated condition and boarded windows indicated it was also abandoned.

Her throat choked tight. She'd get no help here.

Tying her mount up cautiously, Meredith approached the cabin and pushed the door open. Her nostrils flared at the smell of mold and decay. She fumbled around in the darkness and found a candle and a box of matches that had obviously been left by the previous occupant. She lit the candle with a shaking hand and scrutinized her surroundings more closely.

The cabin was filthy and cold. It had obviously been unoccupied for a long time . . . but she was safe at last.

Meredith looked down, realizing for the first time that she was clad simply in a thin chemise and cotton underskirt.

The incredulity of her circumstances suddenly too much to absorb, Meredith stumbled toward a dusty bunk littered with debris and sat down. Fatigued and shivering, she then swept the bunk free of clutter, lay back, and pulled a stained coverlet up over her seminakedness.

She needed to sleep. If she did, she was somehow certain that when she awakened, she would discover that the day had been nothing more than a horrendous dream.

Yes . . . a terrible, horrific dream.

Meredith closed her eyes and forced her mind free of thought. She drifted into oblivion to the sound of a wolf's haunting howl.

Chapter Two

"Of course, I understand, Aunt Letty." Seated beside Letty Wolf in her elaborate living room, Mason Little placed his teacup back down on the silver tray that had been brought in earlier by Millie, Letty's uniformed maid. His raspy, educated voice reverberated on the uncomfortable silence as he looked at her sympathetically. Of medium height, his physique carefully maintained, his apparel the latest fashion, his thinning hair groomed by the most expensive barber in New York, Mason Little was the epitome of the well-dressed cosmopolitan solicitor. Few looked any further than his surface appearance to note the small, tight lines around his mouth, or notice that the sympathy in his voice was seldom reflected in his eyes.

His expression sensitive and filled with compassion, Mason took Letty's hand. "I understand how you feel. You're a mother who has lost her children and you need to find them."

"You're so understanding, Mason." Truly uncomfortable with the situation, Letty continued, "I thought when you made contact with me a few years back that the contact would be brief, but it was not. I've appreciated the fact that you've never attempted to judge me during the time since, and that you've chosen to consider me family despite Archibald's demise."

"It isn't my place to judge anyone, Aunt Letty."

Her eyes briefly bright, Letty swallowed and said, "I felt it was important to explain the situation to you personally. I hope you agree that although awkward, present circumstances have necessitated these changes in my will."

"Of course I do."

"Needless to say, although the bulk of my estate will go to my daughters if they agree to the stipulations I've made, I will be generous in my bequest to you."

"Aunt Letty . . . please. I don't want to talk about wills. You have a long life ahead of you."

"You do understand that I would have asked you to handle all the intricacies of my will if not for my long-standing association with Wallace, Pittman, and O'Brien."

"Of course, Aunt Letty."

"Archibald was a dear man, and I have sincere affection for you."

"And I for you."

Letty said with relief obvious in her tone, "That's settled, then. I'm glad. I was so worried that I—"

Standing up abruptly, somehow unable to continue, Letty extended her hand and said softly, "Thank you for your thoughtful support, Mason. I regret having to bring this conversation to such an abrupt close, but—as you know—I have a long night ahead of me, and I must rest now. But before I do, I want to say that you've made difficult circumstances very easy for me. I thank you for that and I apologize for any discomfort I may have caused you."

"Dear Aunt Letty . . ."

Accepting Letty's warm adieu with a smile, Mason closed the hallway door of Letty's luxurious apartment behind him. The lock clicked closed, and his smile faded.

I thank you, Mason. . . .

I apologize for any discomfort I may have caused you. . . .

Mason's lips curled expressively. Damn Letty Wolf and damn her darling daughters! He had actually celebrated the day that his *dear aunt Letty's* spoiled children had chosen to sever their connection with her. He had forced himself to renew his acquaintance a few years earlier with the rumored half-breed tart that his senile uncle had picked up in his travels. He had realized it might be beneficial to cultivate his vague connection to her when her social club started to succeed so handsomely. He had hoped that connection would pay off somewhere along the line, but the fact that his dear aunt Letty became angry enough with her daughters to make him her sole heir in her will was a windfall he had not expected.

That windfall had come just in time for him—during a period when his penchant for gambling had driven him so deep into debt that he had been uncertain how he could possibly extricate himself. When the news that he was to be his aunt Letty's sole heir became common knowledge, everything changed. His markers were again accepted freely—markers that he would soon be pressured to pay.

Mason's rage heightened. How dare she shatter his world like this? How dare she place his whole future in jeopardy? Aunt Letty somehow felt she had the right to play God with her questionably obtained wealth, but he would not allow it! Nor would he allow her vacillating, menopausal temperament to result in the possible spilling of his own blood.

So "understanding," was he?

She had "sincere affection" for him, did she?

A flush transfused Mason's face as he mumbled, "No, you won't get away with this, *Aunt Letty*. I promise you that!"

Taking a moment to draw his emotions under control, Mason then walked stiffly down the hallway.

Standing in a dark alleyway beside an all-night club hours later, in an area that the better class of New Yorkers did not normally frequent, Mason felt his patience ebbing. It was three o'clock in the morning and he hadn't yet gone to bed. He had spent the entire day after leaving his dear aunt Letty searching for Humphrey Dobbs, the small, rodent-like fellow now standing uncertainly in front of him. He had finally found Dobbs, but the fact that the fellow had imbibed liberally and did not appear to be fully cognizant of what he was saying raised his ire.

Mason said hotly, "Are you listening to me, Dobbs?"

"I always listen when you talk, Mr. Little, because I know you don't seek me out unless you have something important to say."

"I have something to say, all right. What I'm wondering is if you're in a condition to listen."

His expression suddenly as hard as the new tone

to his voice, Dobbs said unexpectedly, "If you've got something to say, say it."

Yes, Dobbs was the right man, all right. Dobbs was short and thin with large, pointed features. His clothes hung on him as if made for a larger man, and the hair under the workman's cap he wore was greasy and sparse. His appearance was innocuous. It belied the influence he had in a community where anything could be had for a price. Everyone knew him, and no one dared to be his enemy because Dobbs had *connections* that would make being his enemy extremely dangerous.

Fully aware of those facts, Mason began slowly. "I suppose you've heard of my new circumstances— that my benefactress has already changed her will to reinstate her daughters with the provision that they contact her within the year—in which case my share of the inheritance will be reduced to a 'generous bequest.'"

"Yeah, I heard. Mr. Charles didn't like the sound of that at all."

Mason took a nervous breath. Mr. Charles. He knew who that infamous fellow was. He was the man who made sure debtors paid their gambling bills . . . one way or another.

"That's why I came to you." Mason forced himself to smile. "I'll need three fellows who don't mind traveling to take care of a job that will correct the potential difficulty of my situation. I will, of course, provide a significant reward for their efforts."

"That sounds interesting."

"Their tasks won't be difficult. Miss Wolf has three daughters. As you know, she's hired three detectives from the Pinkerton Detective Agency to find them and present them with the stipulations for reinstatement in her will. It didn't take much effort to learn that the men Pinkerton sent after them are Trace Stringer for the eldest daughter, Larry Worth for the middle daughter, and Tom Cooley for the youngest daughter."

"Stringer and Worth can probably handle the job, but Tom Cooley—he's an old bugger, ain't he?"

"Yes, well, Pinkerton must have confidence in him or he wouldn't be using him on this assignment. In any case, these men need to find Miss Wolf's daughters and either convince them to return with them or have the young women sign a statement stating that they know the conditions of the will and don't intend to abide by them."

"So?"

"So, I want you to make *sure* Miss Wolf's daughters don't return."

"Meaning?"

"Meaning?" Mason's ire rose again. "Do I have to spell it out for you? I mean that anything your men deem necessary in order to stop Miss Wolf's daughters from returning is all right with me. *Anything* . . . do you understand?" Pausing to emphasize his unspoken meaning, Mason continued, "I will, of course, make sure that the financial compensation suits any solution your men feel is necessary."

"Yeah . . . well . . . from what I hear, that ain't the problem. Rumor has it that Miss Wolf's daughters have disappeared."

Mason replied impatiently, "All your men need to do is to follow the Pinkerton detectives. Those fellows have a head start on your men and they won't have any problem finding Letty's daughters because that's their job. That should be easy enough since the Pinkertons won't have any idea that your men are a few days behind them and won't have covered up their trail."

Mason handed a manila envelope to Dobbs without waiting for a reply. "The information in this envelope is all I have on Letty's daughters. Don't ask me where I got it, but it's the same information that the Pinkerton detectives have, too, so that should start your men in the right direction."

Dobbs paused a tense moment before accepting the envelope. He then said with a flicker of his brow, "My fellas are always happy to work when there's the potential for a big payday involved."

"That's what I like to hear."

"Of course, their dispositions—and mine—would suffer greatly if they found out there wasn't a big enough reward waiting for them when they finished their work."

"There's no chance of that." Mason's mouth twitched noticeably at Dobbs' implied warning. "I'll advance you a sizable sum from my own funds, and the rest will come from Miss Wolf's bank account. It'll be mine soon enough."

"Is that so? It seems to me that Miss Wolf ain't that old. It may be years before her bank account is yours, no matter how this all works out. My men and me don't expect to wait for our money."

Mason responded coldly, "Miss Wolf isn't old, but she won't have the potential for a long life span if your men make sure that I'm her only heir. I can't take the chance that she'll change her mind again."

Mason paused to assess Dobbs' reaction to his

statement. When Dobbs did not even blink, Mason added, "But one step at a time. I need to be sure none of her daughters come back."

"I can see to it that's taken care of."

"One stipulation . . . I need to be kept apprised of what's going on with your men. I don't like being kept in the dark."

"I can take care of that, too."

"It's settled, then."

"It will be, if the advance you're talking about is good enough."

"You can count on it. I'll make sure we agree on the amount tomorrow."

Dobbs smiled. "If I do, my men will be on their way."

Mason nodded. "Tomorrow, then."

Mason waited for Dobbs' nod of final consent before starting back down the alleyway toward the darkened street. It annoyed him that Dobbs knew he would pay whatever Dobbs' men demanded in advance, but he knew he would meet their price even if he had to empty his accounts to do it. The reason was simple. Dear Aunt Letty had left him no choice.

Grateful to immediately hail a passing carriage when he emerged from the alleyway, Mason did not look back. As far as he was concerned, his future would soon be secure, and the sooner he got out of that side of town, the better.

Trace squinted at the silver light of dawn edging through the window shade, and then glanced around. He hadn't slept well. As a matter of fact, he had hardly slept at all. The Red Willow Hotel's accommodations were less than perfect, but he could not blame the room or the bed for his sleeplessness.

Trace sat up on the lumpy mattress, and then threw his legs over the side and reached for his pants. It still didn't make any sense. He had conversed with the talkative deputy the previous evening, and everything that the hotel clerk had said was true. A red-haired woman had walked through the doorway of the bank beside a slovenly, dark-haired wrangler with a drawn gun. After announcing that he was there to rob the bank, the fellow whispered to her, and she went directly to the tellers to collect the money from their drawers. When the second teller prepared to fight back, she warned him that his life hung in the balance, and she then thanked him after he emptied his drawer into the sack.

The bank robber then spoke to her again and she accompanied the bank manager into the vault to add its contents to the money bag. They left the bank together—both on the same horse—and no one remembered her even looking back when her partner shot to kill as they escaped.

He had confirmed that the red-haired woman was indeed Meredith Moore. Beside the fact that very few women seemed to look like her, her name was clearly embroidered on the carpetbag that she left behind. So the question was, why did she leave her bag behind when it could identify her? Even more importantly, why would she bother to rob a bank in the first place? She could get all the money she would ever need simply by visiting her mother.

No, none of it made any sense. There were too many unanswered questions, and no one to help him answer them. The inexperienced deputy had lost the trail after the bank robber's dramatic escape, had ended up leading the posse on a wild-goose chase, and had already made up his mind that Meredith Moore was as guilty as her slovenly partner. It looked as if Trace was going to have to get to the bottom of things himself before he settled his own business with the elusive Meredith.

His frown darkening more by the moment, Trace dressed and left the Red Willow Hotel before the sun began its ascent in the morning sky. His saddlebags in hand, he made his way to the livery and told the stable hand to ready his horse. After a short trip to the mercantile, he headed out of town. Unlike the inexperienced deputy, he did not intend to allow emotion to cloud his vision, and there was one thing he knew for sure. Despite the deputy's failure, he knew everyone left some sort of trail that the right person could follow.

He was the right person.

It was just a matter of time.

Meredith awakened slowly. Somehow unwilling to open her eyes, she mumbled a soft plea, and then slowly raised her eyelids.

Oh no!

Meredith squeezed her eyes shut again. It couldn't be true! She couldn't be stuck in a filthy, moldy cabin in the middle of nowhere with the memory of the previous, terrifying day haunting her.

She opened her eyes again.

It was all true.

Panicked, Meredith sat up. She had always been so resourceful. It had been she who was the spokesperson for her sisters and for herself when their nannies treated them unfairly. It had been she who spoke up to their mother during the years when it seemed that her sisters and she were the last thing on their mother's mind. Finally, when her mother separated the sisters so they could not present a united front, it had been she who maneuvered a way to maintain contact with them.

Meredith's throat closed momentarily tight at the memory of those difficult years. She supposed it wasn't hard to understand why *Grandfather* first appeared to her about that time, but the rest . . . she didn't really understand it. She had at first thought Grandfather was merely a figment of her need, but although his appearance was strange and his tongue foreign, there was something about him that made her trust him . . . that somehow made her care about him in the same way that he seemed to care about her. She did not comprehend how she understood the language he spoke, but his advice was sound. He comforted her with his mere presence and instilled confidence when hers waned. His guidance showed her the way to stolen hours with her sisters that were still the brightest moments in her memory.

Strangely, Grandfather's approval had been even more important to her when her sisters and she made their final decision to separate. She had never questioned it, but now as she lay abed on a filthy cot with fearful memories her closest companions, Meredith wondered how everything had gone so wrong.

The rumbling of her stomach interrupted Meredith's introspection, reminding her that she had a more immediate problem to solve. Throwing back the coverlet, she stood up and glanced around her. She hadn't eaten since the previous morning. That was almost twenty-four hours earlier, if she were to judge by the rays of the morning sun slipping through the boarded-up windows of the cabin.

Glancing down at herself, Meredith felt humiliation soar. Her fashionable attire was now gone. Instead, she was clad only in revealing undergarments that she could only describe as indecent, thanks to the devious intent of the bank robber who had captured her.

The bank robber.

Meredith shivered at the memory of the powerful, yellow-eyed animal that had sprung out the darkness to save her. She remembered the bank robber's screams, and she recalled the wolf's howl that had sounded in the sudden stillness as she made her escape. She had heard that same mournful wail again before she fell asleep. She wondered, almost fearfully, if the appearance of that vicious animal had anything to do with the howling of a wolf that had seemed to forecast all the momentous events of her life—the same howling that seemed somehow intertwined with her thoughts of Grandfather.

Meredith unconsciously negated that idea with a shake of her head. Her emotions were playing tricks on her. At that very moment, the bank robber was probably nursing his wounds, making his way through the wilderness on foot, hoping to escape the posse that was probably still hunting him.

In any case, she needed to concentrate on her present problems—the need to find food, drink, and some kind of clothing to cover her before she could start back to civilization.

Meredith studied her surroundings more closely. The dusty, web-laden shelves were empty, but she spotted an ancient pump and a rusty pan that appeared to have been an effort to construct a dry sink. She approached the pump and primed it warily. Once, twice, then three times, and water began trickling out of the spout. At first elated, Meredith then noted that despite her continued efforts, the water remained rusty and brackish. Tears rose unexpectedly to her eyes. She was so thirsty.

Forcing herself to blink back her tears, Meredith suddenly remembered that she had left the robber's horse tied up outside the previous night. She rushed to the door and came to an abrupt halt at the sight of the sorry-looking animal still tied to the tree where she had left it.

Damn, how could she have been so thoughtless?

Spotting the canteen on the horse's saddle as she approached, Meredith shook it, then opened it with shaking hands and drank freely. Guilt then rising, she cupped a few handfuls in her palms and offered them to the horse. She hungrily chewed a piece of rolled jerky that she had found in the saddlebags as she tied the horse up behind the cabin in a spot where he could easily graze. Taking the time to search the saddlebags more carefully, she then found a sack with what appeared to be some flour . . . or cornmeal . . . but little else. She carried it back into the cabin remembering what Mrs. Dunbar had said in the school kitchen.

A little flour and water and a person could make herself a meal.

Well, she'd see.

* * *

51

Trace looked up at the position of the sun in the cloudless sky. It was almost noon and he had been tracking Miss Meredith Moore since dawn. He supposed the excitement of the moment and the deputy's inexperience was to blame for his losing the trail, but he'd had no problem—until . . .

Trace swallowed against the bile suddenly rising to his throat. He had come upon the site of the abandoned cabin where Meredith and the bank robber had briefly stopped. There was no evidence of their having prepared a meal or having slept there. That had originally confused him until he had found Meredith Moore's ripped dress on the floor of the cabin and had then followed a bloody trail that led into the brush, hoping desperately that he would not find the beautiful Miss Moore at the end of it. Instead he had been stunned to find the torn body of a man who could be no other than the bank robber, lying in a pool of his own blood.

The grisly sight had turned his stomach. There was no doubt in his mind that nothing other than a wild animal could have been responsible for such butchery. The attack had probably been a surprise, considering that the fellow's gun was still in his holster. As for Meredith Moore, there had been no sign of her except for the tracks of the bank robber's horse making a fast exit. Nor was there any sign of the money that had been stolen from the bank.

He had buried the fellow hurriedly and had gotten back on the trail immediately afterward, following the very clear tracks that he could only assume that the surprising Miss Moore had left behind.

Trace paused as he approached what appeared to be another abandoned cabin. The tracks led directly to it, and a saddled horse was grazing peacefully behind it. He knew that despite the tranquility of the scene, he needed to be prepared for any eventuality—simply because Meredith Moore seemed to be more than he had expected. The brief background sketch he'd seen indicated that she had been born in this part of the country, but that she had been citified from early childhood. It was inconceivable to him that she had managed to elude a posse, and then to escape the wild animal that had attacked the bank robber. He could only assume that aside from being the indulged, runaway daughter of a wealthy mother, the beautiful Miss Moore was also resourceful, determined . . . and dangerous.

With those thoughts in mind, Trace quietly dismounted and tied his horse a distance from the cabin. He approached the structure on foot with his gun drawn, careful not to be seen. He paused at the doorway of the cabin, then took a breath and kicked it open.

The door of the cabin banged back against the interior wall as he entered. A quick glance revealed that it was empty except for a small fire burning in the fireplace. At a sound behind him, Trace turned just as he was struck a painful, staggering blow to the head.

Momentarily disoriented, Trace slumped heavily to the floor of the cabin. Groaning, he struggled to regain his senses as he blinked almost comically at the woman standing over him. Hair brighter than the flames behind her spilled in riotous curls onto her shoulders. Great, darkly fringed eyes stared at him from a face with features so fine as to appear almost unreal. Her bared shoulders were narrow and her breasts were rounded appealingly in the sheer chemise covering them. Long, slender legs were clearly outlined in the revealing underskirt that was her only other attire.

She was beautiful.

She could be no other than Meredith Moore.

And she was pointing his own gun directly at him.

Abruptly breaking the strained silence between them, the woman spoke first. "Who are you?"

Trace rubbed his throbbing head as he stared at the muzzle of his six-shooter. He didn't know what the surprising Miss Moore had hit him with, but she had certainly accomplished her purpose. He was helpless, and he didn't like the way she was holding his gun. Her finger was too tense on the trigger. He had the feeling that she wouldn't hesitate to pull it if she didn't get the right answers from him.

Regaining his voice, Trace replied flatly, "Hold your horses, lady, and don't do anything you might be sorry for." He rubbed his head again, grimacing as he added, "You are Meredith Moore, aren't you?"

The young woman repeated, "Who are you?"

Trace drew himself slowly to his feet, noting as he did that Meredith's finger trembled on the trigger as she took a defensive backward step. She was nervous. One little twitch and he was done for. If he didn't do something quickly—

Moving as quickly as lightning, Trace swatted the gun from Meredith's hand and grabbed her arm. As slippery as an eel, she slid from his grip, swinging her fist with all her might as she struck his chin hard. She had almost retrieved his gun when Trace tackled her with a flying leap, taking the brunt of the fall as they hit the floor with a loud *crack*.

Appearing momentarily stunned, the redhead twisted and turned furiously as Trace rolled atop her, imprisoning her with the weight of his body. Her soft, womanly flesh rubbed tightly against him as she struggled, making Trace even more aware that he was straddling a beautiful, scantily clad, voluptuous woman who was looking up at him with more fire in her eyes than he had seen in a month of Sundays.

Trace felt a perverse, disconcerting urge to smile at the thought that he had finally gotten the best of the bargain.

But that thought was short-lived.

"Get off me!"

Ignoring her command, Trace leaned over to retrieve his gun. He dropped it into his holster and responded coldly, "I've got the gun now, and whether you realize it or not, that means one thing. *I'm* the one who gives the orders."

Meredith stared at the big man sitting astride her so arrogantly as she lay flat on her back on the filthy floor. How had this happened? A few minutes earlier, a strange sound in the yard had caused her to peer out through a crack in the boarded window just as the fellow moved briefly into sight with his gun drawn. Panicking, she had searched her immediate surroundings for something to defend herself with. Her eyes had alighted at the last minute on a rusty poker lying beside the fireplace. She had managed to slip behind the door only moments before he reached it. She had stifled a gasp when he kicked the door open as he entered and had remained instinctively silent until the moment when he turned toward the fire. Seizing the opportunity with shaking hands, she had then slipped out behind him and swung the poker hard.

She remembered scrambling for his gun when he fell—then wondering when he lay momentarily motionless on the floor, if she had possibly *killed* him.

But he wasn't dead, and because of her hesitation, he was now holding her helpless with the weight of his powerful body.

Too incensed at her own stupidity for caution, she ordered, "I told you to get off me!"

The big man leaned closer. She saw the dark flecks of color in his light eyes as he said with a note of threat to his tone, "And I told you that I give the orders now. So answer me. Are you Meredith Moore?"

Meredith went still. "How do you know my name?"

Stunned into speechlessness when the fellow stood up abruptly and swung her to her feet, Meredith took a ragged breath and assessed him more closely. He was even taller than she had thought. His hair was thick and black, although a bit long to be stylish, and his features were strong but too irregular to be called handsome. The stretch of his shoulders was wide, his chest deep, and his light-eyed gaze was sharp. His appearance was powerfully formidable, but there was an unnamed quality about him that left her shaken in a way that had no relation to threat.

He said unexpectedly, "So your name *is* Meredith Moore."

Resenting his effect on her, Meredith replied, "Yes, it is, and I suppose now that you have the gun, you feel you have the upper hand." She taunted, "Of course, if you were a real man, you wouldn't need a gun since I'm only a woman and I'm unarmed."

The fellow's light eyes swept her with an almost insultingly intimate glance that lodged deep inside her before he replied. "If there's one thing I'm certain of, a woman who looks like you is never *unarmed*—but in your case, since you managed to elude the posse pursuing you after you robbed the Winsome Bank with your partner yesterday and—"

"Wh . . . what?"

"I said—"

"I heard what you said!" All other thought thrust from her mind, Meredith gasped. "My partner? I'm a victim here, not a criminal." To the fellow's skeptical gaze, she continued hotly. "You came into this cabin with your gun drawn, knocked me down, and now you stand there threatening me, and you claim *I'm* a lawbreaker? Who are you, anyway?"

Pausing to assess her for a silent moment, the fellow said, "Look, Miss Moore . . . the lump on my head where you hit me is still throbbing, and I buried the fella you robbed the bank with a few hours ago, so I'm not in the mood for your games. I want to know what's going on."

"Buried him . . ." Meredith swayed. She shook off the fellow's hand when he gripped her shoulder to support her and said, "He's dead?"

"He's dead, all right. I followed your trail from town to the abandoned cabin that you two stopped at. I found his body."

"His body . . ." The fellow gripped her shoulder again as her color paled. This time she did not shake it off as she asked haltingly, "That animal killed him?"

"I guess. Considering what the fella looked like, I figured nothing human could have made that bloody a scene."

Meredith did not realize she had almost lost consciousness until she was suddenly swept up into the stranger's arms and carried to the cot. Regaining her stability when he attempted to lay her down, Meredith forced him to release her and stood unsteadily on her feet as she stammered, "I told myself that he must have escaped that animal's attack. He was despicable, but to die that way . . ."

Meredith breathed deeply and then raised her chin. Her gaze direct, she said with a shudder, "He tried to force himself on me. If it wasn't for the animal's attack, he probably would have used his gun on me when he was done."

"That isn't the way Winsome sees it."

"What are you talking about?" Shaking her head confusedly, Meredith demanded again, "Who are you, anyway?"

Trace stared at the young woman standing beside him. Her gaze direct, she seemed to have no realization of how she looked with the shadow of her erect, rounded breasts quivering with emotion underneath the sheer undergarment she wore. The heat of her still warmed his arms, and the memory of her female softness was still strong and clear. Even in her disheveled state, she was the most beautiful woman he had ever seen.

Too beautiful. She probably knew better than anyone else that her skin was creamy . . . smooth . . . flawless, that it probably tasted as sweet as honey and—

Aware of the danger of indulging those thoughts, Trace halted them cold. "My name is Trace Stringer. I'm a Pinkerton agent. Your mother hired the Pinkerton Agency to track you down."

Her expression suddenly guarded, Meredith responded with a single word. "Why?"

"Why what?"

"Why did she hire your agency?"

"I don't think that matters right now, since as far as Winsome, Texas, is concerned, you're now a wanted woman."

"I don't believe it." Meredith shook her head. "That can't be. I don't even know the bank robber's name. All I know is that he threatened me with a gun when I went to the bank to pick up the draft I had sent there, and forced me to take the money from the tellers and from the vault while he held his gun on everybody."

"You thanked the teller when he put money in the money bag."

"The teller looked like he was going to refuse. I didn't want the bank robber to shoot him or me."

"The bank robber called you sweetheart . . . darlin' . . . dearie."

"What else could he call me? He didn't know my name."

"You rode off with him and the money bag from the bank."

"I was his hostage!"

"That fella's dead, so where's the money?"

Meredith hesitated a moment. Raising her chin, she replied flatly, "I don't know."

Silence.

"I don't know where the money is!"

"Really?"

"The bank robber lost it."

Silence again.

"It's the truth! Whether you believe me or not, the money bag fell off the bank robber's saddle while he was making his getaway."

"While you were *both* making your getaway."

"I'm a victim, I told you!"

Trace did not reply.

"Search the cabin," Meredith said defensively. "Maybe that'll prove to you that I'm telling the truth. I don't have the money. If I did, I'd return it to you so we could clear this whole thing up once and for all."

Meredith continued with a narrowing gaze. "Wait a minute. How do I know you didn't find that money while you were tracking me here? How do I know you don't have it hidden somewhere and are just pretending that you don't know where it is?"

"The answer to that is simple. If I had that money, I'd be too busy spending it somewhere to bother following you." Annoyed that he had actually answered that outlandish question, Trace added, "Let me get this straight. The bank robber was waiting at the door of the bank when you got there. He forced you to help him rob the bank, and he then forced you to leave with him."

"He said nobody would shoot at him with me on his saddle, but he was wrong."

"The sheriff didn't have that reservation."

"He hit somebody when he fired back."

"The sheriff."

"Is . . . is he dead?"

Mimicking the hotel clerk, Trace replied, "Not yet." Meredith closed her eyes. Snapping them back open abruptly, she said, "I have to go back to Winsome to explain what happened."

"That would be a good idea . . . if you could return the bank's money."

"I told you, the money bag fell off the saddle during the escape."

"Right."

Meredith glared at him with her startling eyes. Trace's heart jumped a beat despite himself. "The money bag has to be on the trail somewhere," she said. "We'll just have to go back to look again so I can take it back to Winsome and clear all this up."

"*We?*"

Meredith replied haughtily, "You did say you were hired by my mother to track me down and take me home, didn't you? Well, I couldn't go home before I cleared my name here, even if I wanted to."

"Not unless you wanted the Texas Rangers following you." Trace knew that his response had stopped her cold. "There's one thing I need to know. If you were so anxious to get back to civilization, why are you still here in this cabin?"

"The answer to that should be obvious, Mr. Stringer." Her jaw twitching at an admission that she deigned to make, Meredith replied, "I'm lost in this damned wilderness! And in case you haven't noticed, I'm practically undressed!"

Trace frowned. He had noticed, all right.

Meredith continued hotly. "I'm also famished, and I haven't been able to turn anything I found in the bank robber's saddlebags into anything that even resembles being edible."

Trace looked at the riotously beautiful, barely clad woman standing in front of him. Strangely, he had almost forgotten . . . *a spoiled, runaway rich girl. . . .*

Trace turned wordlessly toward the door. He walked back into the cabin minutes later, dropped a few packages on the nearby table, and said simply, "I'll do the cooking."

"You always were luckier than you deserve."

"Rita . . ."

Howard Larson, the Winsome Bank manager, looked at his wife as they sat in their extravagantly decorated parlor. The rugs were Aubusson. He'd had them shipped directly from New York City for their home because Rita enjoyed beautiful things. The furniture had all been made expressly for their house—a contract he had entered into with a New York artist who was exceedingly expensive, but whom his wife adored. Their everyday dinnerware was imported from England, their crystal was delicate and individually hand blown by masters in Germany. There was not a single piece of kitchenware that had reached the market in the big city that they did not possess, and he had made sure that his wife's servants handled all her treasures with care. He spoiled her, but the truth was that he had no choice.

Howard remembered the first day he saw his wife, almost fifteen years earlier. She had been lovely then. Although his own physical appearance was common, he had been an excellent student in college. He had been considered almost a genius in accounting, and had always been told that he had a bright future—yet his appeal to the opposite sex had been limited. He had believed that despite his superior abilities, he would have to be satisfied being average all his life . . . until he saw Rita.

Rita was the younger sister of one of his classmates, and he had been immediately smitten. He had been so much in love that he had been determined to do or say anything he needed to do in order to gain her attention—and he did. He courted her attentively with presents he could not really afford. He regaled Rita and her family with stories of his promising future. He expounded on countless opportunities that never materialized, and claimed that his exceptional talent with numbers had come to the notice of men in high places.

In short, he had lied, while refusing to consider the consequences of his lies until they caught up with him.

But that did not happen immediately. Rita married him and they traveled west to the land of opportunity—opportunity that did not come knocking at *his* door. Instead, he accepted a common job in a bank while Rita kept house for him and consoled herself with food until she was no longer the slender young woman he married.

Rita did not hesitate to remind him, however, that *he* was not the man she had believed she married. His ultimate rise in the banking industry was tediously slow, while his weight gain was not. Nor was his rapid loss of hair, or the stammer he developed when Rita continually outlined his shortcomings. They did not have children—which Rita blamed on his obese condition. They did not own their own home—which Rita blamed on their meager circumstances. They lived in a small town far from the conveniences of the city—which Rita blamed on his poor job performance—while never hesitating to complain that she was bored . . . bored . . . bored. The only things that seemed to end her boredom, even temporarily, were presents—jewelry, stylish clothing, and luxuries that they could not afford.

It had been so easy to take the first few dollars from the bank vault when he was short of funds. Everyone trusted him. His creative accounting increased dramatically as the sums he "borrowed" grew larger.

The news that his bank was the next one that the central bank would audit had been a startling blow to him. He had marked the date of the auditor's arrival in red on his calendar, trembling as it approached. He could not eat. He could not sleep. He could not even seem to think. He finally confessed the truth to Rita, and her vicious harangues had exploded.

Howard looked at his wife as she stared at him, awaiting his response. She was no longer lovely. She was not the woman he had married in any way, but to lose her would only prove his failure was complete. He could not abide that thought.

"Howard . . ."

"I heard you, dear. You said I was always luckier than I deserve."

Howard saw his wife's face tick. She was struggling to control her anger—a bad sign. Her voice quivered with the effort as she said, "You have no idea how opportune this robbery was, do you?"

"Opportune?"

"The bank was robbed. Your shortages will never be discovered. You should be thankful!"

"I suppose."

A blood rage flooded Rita's thickening features.

"Fool! You've been saved, and you don't even have the sense to realize it."

"Perhaps." When Rita's face turned a purple hue, Howard hastened to add, "But if the bank robbers are found and the funds recovered, the truth will come out."

"Sheriff Keller has been shot, and his deputy is an ass! They'll never find the bank robbers."

"I agree, but Deputy Cobb isn't too stupid to call in the Texas Rangers."

"He'd never do that. That would be admitting he can't handle his job without the sheriff."

"Sheriff Keller won't hesitate to call them in. He's a determined old cuss. If he sees that his deputy is out of his element, he'll ask for help."

"Sheriff Keller is unconscious."

"If he regains consciousness."

"If . . . if . . . if!" Rita covered the distance between her husband and her in a few heavy steps. Almost nose-to-nose with him, she hissed, "Stupid, that's what you are. An idiot! You're always telling me you'd do anything for me. If you really meant it, you'd stop talking about Sheriff Keller and take care of him so he won't be a threat to us any longer."

Howard gasped.

"That's right," Rita warned softly, "I said *so he won't be a threat to us any longer*, because I'm telling you now, I've sunk as low as I intend to as a result of your stupidity. I will not allow you to drag me down any further. I'll leave you first."

"No."

"I'll go back to my family and I'll tell them the truth, that you are a liar and a thief, and that I want no part of you."

"No!"

"You wouldn't like that, would you, Howard?"

"You know I wouldn't, Rita. I love you."

"Then prove it to me. Make this whole fiasco go away."

"You know I meant it when I said I'd do anything for you, Rita."

"And if the bank robber and his accomplice are caught?"

"I'll . . . I'll deny everything, that's what I'll do. After all, who is more credible, a bank robber and his girlfriend or a bank manager?"

"What about Sheriff Keller?"

"Rita . . . he's a friend."

Rita's face flamed hotly. "A friend who will be the end of us both if you allow it."

"But—"

"Sheriff Keller is an old man. He's badly wounded and his time is limited anyway. Don't force me to do something you'll regret."

Howard stared at his once lovely wife. It occurred to him that he had never seen his dear Rita more clearly than he did at that moment. No, she wasn't lovely anymore.

"Howard . . ."

He did not reply.

"Here, put these on."

Trace looked at Meredith—the spoiled, runaway rich girl who was consuming the last of the food he had cooked—the *beautiful*, spoiled, runaway rich girl who had eaten so hungrily that she seemed to have completely forgotten her state of near nakedness.

I'm not a babysitter, Robert.

Trace silently revised that thought. He had seen to it that Miss Meredith Moore was safe from any immediate threat, that she had been fed, and that she would soon have her reputation restored— accomplished without a civilized word of thanks. All he had to do now was to clothe her.

Trace attempted to stabilize his vacillating emotions. He had been warned that Letty Wolf's daughters were beautiful. Well, this one certainly was. He also knew that Letty had sent her daughters to the best boarding schools and had provided everything that money could buy. He had come to realize, however, that in doing so, Letty had educated her daughters without providing them with any of the skills that might prove valuable in life. He had also learned the hard way that Letty had managed to foster in her daughters an irritating sense of superiority that seemed to be his only protection against the bold Meredith Moore's female aura. He supposed he should be grateful for that reality, but at the moment, gratitude was beyond him.

Indicating the spare shirt and pants that he had dropped on the table, Trace said, "These clothes may not be exactly what you're accustomed to, but they'll have to do at present." Noting that Meredith looked askance at the wrinkled garments, he warned, "Like I said, you don't have any choice, so put them on."

Meredith looked up frigidly from her empty plate. "I don't like taking orders." Hesitating a moment longer, she continued with a trace of lingering hauteur, "But I suppose I can purchase more suitable clothing after I straighten things out in Winsome."

Typical.

Trace replied equally coldly, "You're welcome."

* * *

Forcing his gaze intently on the trail as the morning sun reached its apex a few hours later, Trace remained intensely aware of Meredith Moore riding beside him. She had emerged from the cabin looking very unlike the woman she had been earlier. His shirt was drastically oversized on her womanly frame, and with his pants rolled up to her ankles and a piece of rope used as a belt, Meredith Moore looked like a scarecrow that was inadequately stuffed.

Yet . . . strangely . . . with her unbound hair glittering in the sun, and with those amazing eyes set in that incredible face, she was still the most beautiful woman he had ever seen.

Apparently, she was also the most obnoxious. "Did you find the trail that the bank robber and I took from the bank yet? What's taking you so long? It's getting late. We need to find that money before someone else does."

Trace looked up from the hard-packed ground their horses trod. "We've been following the trail for the past hour. I bypassed the abandoned cabin where I buried your 'partner' because you said you had lost the money bag before you reached it, and I figured on saving some time. If you want me to go back and show it to you, though, I'll be happy to do you that favor."

Trace frowned, noting that Meredith's steady gaze flickered. That thought obviously unsettled her. He couldn't figure her out. She expected things to work out exactly as she had planned, yet when he saved her from a predicament that she apparently couldn't handle, she treated him as if he were the enemy.

Trace's frown tightened when Meredith replied, "Unfortunately, everything looks the same to me around here. A tree is a tree. We could be traveling in circles for all I know." She hesitated, and then asked, "You are sure we're not traveling in circles, aren't you?"

Trace's darkening expression responded more clearly than words, and she added, "All right . . . we aren't. In that case, you should tell me when to start looking for the money bag that the bank robber dropped."

"I've been looking for it for the past hour."

"Oh, thank you very much for imparting that information to me." Meredith's lips tightened. "Even if it is belated."

"As belated as your thanks, you mean?"

Riding in silence a little longer, Meredith said abruptly, "I don't see the depression, the crevasse, or whatever you call it out here where the bank robber almost lost control of his horse. That's probably when the money bag started to come loose from the saddle."

"We should reach that spot soon."

A few moments more of silence was broken when Meredith said, "If that's true, we should've found the money bag already. What if we don't find it? Do we assume someone else found it? Do we go back to Winsome anyway? Will the deputy believe me if I don't come back with the money? Should I—"

Trace interrupted Meredith's litany of questions as he asked, "What's that lying in the bushes over there?"

Meredith watched as he halted his horse and dismounted. She caught her breath when he pushed aside the heavy foliage and picked up a money bag clearly marked WINSOME BANK.

Meredith blinked. Trace thought he saw a mist momentarily fill her eyes before she raised her chin and said abruptly, "What are you waiting for, Mr. Stringer? Let's get going."

"Well, if it ain't Trace Stringer again. Put your hands up!"

Behind Meredith as they entered the Winsome sheriff's office, Trace halted abruptly. He raised his hands as the deputy pointed his gun directly at them. Refusing to surrender to the indignity despite the fear that set her to inwardly quaking, Meredith did not.

"I know who you are, lady, so put your hands up, too. I ain't going to warn you again."

The thin, dark-haired deputy with the outlandishly hand-tooled boots glared at Meredith with small eyes set in a narrow flushed face. His hands were shaking and with one glance at him, Meredith could tell he didn't realize he was making a big mistake.

Trace's voice in her ear ordered, "Do what he says, damn it! He's just one step away from shooting you."

Meredith raised her hands. She glanced at Trace, whose gaze was intent on the fellow's gun, and her heart jumped a beat. She could tell from his expression that he had meant what he had said—another moment's hesitation and the deputy would have shot her.

Meredith instinctively raised her hands a little higher as Trace said with an attempt at a smile, "You're making a mistake, Deputy."

Ignoring Trace's comment, the deputy responded, "When you came in here yesterday, I figured you were just making conversation and being nosy about what happened at the bank, but you found this lady when I couldn't. I got to give you credit for that, Stringer, but I got to say, too, that wearing them clothes, she don't look much like the woman folks described. I ain't asking what happened to that citified outfit she had on, but I figure she gave you a run for your money."

The deputy added, "You can put your hands down, Stringer—but not you, lady. You got away on me once and I ain't taking the chance of losing you again."

Meredith watched perspiration ooze through the pores of the deputy's forehead as he asked abruptly, "Where's the fella who robbed the bank with you?"

Incensed, Meredith was about to reply when Trace responded in her stead, "Miss Moore wasn't a part of the robbery, but the bank robber is dead. Some kind of wild animal got him. I buried him at an abandoned cabin a ways from here. You can go out later and dig up his body if you doubt what I'm saying, but you don't need to, since I found Miss Moore and the money, and she just wants to make sure that the money gets back where it belongs."

"What are you saying?" The deputy glanced at the money bag Trace tossed on the desk. "You're saying this woman gave herself up to you willingly?"

Meredith's patience was short. She had slept poorly the night before and she was all too aware that Trace Stringer challenged her in ways she did not fully understand. She was tired. All she wanted was a bath, a change of clothes, and a clean place to lay her head.

Accordingly, Meredith responded sharply. "I came back with Mr. Stringer of my own accord because I didn't have any part in the robbery, just as he said. I was forced to help the bank robber, and then I was kidnapped by him."

"Yeah, sure—*dearie, darlin', sweetheart . . .*"

Incensed at the deputy's tone, Meredith turned toward Trace and said, "Isn't there someone other than this ignoramus that I can talk to?"

"Ignoramus . . ." The deputy's face flamed as he waved his gun in the direction of the cells behind him. "I ain't stupid enough to let you get away again, so you can get yourself right through that doorway and behind those bars . . . *pronto!*"

"I want to talk to the sheriff," Meredith demanded.

"The sheriff ain't in no condition to talk."

"When will he be able to talk to me?"

"The doc ain't sure. Maybe never. He ain't regained consciousness yet, and I'm the man in charge."

Exasperated, Meredith turned again to look at Trace. "Say something!" she demanded. "Do your job. This man thinks I'm a bank robber!"

His glance deprecating, Trace replied, "You may be many things, ma'am, but you're not a bank robber." Turning to the deputy, he said, "I admit this lady isn't what either of us expected, Deputy, but she's telling the truth. She's just an innocent bystander. That money is in the money bag just the way it was taken from the bank."

"I ain't going to count it." His eyes small pinpoints of light, the deputy's tone grew more threatening by the moment. "Get yourself into that cell, lady. I ain't going to tell you again."

72

Meredith opened her mouth but no sound emerged. She glanced at Trace, only to hear him say, "Do what the deputy tells you to do."

"Wh . . . what?"

Incredulous, Meredith stared at him as he repeated, "Do what the deputy says." He took her arm and ushered her toward the door to the back room as he whispered, "I'll get somebody over here to count the money in that sack and it'll all be over."

Balking, Meredith demanded, "Do you mean you're actually going to let that idiot lock me up? Aren't you supposed to protect me? Aren't you supposed to make sure that I'm returned to my mother safe and sound?"

"No."

"What?"

"I'll discuss what your mother wants from you later—but first, get into that cell."

Aware that Trace Stringer had maneuvered himself between the deputy's gun and her, Meredith said adamantly, "I won't do it! I won't go into that cell. I'm innocent and I—"

Gasping when Trace swept her up into his arms and walked toward the cell, Meredith kicked and squirmed in her protests. Amused, the deputy watched as Trace carried her through the doorway, pushed open the cell door with his shoulder, dropped her onto the cot, and exited, slamming the barred door behind him.

Meredith scrambled to her feet to the sound of the cell door locking closed. She gripped the cell bars as Trace and the deputy strode back into the outer office. "Don't you dare leave me here, Mr. Stringer!

Even if that fool deputy refuses to accept the truth, I'm innocent. I will not be incarcerated! I will not allow anyone to—"

The slamming of the inner door halted her protests, and Meredith stood still with shock. She had been a free woman with a well-conceived plan for discovering her past only a few days previously, and now—

Meredith's introspection paused as the sound of deep voices in the outer office faded. She heard the street door open and close, and then saw the deputy peer at her through the peek hole in the inner door moments later.

Had Trace Stringer abandoned her? Had he left her to rot in a filthy cell?

Meredith took an involuntary backward step. No, he couldn't have. He was a Pinkerton. He could not possibly know that she didn't intend to cooperate with any effort he made to take her back to her mother—not that her mother would really care.

Refusing to surrender to desperation, Meredith sat down abruptly on the cot behind her. It was spotted and smelled of mold, but she was beyond caring. Trace Stringer was gone and she was alone.

Meredith swallowed, and then closed her eyes. She wiped away a straying tear as she whispered desperately into the stillness, "Grandfather, where are you now? I need you."

A late afternoon sun shone on the boardwalk outside the bank doorway as the tall fellow approached Howard Larson's desk. Larson stood up instinctively. The heels of the fellow's boots had made a familiar sound against the hardwood floor of the bank, but when he had looked up, he had known immediately that although the fellow was dressed like a wrangler, he was too intense, his gaze too keen, and his step too deliberate to mean ordinary business.

His heart pounding, Howard attempted a smile that fell the moment the fellow asked, "Are you Howard Larson, the bank manager?"

"Yes, I am. May I help you?"

"My name is Trace Stringer. I just delivered the money bag robbed from your bank yesterday to Deputy Cobb in the sheriff's office, and I want you to verify that it's intact."

Howard replied unsteadily, "I'm sorry. I don't really know you or what you're talking about."

"That's not important right now. I found the money bag on the trail and Deputy Cobb won't allow it out of his sight. I'm saying that if you want that money back any time soon, you'd better come with me right now."

Silently panicking, Howard replied, "I'm sure Deputy Cobb will inform me as soon as possible if the money bag has been returned as you claim."

Stringer's expression darkened. "Look, there is a hysterical, *innocent* young woman in the sheriff's office who is waiting for you to verify that all the money is in that money bag so the deputy will let her out of the cell he put her in."

"An innocent young woman ... you mean the red-haired bank robber?"

Stringer advanced a step closer and growled, "It's to your advantage to come to the sheriff's office with me now, Mr. Larson, but I'm warning you—if you don't come willingly, I'm prepared to *make* you come with me."

"Mr. Stringer . . ."

Stringer's hand moved toward his gun.

Smiling shakily, Howard turned toward the clerk nearby and said, "I'll be back shortly, Davis."

Howard left the bank with his heart pounding.

"What do you mean some of the money is missing?"

Incredulous, Trace stared at Howard Larson as Larson replied, "J . . . just what I said. The amount that the tellers calculated they had in their drawers is in there, but most of the money from the vault is missing. *Thousands* of dollars. . . ."

"That's impossible."

Larson had just finished counting the money that was spread out on the sheriff's desk in front of them, and Trace shook his head incredulously. Thousands of dollars was missing? He glanced at the inner office door, uncertain if Meredith could hear their discussion. "I found the money bag where it had fallen from the bank robber's horse when he was making his getaway. It was almost hidden in the foliage. No one would have seen it if he weren't already looking for it. Besides, no one would have taken only part of the money and left the rest. There has to be another explanation."

Deputy Cobb snickered. "Looks like you ain't as smart as you think you are, Mr. Stringer. Looks like that pretty lady in there put one over on you. You say her partner was dead when you found him?"

Trace replied patiently, "He wasn't her partner."

"Well, she probably killed him and hid most of the money somewheres before she took off again—before you found her."

"Why would she do that?"

"Mr. Larson here says that thousands of dollars is missing." The deputy shrugged a bony shoulder. "A lady would be real happy with thousands of dollars to spend, especially if she could claim that the money bag was lost on the trail if somebody caught up with her. She probably figured she could claim that turning it in proved she was telling the truth. She probably figured that the bank would be so happy to get part of the money back, they'd let her go free."

"That doesn't make sense."

"It makes sense to me."

Trace frowned as he said, "Deputy . . . Mr. Larson . . . something is wrong here. Miss Moore's dress was on the floor in shreds when I entered the cabin where the bank robber attacked her. If she was his partner, she wouldn't have resisted his attentions."

"Maybe . . . maybe not."

Trace glared at the grinning deputy. It was obvious that Deputy Cobb was determined to be able to say he had at least one of the bank robbers in custody, and the truth be damned.

Turning toward the sweating Howard Larson, Trace said, "You're sure of the amount that was in your vault?"

"Of course I'm sure." Larson's expression grew rigid. "I'm a professional. It's my business to be sure how much money is in that vault at any given time. Deputy Cobb can check my books if he likes. It's all there in black and white." Drawing himself up to his full, portly height, Larson added, "I resent your implication that there could be any confusion on my part, Mr. Stringer."

"Don't take it personal, Mr. Larson," Deputy

Cobb commented. "I'm thinking that Stringer here has a special liking for redheads and maybe too much time on his hands. I figure he'll make himself believe anything she tells him if he thinks it'll make her more appreciative toward him. Me—I don't believe a single word of that innocent act she's putting on, even though I got to admit that the lady is real good-looking."

Trace did not bother to respond that he was a professional, too—a Pinkerton—and that he didn't allow personal feelings to influence his professional judgment. At least he wasn't supposed to. Somehow uncertain at the moment, he decided to play along. He shrugged. "Maybe you're right, Deputy. Miss Moore sure is a lot of woman. But, who knows, maybe when Sheriff Keller regains consciousness, he'll believe her, too."

The deputy frowned. "I don't know if I like the sound of that."

"Come on, Deputy," Trace chided. "If Sheriff Keller believes her and lets her go, you'll still get credit for being cautious about her while he was recuperating."

Deputy Cobb did not reply.

"What about the rest of the money?" Larson asked nervously. "My auditors are due here in a few weeks. They'll want to know what's being done about this. What am I supposed to tell them?"

The deputy responded, "I guess that'll be up to Sheriff Keller. He'll call in the Texas Rangers if I know him."

Larson gave a short, jerking nod. "The Texas Rangers . . . but what if Sheriff Keller doesn't regain consciousness?"

"Well, *I* ain't going to call in the Texas Rangers,

that's for sure!" Adamant, Deputy Cobb added tightly, "I know what they're like and I don't want them nosing around here without the sheriff on hand. Dealing with them ain't my job. I done my job by locking up that red-haired woman, and as far as I'm concerned, if her partner's dead, she can pay the price."

Trace unconsciously shook his head.

"What's the matter with you, Stringer?" The deputy's face flushed. "You got some objections to what I said?"

"No, I—"

"*Mr. Stringer . . .*"

Trace turned briefly toward the sound of Meredith's voice calling from her cell, and Deputy Cobb stated flatly, "If I was you, I'd forget how good-looking that woman in there is because she's going to stay right where she is. You done your part when you brought her back here. Sheriff Keller was well liked in this town, and there ain't nobody who's going to object to seeing that she stays behind bars until we're sure what way it's going to go for the sheriff." He muttered with a frown, "If he don't make it, she might be in real trouble, too, figuring how many hotheads there are in these parts—but I ain't going to worry about that now."

"What about my auditors?"

The deputy looked at the perspiring bank manager and shrugged again. "Tell them the truth—that Sheriff Keller will handle everything. If the sheriff don't make it, just tell them that the redheaded woman got away with some of the money and won't give it up, and they should be glad to get back as much as they did."

Larson nodded stiffly. "What about this money I just counted?"

"Just give me a receipt and take it. I don't want that much cash hanging around here anyways."

When Trace made no comment, Deputy Cobb turned toward him and said, "As for you, Stringer, my advice stands. That woman in there ain't going to do you no good nohow." Pausing, the deputy added, "Come to think of it, I don't rightly remember what you said you was doing in Winsome when you first came in here. Are you planning on staying long?"

"No longer than I need to." Carefully hedging his response, Trace continued. "I have to wait for that fella I was supposed to meet up with at the end of the week, and then I'll be heading out. I don't want to get mixed up in anything that might involve the Texas Rangers. They're not my favorite people. As far as that lady in there is concerned, she's on her own."

Tipping his hat, Trace turned abruptly toward the door. He was about to pull it open when he heard again, *"Mr. Stringer . . ."*

Momentarily tensing at the tremor of anxiety in Meredith's tone, Trace pulled the door open and closed it firmly behind him.

Chapter Three

"Tell me exactly what happened—exactly, do you hear me?"

Rita Larson stared at her husband with her dark eyes contemptuous. He had returned late from work at the bank. Their resources recently curtailed, she had been forced to fire her cook and she had made a halfhearted attempt to fill the void. She had prepared a roast for supper—a roast that had become spoiled as she had waited for her husband to return. One look at him as he appeared at the kitchen door in the darkening twilight, and she knew something was terribly wrong. He stood silent, unmoving, perspiring heavily, and his expression had been so anxious that he had appeared a sniveling caricature of the man she had believed him to be those many years ago.

Rita strove to maintain her composure as Howard's lips trembled. She had been so certain that she had married wisely. She had been young and beautiful, with so much to offer a man. She had not been attracted to Howard when she met him. Actually, she had considered him an uncommonly vapid fellow with little to recommend him as a suitor, until overhearing her brother marveling at Howard's expertise in accounting. He had a reputation as some kind of genius. She had then allowed Howard to enter the field of suitors for her hand. She had weighed his efforts carefully as he had lavished her with elaborate gifts and surprises. Finally convinced that he was mad about her and that he would provide her with the future she had always dreamed of, she had ignored her personal distaste for him and had accepted his proposal. She had then accompanied her new husband on his move west to the "land of opportunity" with a certainty that the world was her oyster.

She could never have been more wrong.

Howard had proved to be exactly what she had believed he was at their first meeting—a man who was common in every respect, and a man whose "expertise" would never be realized because he was totally lacking in *gumption*.

With one common job after another, with each failure followed by the next, she had become humiliated by the fact that she was Howard's wife. Had she not been embarrassed to reveal to her contemporaries how great a failure the man of her choice had become, she might have left him countless times.

But she hadn't.

Explaining his fiascos with excuses too lame for her to recall, Howard had showered her with gifts and glorious luxuries that had briefly soothed her. It was only when the situation became dire that Howard confessed to her that he had used his "expertise" to cover his theft of bank funds—a theft that an approaching audit was bound to unearth.

Rita's own image flashed briefly in the mirror as she turned, and her anger heightened. She had spent fifteen years with a husband who had disappointed her from the first day of their marriage, and those years had taken their toll. Her beauty and feminine appeal had disappeared, the glorious future for which she was destined had become no more than a youthful fantasy, and she appeared to be stuck for life with a mewling, overweight pretender who now shuddered with fear at the thought of telling her what was evidently the next episode in their march toward disaster.

Rita waited for Howard's reply. She glared at the perspiration visible on his balding head. She watched as he wiped away the glistening beads that dripped from his temples and lined his upper lip.

Her patience expired, she demanded, "Well?"

"I was afraid this would happen. I was afraid the bank robber and the money bag would be found and the missing funds in it would become evident."

"What are you talking about?"

Howard took a shaky breath. "A big fellow came to the bank and demanded that I accompany him back to the sheriff's office. He said he had found the money bag that had been stolen. He claimed that the red-haired woman had nothing to do with the robbery, that she was a victim, but that the bank robber had been killed and that she had come back with him to return the money and prove her innocence. He said the deputy didn't believe her and he had put her in a jail cell anyway."

"Who is this fellow?"

"His name is Trace Stringer. He seemed to believe everything the redheaded woman told him, and that the whole episode could be cleared up as soon as I counted the money and told the deputy that it was all there. I went with him because I didn't have any choice. He threatened me."

Rita urged again, "So?"

"So I counted the money, and I told them that thousands of dollars was missing."

"What was their reaction?"

"Mr. Stringer was stunned, but I really think Deputy Cobb was glad. He seemed to think that he had redeemed himself for losing the bank robber's trail by getting the red-haired woman into custody, even though the bank robber was supposedly dead and some of the money was still missing."

"And . . . and . . ."

"It's all going to fall down around us, Rita." Howard took a step toward her as he added meekly, "I should have known it would end this way, but I didn't want to lose you."

Disgust rampant in her gaze, Rita said, "Just tell me what the deputy decided to do!"

Howard responded in a quivering voice, "The deputy is going to keep the red-haired woman in custody until the sheriff regains consciousness. He said it's up to the sheriff to do what he thinks is best then. He said the sheriff will probably call in the Texas Rangers."

"No!"

"That's what he said." Perspiration streaming from his temples, Howard claimed in a desperate voice, "We're doomed!"

"We?" Rita advanced a threatening step as she repeated in a voice gradually accelerating in volume, "We? I had nothing to do with your thievery, yet my reputation will be ruined along with yours if this is found out. I will not allow that to happen, Howard. I will not allow people to talk about me and comment how far I have fallen."

"Rita . . ."

Resuming control of her emotions with sheer strength of will, Rita said more softly, "You said Deputy Cobb won't do anything until Sheriff Keller regains consciousness."

"That's right."

"But Doc Gibbs can't be sure that Sheriff Keller will recover."

"No."

Her patience almost expired, Rita prompted, "What does Deputy Cobb intend to do if Sheriff Keller doesn't recover?"

"He said he won't call in the Texas Rangers. He doesn't like them. I think they make him feel inept in some way. He said that Stringer and he had done their part by putting the red-headed woman in jail, and as far as he's concerned, she can pay for the robbery."

"Did you tell them that auditors were coming to the bank?"

"Yes, I did, but he said that didn't make any difference—they should just be glad to get back part of the money. Then he gave me the money bag and told me to take it back to the bank."

"So Sheriff Keller is the key. Deputy Cobb intends to hold the redheaded woman for trial, and if the sheriff doesn't survive, she'll pay the price and that'll be the end of it."

"*If* Sheriff Keller doesn't survive. Doc Gibbs

claims that although the sheriff isn't out of danger yet, he's improving every day. And *if* the auditors don't demand a more thorough investigation when they come, in which case the Texas Rangers—"

"If . . . if . . . if! There you go again, Howard! You're afraid of your own shadow!"

"No, Rita, I'm just realistic."

"Not realistic enough to have kept your hands off money that wasn't yours!"

"Rita . . ."

Pulling herself up rigidly erect, Rita demanded, "So what are you going to do about it all, Howard?"

"What am I going to do?"

"I won't run away! I won't become a fugitive for you."

"I wouldn't ask you to do that, Rita."

"You're telling me what you wouldn't do, Howard. What *will* you do to put this situation right? Everything hinges on Sheriff Keller's recuperation. What if he *doesn't* recuperate?"

Howard went still. "We've been through this already. I told you, Sheriff Keller's my friend."

"And I'm your wife! Tell me, Howard, which of us do you choose?"

"Neither. I won't choose either one! If Sheriff Keller survives and he starts an investigation that reveals my thefts, it . . . it'll be what I deserve."

"But not what *I* deserve, Howard."

"Rita . . ."

"When we were married, you vowed to protect and care for me—but you are not fulfilling your vows. The solution is simple. This whole fiasco will come to an end if Sheriff Keller doesn't survive."

"No."

"Yes."

"No!"

"Howard . . ."

His eyes wide, Howard said incredulously, "I will do anything for you, Rita—anything but that." He dismissed any further discussion by turning abruptly toward their room as he muttered, "Anything but that."

The bedroom door closed behind him, and Rita seethed as she stared hotly in its direction. Her gaze dark, she mumbled, "Fool . . . mewling coward."

She paused, and then added, "I'll do it myself!"

Meredith sat silently in her jail cell. She stared down at the oversized shirt she had pushed up to her elbows, at the ridiculously fitting men's pants rolled up to her ankles. If anyone had told her she would even be seen in garments like this, she would have told them they were insane. For that matter, if anyone had told her that she would be sitting in a jail cell as twilight darkened on a warm, Texas night she would have told them—

Meredith strained to retain control of her emotions. She had only been able to hear bits and pieces of the conversation that had progressed in the outer office earlier, but what she had heard had astounded her. Thousands of dollars was missing from the money bag? That couldn't be true. She had helped to fill that money bag from the vault herself. She had given it to the bank robber, and the weight was approximately the same as when they brought it back to the deputy. She couldn't believe that thousands of dollars was missing from the bag.

Something was terribly wrong. She had known

the moment she stepped into the sheriff's office, however, that it didn't matter to the deputy if the situation didn't make any sense as long as he could satisfy the townsfolk by saying he had her in custody.

Meredith looked around her at the barren, cracked walls of her cell as a bleak reality loomed. Twilight was darkening into night outside her cell window. The deputy had brought her a meager supper on a metal tray that was nicked and stained. When she refused to accept it, he placed it on the floor outside her cell with a few angry comments and left. In the time since, she had been allowed to visit the facilities outside to relieve herself—an embarrassment she would not easily forget—and she had been brought back to her cell, which was when her untouched, fly-ridden tray had finally been removed. The deputy had since gone home, leaving only an old fellow who was now snoring loudly, to watch the office. She was now alone in her cell with the prospect of a long night ahead of her, when she was supposed to sleep on a hard cot, with a threadbare coverlet her only shield against the darkness.

Meredith swallowed tightly. She was alone and the situation was out of control.

Strangely, everything seemed to have fallen apart the moment that Trace Stringer had deserted her. He shouldn't have, should he? He was a Pinkerton hired by her mother to bring her home. He'd had an obligation to see her through her present travails. Her acute sense of being forsaken went deeper than that. There had been something about him . . . the way he looked at her . . . his tone of voice . . . that had given her an instinctive feeling that despite everything he would keep her safe from any threat.

She had thought he believed what she told him about the robbery and that he'd help her sort it out. Instead, he had deserted her at the first sign of opposition—not unlike her own mother, who had abandoned her children when reality became too much for her to bear. She supposed she should have become immune to that kind of disappointment; but, contrarily, she was actually—

"Meredith, can you hear me?"

Meredith caught her breath at the sound of the male voice coming from the darkness beyond her barred window. Her heart jumped a beat when the voice sounded again.

"Meredith . . ."

Uncertain if her imagination was playing tricks, Meredith stood up on her cot and peered cautiously out the window. Her heart began thudding when she recognized the shadowed figure of Trace Stringer. Swallowing, determined not to reveal the emotion that the sound of his voice raised, she said, "Yes, I hear you." She then added in a voice totally lacking her former hauteur, "Get me out of here!"

"It isn't that easy." Trace moved into a shaft of moonlight that illuminated his sober expression as he whispered, "Something is going on here that I don't understand yet."

Meredith gasped, "Don't tell me you expect me to stay in this . . . this *prison* until you figure things out. I'm innocent! I don't have the thousands of dollars that Mr. Larson claims is missing from the money bag, and I don't know who does."

"Calm down, Meredith. It won't do any good to lose control."

"Lose control?" Meredith strained to see Trace's

face. "I hate it in here! It's damp and dirty, and there are tiny scratching sounds in the darkness that I won't allow myself to identify. I didn't come to Texas to be confined in this cell. I came here with a greater purpose in mind—which I can't accomplish in here." She paused, and struggled to keep her emotion under control. "Please . . . please get me out of here."

The desperation in Meredith's voice tore at Trace as he stood below the cell window in silence. He could barely make out her face where she peered at him from the shadows. Still, the desire to force his way into the cell to hold her close and calm her fears was more powerful than any emotion he had ever experienced.

Hardly aware that he had spontaneously slipped into the use of her first name, Trace knew only that the panic in her tone raised a need in him that he could not ignore. "Listen to me, Meredith, I need a few days to look into things so I can find out exactly what's going on here. Meanwhile, you're safe in there."

"Tell them who you are . . . that you're a Pinkerton," Meredith insisted. "That name commands respect in some quarters."

"Tell them so I can then explain why I'm here—that you're a runaway, and your mother hired the Pinkerton Agency to find you and take you back north if possible? Do you really think that will inspire the locals' confidence in you? Besides, knowing that I'm a Pinkerton will only complicate matters and put the deputy on his guard against me. I don't want that."

"I don't want to stay in here, either!"

The need to be closer to her, to touch and reassure her was almost more than he could bear. Trace searched the shadows with his gaze. Seeing a large rock a distance away, he rolled it underneath the window and then stood on it. Meredith drew back spontaneously when his head appeared opposite hers outside the elevated cell window. A few words from him brought her closer to the bars as she pleaded, "Please get me out of here."

"Look at me, Meredith." Despite the bars between them, they were so close that Trace could feel the brush of her breath against his lips as he whispered, "Do you believe me when I say I'll get you out of that cell?"

Meredith's scrutinizing gaze was almost palpable in the darkness. He felt its heat . . . its urgency. The knot inside him tightened in the few moments before she replied, "Yes, I believe you."

"Then try to be patient a little longer." He added hoarsely, "I don't want to see you in that cell any more than you want to be there."

Trace saw Meredith's lips tremble as she struggled to retain control of her emotions. His gaze touched them with a driving hunger as she whispered, "How long do you think it will be?"

"A few days, no more."

"I don't know if I can stand it here that long."

"I won't leave you here. I promise you that."

Momentarily silent, Meredith whispered, "I don't believe in promises."

"You can believe in mine."

Meredith briefly closed her eyes. She nodded her assent despite her obvious reservations, and Trace's throat tightened. He whispered, "Try to sleep now. I'll straighten this whole thing out as quickly as I can." He added with a frown, "But as far as anyone else knows, I've washed my hands of you and I'm just waiting for the fellow I'm supposed to meet in Winsome at the end of the week."

Meredith could not seem to reply and Trace heard himself add in a tone that he hardly recognized as his own, "I won't let them hurt you in any way, Meredith. You believe me, don't you?"

"Yes."

Meredith's reply was a rasping whisper that touched Trace's heart. He reached through the bars to stroke the soft contour of her cheek. She touched his hand, and a jolt of need shuddered through him.

The silence between them almost tangible, Trace could do no more than nod a good-bye. Stepping down off the rock, he rolled it back to its original position. He looked back for a last, fleeting glance at the small face barely visible at the cell window before slipping into the shadows.

Sounds of frivolity from Winsome's only saloon echoed on the stillness, drowning out the sound of Rita's footsteps as she moved slowly through the backyards of the few houses that lined the lower portion of the main street. A full moon relieved the shadows, allowing her to make her way without being seen as she glanced around her. She tripped over a discarded can and stopped momentarily, her heart pounding at the thought that someone might have heard her. When there was no reaction to the sound, she continued on.

Rita's features drew into a frown as she recalled

Howard's reaction to their conversation a few hours earlier. Coward that he was, he had delivered the message of their doom, and had then retired to their bed without supper. He had fallen into a deep sleep as if he hadn't a care in the world, while she had wrestled with her anger.

Sheriff Keller is my friend, Rita.
I'll do anything for you—anything except that.

He was still sleeping soundly when she made her final decision. If her husband wasn't man enough to secure their future, she had no choice but to take over that responsibility—and there was now only one way to do it.

Just a few more yards and she would be there.

Rita came up behind Doc Gibbs' house at last. The town's only doctor had a well-established routine that allowed everyone in town to know his whereabouts at any given time. That fact served her well. Doc Gibbs never left his office to visit a patient without informing Hilda at the mercantile where he was going—just as he never let a night pass without walking across the street from his house to the Last Chance Saloon for twenty minutes of nightly fortification before going to sleep.

It was common knowledge in town that Doc Gibbs went to great lengths to maintain his routine. If past performance were any indication of his behavior, he would check on Sheriff Keller and make sure his patient was comfortable in the front room of his house that he used as a hospital. At nine o'clock, he would then walk across the street to the Last Chance, making sure to return promptly to check on his patient before going to bed.

Rita looked down at her expensive pendant watch

as she stood in the shadows behind Doc Gibbs' house. The watch was another of the meaningless presents Howard had given her—but at least this one was useful. It was five minutes to nine. She would not have to wait long.

Standing silently in the darkness, Rita saw movement at the front door of Doc Gibbs' house the moment before he exited and started across the street toward the Last Chance Saloon. He was right on schedule. She had twenty minutes to accomplish her purpose. She could not waste time.

Doc Gibbs disappeared through the saloon's swinging doors as Rita pulled open the back door of his house. It was unlocked, as she knew it would be.

Rita walked quietly up the hallway and entered the room serving as Doc Gibbs' hospital. She was familiar with his house. She had spent considerable time there while visiting a female member of her church whom Doc Gibbs had operated on—a mission of mercy totally different from her present task.

Standing beside Sheriff Keller's bed minutes later, Rita looked down at the aging lawman. Still and unmoving, the sole occupant of the room, Sheriff Keller looked old and pale—almost colorless. She had heard he had lost a lot of blood and that his chances of survival were slim. It appeared to her that each breath might be his last. She hadn't expected the sheriff to look that bad. Yet Doc Gibbs had said the sheriff was improving, and the truth was that she couldn't afford to take the chance that he would.

In a moment of arrant rationalization, Rita told herself that Doc Gibbs was being overly optimistic, that Sheriff Keller was going to die anyway, and that she was actually doing the sheriff a service by saving him from further suffering.

She was performing an act of mercy. She smiled at the thought that this time was not so different from her former visit after all.

With that thought in mind, Rita moved closer to the bed and mumbled a few words of solace before taking the pillow out from underneath the sheriff's head and pressing it down firmly on his motionless face.

She felt a surge of panic when the sheriff's arms began flailing in feeble protest, and she forced the pillow down more tightly. Her breath came in deep, uneven gasps as she maintained the pressure until his struggles ceased. She was more disturbed than she cared to acknowledge when he was still at last. She made certain he was no longer breathing before she then slid the pillow back under his head, re-arranged his coverlet, and repositioned him carefully with trembling hands.

Stepping back, Rita looked at Sheriff Keller a moment longer. The need for force had shaken her.

Rita's lips ticked. She would never forgive Howard for that.

Leaving the house unseen, Rita made her way back through the backyard shadows and arrived at her house a few minutes later. She breathed a relieved breath when she entered her kitchen at last. She had accomplished her purpose. The threat had been handled. She did not expect any further problem.

Rita undressed in the shadows of her room and climbed into bed beside her sleeping husband. She took a stabilizing breath as she closed her eyes to sleep, secure in the knowledge that he hadn't even realized she was gone.

* * *

Still standing on the cell cot, Meredith stared at the spot where Trace had slipped into the shadows outside her cell window. She had been somehow unable to move after he disappeared from sight, and the magnitude of the situation had loomed more darkly.

She was alone and helpless again.

Finally climbing down, Meredith lay back against the cot and pulled the threadbare coverlet up over her.

I'll get you out of there. I promise. Try to sleep.

Meredith remembered the sound of Trace's voice. It was deep and vibrant. It had rung with a determination and conviction in direct contrast with her own desperation. Strangely, at the touch of his hand on her cheek—that brief caress—she had believed him completely.

Now, however, removed from the emotion of the moment, she did not understand why she had believed him. With the exception of her sisters, no one had ever kept a promise to her. Her mother had been too busy, and her teachers had considered a promise merely a means to an end. What had made her believe Trace Stringer was different?

With that question somehow too difficult for her to answer, desperation surged anew as she struggled to empty her mind of thought. She needed to sleep. It was her only escape from the fears haunting her.

Her mind drifted.

Suddenly realizing that she had dozed, Meredith snapped awake again with a start. Uncertain what had brought her back to full wakefulness, she then heard a lingering wolf's howl. She stared into the darkness of her cell, where she saw a silver-haired image gradually growing clearer before her eyes. His long hair lay against the aged, narrow line of his bared shoulders, and his small, penetrating eyes looked at her from a deeply wizened face baked by the sun.

Grandfather!

A sob escaped Meredith's throat as he spoke softly in a reassuring tone. His words resounded clearly in her mind.

Trust, Meredith.

Believe.

Do not allow your fears to assume control.

Meredith whispered, "How can I make myself believe, Grandfather, when the person I believed in most always failed me?"

Trust . . . him.

"Grandfather . . ."

Trust him.

"Grandfather . . . !"

The image faded all too soon and Meredith caught her breath. She remained silent as the echo of a wolf's howl sounded, and then trailed into the stillness of the night.

Chapter Four

"What do you mean, the sheriff's dead?" Trace went still. He looked up at Sally Weiss as the middle-aged waitress placed his breakfast platter on the table in front of him. Short and stout with graying hair and a face that bore the marks of a difficult life, Sally had the distinction in town of being a person who could be depended upon to convey the news of the day quickly and with a minimum of inaccuracy.

Taking that distinction seriously, Sally leaned closer as she continued. "That's what John Slaughter from the undertaker's parlor said when he came in this morning. He said that Doc Gibbs found the sheriff dead when he returned from his nightly visit to the Last Chance. He said Doc Gibbs felt real bad about it, too. It seems that Sheriff Keller had opened his eyes a few times before that. He seemed to be getting stronger, and Doc thought he was on his way to recuperating."

Trace was momentarily speechless. "What happened?"

"Doc said there was no sign that the sheriff struggled for breath or anything like that, so he figured that Sheriff Keller just died in his sleep from complications of his wound. I got to say that makes the townsfolk look at the red-haired woman that the deputy is holding in jail a little differently. She ain't just a bank robber now. She's a murderer."

"I thought the fellow who robbed the bank was the only one who had a gun."

"Yeah . . . well, that fella ain't around no more to pay the price. You're the one who said he was dead, ain't you?"

"He was dead when I found him. I buried him. I figured it wasn't right to leave him out there for wild animals to finish the job, but the deputy can check on it if he wants to."

"If I know Deputy Cobb, he ain't about to go digging up no corpse, no matter how important it might be. He believes what you told him, anyway. He figures you wouldn't have been able to bring back that money bag if he was alive." Her gray brows knitting, the woman asked unexpectedly, "Whatever made you follow them bank robbers like you did, anyway?"

Trace shrugged. "I don't rightly know. I had time on my hands and I've done a lot of tracking. With everybody talking so much about that red-haired woman, I was curious. It isn't often that a fella gets to see a woman who looks like that."

"Yeah, well, curiosity killed the cat, you know."

"Don't worry about that." Trace gave a short laugh. "I washed my hands of her the moment Deputy Cobb put her in that cell."

"From what I hear, you're the one who put her in that cell."

Trace forced a smile. "Well, there may be some truth to that."

Sally drew back and stared at him more intently as she wiped her callused hands on the apron stretched around her bulging middle. "If you want my advice, you'll make sure you stay out of things from here on. Sheriff Keller was real popular in Winsome. Folks ain't going to take his dying lightly."

"What's that supposed to mean?"

"It means you should listen to what I said if you want to leave this town without any problem when that friend of yours finally gets here."

"You're saying the red-haired woman might be in for some trouble from the local folks here?"

Sally shrugged offhandedly. "We've got a lot of hotheads in this town who would want to serve on any jury that might be formed for her trial . . . if she makes it that far."

Trace replied just as offhandedly, "I'm glad to be out of it, then."

"Well, you ain't exactly out of it. There's some who think your bringing that redhead back here sounds a little strange . . . especially with some of the money still missing."

A call from a nearby table turned Sally away with the final warning, "You'd be smart to listen to what I said."

Frowning, Trace turned his attention back to the breakfast in front of him and picked up his fork. His appetite had disappeared with the thought that this assignment and the lovely Meredith Moore were far more complicated than he had ever thought either of them would be. Sighing, he forced himself to eat. He had the feeling it was going to be a long day.

* * *

"Eat up, *darlin'*. You never know when a meal might be your last."

Meredith looked at Deputy Cobb as he delivered her breakfast with that message and an irritating smile. The thin, smarmy fellow had arrived at her cell door with the same stained tray in hand as the previous night, this time bearing a plate of sorry-looking eggs and two slices of old bread. His glances were becoming increasingly heated when he looked her way, and revulsion swelled inside her.

Refusing to accept his offering, Meredith waited until he placed it within her reach on the floor before she said, "Don't call me *darlin'*. My name is Miss Moore. And I want to know if there's a lawyer in this town that I can hire to speak up for me."

Obviously annoyed by her tone, the deputy replied tartly, "There ain't nobody in this town who'll take on that job, lady, especially now."

"What do you mean, 'especially now'?"

"I mean now that Sheriff Keller is dead."

Meredith gasped. "The sheriff died?"

"That's what I said."

Meredith went still. She had heard the wolf's howl the previous night. She should have realized that Grandfather's visit wasn't just coincidental. She should have known—

"What's the matter *darlin'*?"

Her face flaming at the deputy's obvious determination to demonstrate that he had the upper hand, Meredith asked bluntly, "What happens now, then? Who will handle the investigation from here on?"

"What investigation?"

"To find the money that was missing, to find out how it could be missing in the first place!"

"Oh, we all know what happened to that money. You got it hidden somewheres."

"That doesn't make sense, and you know it."

"Sense or not, that's what everybody's thinking."

"That's crazy!"

"You'll go to trial for what you done, that's for sure now, and if you're lucky you'll get to serve your time."

"What do you mean, if I'm lucky?"

"Meaning, I ain't the kind of fella who'll go against the wishes of the town if they want it otherwise."

Meredith gasped. "You . . . you couldn't be talking about the townsfolk taking their own justice. This is 1882. Nobody does that anymore, and nobody would be stupid enough to take vengeance on a woman."

"Yeah, well, I can't say the townsfolk especially like you."

"No one here even knows me!"

The deputy inched closer to the bars between them as he said, "*Darlin'*, a woman who looks like you do, especially with them high-class clothes you was wearing, and who talks like you do with that way of looking down her nose at folks around here . . . well, she starts people talking about her the minute she walks down the street."

Meredith's eyes widened. "Do you realize what you're saying? You're saying I'm being prejudged to be guilty."

"I'm not saying nothing that ain't true." The deputy inched even closer as his voice dropped to a suggestive whisper. "So, if I was you, I'd take my pleasures wherever it might do me the most good,

because your future don't look too bright from
where I stand."

Allowing a few moments for the full weight of his
statement to register, Meredith said softly, "And
you're figuring *you* could do me the most good right
now, is that right?"

"Maybe."

Meredith sneered. "You are a bastard, aren't you,
Deputy Cobb?"

The deputy's smile faded as he responded, "Did
you ever think that it ain't too wise to talk like that to
the fella who has your life in his hands?"

"Get out."

"What did you say?"

Her voice gaining in volume despite her inner
trembling, Meredith said, "Get out, you poor excuse
for a law officer! It's no wonder you don't want the
Texas Rangers to come in here. They'd strip that
badge off your shirt in a flash!"

"Well, you don't have to worry about that!" Deputy
Cobb's narrow face reddened. "There ain't no way I'm
going to let the Texas Rangers stick their noses into
this situation. As far as I'm concerned, I found the person responsible for robbing that bank, and that's
you—and you're the one who's going to pay for it."

"Even if I'm not guilty?"

"Lady, it don't make no difference to me as long as
it's no skin off my nose."

Stunned and incredulous, Meredith could only
watch as Deputy Cobb walked away, pulling the office door closed with a jarring snap behind him.

Trace walked slowly toward Winsome's livery stable, his stride casual. His ultimate goal was to make

sure that his horse and the mount that Meredith had ridden into town were being tended to, but the long walk from one end of the town to the other gave him the chance to judge for himself the reaction of the townsfolk to the news of Sheriff Keller's death.

A few minutes on the street and the reaction was obvious.

It didn't look good.

His first stop had been at the mercantile where Willard, the prematurely balding proprietor, stood behind the counter conducting a hearty argument with a red-faced, heavily armed fellow. They were debating the merits of wasting the town's money on a trial for the sheriff's murderer. The fact that it was a woman being held for the crime did not seem to matter.

After making his purchases, Trace had listened to talk along the main street, and his concern at the malevolence of the town's reaction to the sheriff's death escalated. It seemed Sheriff Keller was a "town father" that everyone liked and respected— bad news for the person suspected of killing him.

He turned into the livery stable and paused when he realized conversations there also centered on the sheriff's demise—conversations that stopped when he entered. The glances he received lent more credence to Sally's warnings.

Taking only a moment to check on the horses, Trace walked back down the street, his objective Doc Gibbs' office. He entered it minutes later, noting that the doc appeared momentarily startled before he asked, "Can I help you, Mr. Stringer?"

"It looks like everybody in town knows who I am. I don't know whether that's good or bad."

Doc responded flatly, "It isn't good if you ask me."

Trace frowned at Doc Gibbs' outspoken response. He said without preamble, "I figure it's to my benefit to learn what happened to Sheriff Keller to make him die so unexpectedly."

"Like I said to everybody else who stopped here to ask, it looks to me like he just died in his sleep. There was no sign of last-minute struggling for breath or anything like that before he died. As a matter of fact, he looked real peaceful with the coverlet tucked so neatly around him like it was."

"Maybe somebody stopped by to see him while you were gone and fixed his coverlet for him."

"No, he didn't have any visitors. Joe, the bartender, was watching the front door for me."

"So you're saying—"

"I'm just saying I never saw a more peaceful-looking death. His arms were folded, and the coverlet was arranged so nice that he—"

Interrupted by the entrance of an excited young man who was breathing heavily, Doc looked at him and said, "What's wrong with you, Henry?"

"It's Mary's time, Doc!" The young, flushed fellow continued nervously. "You'd better hurry up, too. She's feeling the pain real bad now, and I figure it won't be too long before we get us that first baby we've been waiting for."

Doc Gibbs nodded. "That's the only good news I've had so far today. I'll be with you in a minute. I just need to get some things and then tell Hilda where I'm going."

"I already told Hilda, Doc. I stopped at the mercantile before I came here so we could go right on." He urged, "Come on. Mary's waiting for you."

Doc turned back to Trace as he threw a few items into his black bag. "I don't have much else to tell you, Mr. Stringer. Sheriff Keller's dead, and that's it. So if you don't have any other problems that I can help you with, I'll be leaving with this fellow now."

"Go ahead, Doc." Trace nodded. "First things first."

Trace accompanied the two fellows out the front door of Doc's house. He watched from the board sidewalk as they quickly mounted and rode off. He waited only until they rode out of sight before strolling casually back into Doc's house.

Trace paused, aware that the interruption couldn't have come at a better time. Doc hadn't said much and didn't seem to have much more to say, but Trace was struck by the fact that he had commented twice on the neat appearance of the scene when Sheriff Keller died.

His Pinkerton second sense nagging, Trace entered the front room that was obviously used for Doc's bedridden patients. The stripped bed in the corner gave silent witness to Sheriff Keller's former presence, and Trace frowned. Having found nothing to stir his suspicions minutes later, he walked slowly through the house. Sheriff Keller had died while Doc Gibbs was gone. He didn't have any visitors because the bartender was watching for them, which meant any approach that might have been made would have had to come from the back entrance to the house.

Emerging into the backyard a few minutes later, Trace studied the scene carefully. He saw nothing more than a cleared, unkempt portion of land that was no better or worse than those of the few houses nearby. The ground was dry and dusty, and marked with the footprints of boots frozen in time since the last rainfall, which had obviously been months previously. He was turning back toward the house when the morning sunlight glinted on an object in the grass at the rear of the yard.

Retrieving a woman's gold pendant watch from an overgrown spot moments later, Trace scrutinized it carefully. It was still sparkling and relatively free of dust. It obviously had not been lying there long. He had seen watches similar to it before, worn by society women in the city. He could not imagine that any woman in Winsome, Texas, would spend her hard-earned money on such an extravagant item.

Trace realized with a frown that had Meredith not been safely ensconced in jail the previous night, the watch would probably have been presumed to be hers. It would probably also have been the final proof of her guilt for both the bank robbery and for Sheriff Keller's death as far as the residents of the town were concerned.

But she had been in jail, and someone else had been in that backyard.

Trace shoved the pendant watch into his pocket and turned toward the street. He had some work to do.

Howard Larson paled as he sat at his desk in the bank office. He looked up at Jeff Fielding as the stern-face cowman said hotly, "That's right, the sheriff's dead, and as far as I'm concerned, that ain't tolerable. Sheriff Keller was a good man. If it wasn't for him, them rustlers who were hitting my ranch would've put an end to me, but he didn't quit until he got every last one of them." Fielding added with a darkening of his frown, "I can't say I think much of his deputy. It's my thought that the sheriff felt kinda sorry for Billy Cobb because his mama asked the sheriff to keep an eye on him before she died. I can't think of no other reason why Sheriff Keller would pin a badge on him, but that's something the townsfolk can take care of when this is all settled. Cobb's good enough to keep an eye on the bank robber in jail until the law can take care of the rest."

Ignoring Fielding's reference to the jailed woman, Howard asked haltingly, "Wh . . . who told you the sheriff died last night?"

"John Slaughter at the undertaker parlor had to get some things at the mercantile so he could fit the sheriff for a coffin. He told Willard Dread at the mercantile that Doc Gibbs was real upset about it."

"Doc Gibbs seemed to think that the sheriff was getting better."

"Well, it ain't the first time the doc was wrong." When Howard appeared too stunned to reply, Fielding said with a note of regret in his voice, "I'm right sorry I was the one to break the news to you, Howard."

"Oh . . . I would've found out sooner or later." Howard mumbled a few more words in parting before Fielding walked out the doorway. His gaze intent on the angry Texan, Howard saw two fellows engage him in a conversation that darkened the rancher's frown. Feelings were running high at the news of the sheriff's death. The sheriff had been a friend to many—including himself.

Standing up abruptly, Howard wiped his brow with his handkerchief. "I'll be back shortly, Gregory," he said to the teller. "I have an errand to run."

Leaving without waiting for a response, Howard

snatched up his hat from the nearby rack and headed for the door. He nodded absentmindedly to townsfolk in passing, his mind occupied with a rapidly expanding horror. He closed the kitchen door of his house behind him a few minutes later, took a steadying breath, and asked flatly when Rita entered the kitchen with a semismile, "Did you do it, Rita?"

"Do what?"

Howard looked at his formerly lovely wife. Middle-aged and matronly, she had lost all trace of the woman who had so enraptured him fifteen years earlier, but he had accepted that change. He had even blamed himself for her physical deterioration, but he did not blame himself for this.

Howard said emotionlessly, "Sheriff Keller is dead. Did you do it?"

"Sheriff Keller died?" Rita gasped, her plump hand snapping up to the bodice of her blue morning gown. "Howard . . . how could you ask me such a question?"

"Did you do it?"

"Howard, I'm shocked that you could think even for a moment that—"

"Answer my question!"

Rita blinked. She was obviously stunned at his unexpected tone of voice. "No, I did not cause Sheriff Keller's death. The idea is abhorrent to me."

Howard's round face twitched. He replied softly, "The idea wasn't so abhorrent to you last night. Last night you all but asked me to take care of it."

"That was last night. In the heat of the moment, I might have said something that led you to believe I considered Sheriff Keller a threat to our future, but after you went to bed, I thought things over. I knew that you were right. Besides, as you said, who would believe the word of a red-haired stranger over that of a well-respected banker like you? Certainly no one in Winsome would."

"I want the truth, Rita! I won't settle for less!"

"I'm telling you the truth! I had nothing to do with Sheriff Keller's death."

Howard replied slowly, "I'm relieved to hear you say that, Rita, because the truth is, if you *were* responsible, I would walk away from you and never look back."

"Howard . . . what a terrible thing to say!"

"I mean every word. I'm a thief, but I'm not a murderer. And I will not live with a murderer."

Rita took a halting breath before she said with a shaky smile, "Well, we won't have to worry about that, will we?" Her expression taking on a more sober tone, she added, "All we'll have to concern ourselves with right now will be attending funeral arrangements for poor Sheriff Keller." She added almost incidentally, "How did the sheriff die . . . of complications from his wounds?"

"Doc Gibbs said he died in his sleep."

"He had a peaceful death, then, at least."

Howard stared at his wife in silence. Her appearance was striking, if only because of the excellent taste of the understated but exceedingly expensive morning gown that she had ordered directly from New York. Only he knew the actual price he had paid for his wife's fashionable appearance.

But he would have paid any price to keep her . . . any price except one.

Howard turned back toward the door.

"Where are you going, Howard?" Rita took an uncertain step toward him. "You don't look well."

"I'm all right . . . now."

He opened the door as Rita asked, "Will you be coming back here for lunch?"

"I don't know."

"Howard . . ."

But Howard had already turned his back on her and was walking out the doorway.

Stunned, Rita looked at the kitchen door as it closed behind her husband. Her lips separated with surprise in the moment before she suddenly laughed aloud at the irony of the moment. She had waited so long for Howard to show the smallest sign of gumption. To see it so clearly reflected in his eyes now—and directed at her—was a touch of irony that she could not help but appreciate.

Her smile dropped away as suddenly as it had appeared. Rita sneered. Threaten her, would he? Pretend to be shocked, would he? Take the high road, would he? Force her to *lie* to him, when she had merely done what he should've done in order to set his misdeeds right?

Rita raised her chin. Perhaps it was time for her to return to New York, where she would be appreciated for her devotion to excellence. Perhaps it was time to shed the *mediocre* mantle that her *mediocre* husband had forced on her over the last fifteen, empty years. Perhaps it was time to start life anew while she still had a few good years ahead of her.

Yet . . . as a married woman, she could only return to her rightful place in society in one way.

A grieving widow was treated kindly.

A grieving widow was respected by all.

A grieving widow was accepted back into society whenever she was ready to assume its rigors.

Howard's image appeared before Rita's mind's eye, and she ground her teeth tightly shut. She need only wait until the present situation was settled before making her move. Sheriff Keller had died in his sleep. Howard was overweight and under such stress that no one would give a second thought to his own sudden demise in the same manner.

Rita took a deep, unencumbered breath. That was that, then! Having finally made a decision that she had unconsciously waited fifteen long, dreary years to make, she felt suddenly free.

The mercantile store was devoid of customers in the midafternoon lull. Trace had deliberately waited for the heat of the afternoon hours when traffic there would be at its slowest and the proprietor would be free to spend some time in conversation. He had taken the chance of showing the pendant watch he had picked up behind Doc Gibbs' house at several places in town. He had casually flashed it at the haberdashery when he had gone there for a change of clothing, at the pharmacist's shop where he had purchased some muscle liniment, and even at the saloon when he had visited to slake his thirst. His hope that someone might recognize it had been greeted with no more than suspicious glances and a few questions about "the redheaded woman being held in jail." Wary of any further reactions he might receive, he had strolled into the mercantile store on the pretext of filling a list of travel provisions that had raised the proprietor's brows.

"Planning on hitting the trail soon, Mr. Stringer?"

"My name's Trace." Presenting as friendly a demeanor as he could manage, Trace continued, "And the answer is yes, I'll be hitting the trail as soon as my partner gets here at the end of the week."

"That sounds like a good idea to me."

Alert to the proprietor's tone of voice, Trace asked, "Should I consider that a comment or sage advice?"

Glancing around him, the balding proprietor said in an intimate whisper, "If I was you, I'd consider it more in the line of advice." His small eyes intent on Trace's expression, Willard said, "Look . . . I've been living in Winsome for eighteen years, and I've made a place for myself here. It's a nice town, and I like it. What I don't like is what I've seen happening since Sheriff Keller died last night."

"What are you saying?"

"I'm saying that Deputy Cobb has been doing a lot of talking since the sheriff's demise. He's been working up the people in town, telling them how it's too late to get justice from the fellow who fired the shot during the bank robbery, but that the red-haired woman in jail is arrogant enough to believe that no one will touch her for her part in the robbery simply because she's a woman. He's been telling everybody that Sheriff Keller won't get justice if that red-haired woman comes to trial because once she's all dressed up and flashing them eyes at the jury, no one will convict her."

"And people are believing him?"

"That isn't the worst of it." Willard glanced around him again and said, "Deputy Cobb's been saying that he's thinking your bringing the red-haired woman back to town was a plan that you and

113

her worked out together. He's telling everybody that you probably killed her partner. He's saying she had probably already hid most of the money before you two got together, and that she decided to give back just enough to convince everybody that she had nothing to do with the robbery so you both could enjoy yourselves without the law following you later. Cobb said the only problem with her plan was that he saw through it all and stopped it dead. He said he figures the only reason you're still hanging around town is probably that only the red-haired woman knows where the rest of the money is."

Incredulous, Trace shook his head. "That's all a lie. Everything that Meredith Moore and I said when we came back is true. She didn't have anything to do with the robbery, the bank robber was killed by some kind of wild animal, and neither of us knows where the rest of the money is."

"I figure that's the truth. I figure you and she wouldn't have risked coming back to town if it wasn't—no matter what the deputy says."

Frowning, Trace said, "Are you the only fella in Winsome with common sense?"

"This is a nice town, Trace, but Deputy Cobb is feeling his oats now that he's the only fella wearing a badge, and he knows just what to say to get people fired up. What I'm saying is, I wouldn't wait until the end of the week to leave Winsome, if I was you. As far as Meredith Moore is concerned, she'll just have to take her chances."

His stomach tightened at the proprietor's sober gaze. "What about calling in the Texas Rangers?" Trace finally asked.

"Deputy Cobb doesn't want them here. He gave

instructions to the telegraph office not to let any messages get sent to the Texas Rangers without his permission. Besides, it would take them a few days to get here at the very least, and the way he's been talking around town, I'd say they'd probably get here too late to stop anything that might happen."

Trace commented, "I was wondering why townsfolk were looking at me strangely."

Ringing up his purchases with a frown, the proprietor said, "I'm sorry to say this, but the sooner you leave this town, the better it will probably be for you. I'll do my best to take care of things for Miss Moore . . . but I'm not making any promises."

His jaw tightening, Trace reached for his money pouch, then casually removed the pendant watch from his pocket and put it down on the counter as he counted out his coins.

Willard asked, "Where'd you get that watch?"

Trace smiled casually. "I found it near the pharmacist's shop. I don't know who dropped it, and nobody else in town seems to know, either."

"I can tell you whose watch it is. I was here when Howard Larson got it in the mail from New York. He ordered it for his wife. He gave it to her a few days ago. He's always doing things like that for her. He spends his last penny on her. I can't figure it, but I guess he knows her better than I do."

"What do you mean?"

Willard paused, and then said, "She's . . . well, I guess she just isn't my cup of tea, that's all." He concluded abruptly, "But that's her watch. I can vouch for that. There's no other woman in Winsome who would spend good money on a piece of jewelry like it."

Gathering up his bundles with one hand, Trace tipped his hat with the other. "Much obliged for the advice, Willard. I appreciate it."

Willard shrugged off Trace's gratitude when a matron entered the store and glanced at Trace darkly. Addressing her pleasantly, he said, "Nice day, isn't it, Mrs. Williams? What can I get for you?"

Taking the proprietor's hint, Trace scooped up the pendant watch and walked back out into the heat of the day.

Lunch and dinner delivered to Meredith's cell on the same spotted tray hadn't been any better than breakfast, and the heavy air of the small enclosure was beginning to become overwhelmingly humid as twilight darkened into night. Flies buzzed around the remains of her cup of chicken soup and the pieces of dry beef and gravy adhering to the plate. The only other noise was the sound of Deputy Cobb's snoring echoing from the outer office. The day spent in the cell had been endless and quietly terrifying as Meredith had attempted to sort out her confused thoughts.

Unable to bear the afternoon heat, she had pulled a strip off her coverlet and had tied her hair up from her neck. She had then unbuttoned her shirt as far as decency allowed, had folded the sleeves up to her shoulders, and had rolled the trousers up above her knees in the hope of allowing herself some sort of respite from the climbing temperature. Still, she didn't know how much more she could tolerate.

"Meredith . . ."

The familiar whisper raised Meredith's gaze to the barred window of her cell. She saw Trace looking down at her, and her heart leapt to a sudden pounding. He had come back, just as he said he would. One promise kept . . .

Taking only a moment to glance at the outer office to make sure the deputy was still snoring, Meredith stood up on her cot. She spoke softly, her lips only inches from his. "The deputy told me Sheriff Keller died. What's going to happen now?"

"Yes, the sheriff's dead. As for the rest of your question . . ." Meredith saw the way Trace scrutinized her face as he said more softly, "I waited until I knew the deputy was asleep. I needed to talk to you."

Meredith responded with unconcealed fervor, "I hate it here, Trace." Unaware that she had so easily slipped into the use of his given name, she continued earnestly. "Deputy Cobb is obnoxious, the food is terrible, and the hours are endless. How much longer do I have to stay?"

"Until tonight."

"Tonight!" Meredith gasped.

"It won't be safe for either of us to stay any longer."

"Safe . . . for *either* of us?"

Ignoring her question, Trace said, "What's the schedule here? Who takes over when the deputy goes home?"

"An old fellow named Sam Winston comes here after dark. He sleeps most of the time while he's here."

"That figures." He paused, scrutinizing her wordlessly for a few seconds before he said, "We'll wait for the changeover. It'll be dark then, and we'll get out of here with less trouble."

"You . . . you mean you're breaking me out of jail?" Meredith shook her head. "But the old man has a gun. There has to be a legal way to get me released."

"You can wait for the Texas Rangers to come if you

like, but Deputy Cobb is doing his best to see to it that nobody sends for them."

"I want to get out of here, but . . . but . . ."

"Look, Meredith, you're going to have to trust me. We can straighten things out with the law when you're free. In the meantime, I need to get you somewhere safe."

A lingering suspicion flickered across Meredith's mind. Compelled to voice it, she said stiffly, "I won't go back to New York with you, if that's how you think this is going to end up."

Momentarily silent, Trace asked quietly, "Do you really believe that's the reason I'm here right now?" When Meredith didn't reply, Trace said with a darkening of his brow, "Maybe you do. Maybe then I should just ask if you prefer to stay in this cell than to come with me."

"You know I don't! I don't belong here. I'm innocent of the charges that have been made against me, but I know I can't go back to New York with them hanging over my head." Her voice dropping in timbre, Meredith continued. "I just needed to tell you . . . to be truthful with you. I just wanted to make sure you knew that I won't go back to New York with you no matter how this all works out."

"Going back to New York with me isn't what I'm thinking about right now." Trace's lips tightened as he said, "Just tell me, yes or no. Do you want to get out of here tonight? Otherwise I'll leave without you."

"No, don't do that!"

"It's settled, then. We'll give the old man some time to get comfortable and then we'll make the break."

"But . . . you're not going to hurt him? He's a nice old man. He just—"

"Don't worry about it. It'll be all right. Trust me, Meredith."

Trust.

Trust . . . him.

Meredith swallowed as a haunting image briefly returned. Somehow unable to reply, she nodded her acquiescence.

Trace said, "All right, this is the plan. . . ."

Where was it? What could have happened to it?

A slow flush coloring her sharp features, Rita jerked open the drawer on her bedroom chest of drawers and ransacked the contents with shaking hands. She pulled open the next, and the next, and then slammed the last drawer shut with a curse. She had searched the entire house from top to bottom and she couldn't find it.

Rita's lips jerked nervously. She remembered the last time she had seen that damned pendant watch. She had checked the time when she was in Doc Gibbs' yard and she hadn't seen it since.

The implications of that thought set her to trembling.

It was all Howard's fault! He had bought her that extravagant timepiece. He had sent to New York for it, making it one-of-a-kind in this backwater town. If anyone found it in Doc Gibbs' yard, there would be no doubt whose it was.

Rita struggled to control her rioting emotions. No, she could not afford to panic. She would not accomplish anything that way.

Rita took a deep breath. She forced herself to breathe deeply again and again. Her shuddering finally under control, she then reasoned that no one could have found the watch or there would be talk in town about it. Surely Howard would have been one of the first to hear about it, and fool that he was, he would have come running to her for an explanation.

As if she would tell him the truth. . . .

Maintaining control with sheer strength of will, Rita reasoned that the solution to her problem was simple. She would go to Doc Gibbs' house the following day, would make an excuse to go into the backyard, and she would search for her watch. If it was not there, she didn't give a damn where else it might be. If it was, she would simply slip it into her pocket and walk away.

Yes, the solution was simple.

No one had yet found the watch or made the connection to her.

She was sure of that.

Meredith waited impatiently as the night grew darker. Old Sam Winston had shown up shortly after Deputy Cobb had awakened from his snooze. It had been obvious when the deputy came in to check on her that he was raring to go for the night. She had noted a gleam in his eyes when he looked at her that had made a chill run down her spine, and she had rejected his insinuated advances with open disdain. She had also heard the promise in his voice when he whispered that she'd be sorry for acting like she was too good for him. Unable to do anything else, she had simply turned her back on him, and his grating curse had been accompanied by an aggressive step toward her cell that might have amounted to more had Old Sam not walked into the outer office at that moment. She had the feeling that if Trace didn't come as he had promised . . . if she were still there in the morning when the deputy returned, she might not be as lucky.

Meredith refused to consider that thought a moment longer. She listened to the sound of Sam's snoring as it reverberated in the small office. He had come in to say hello and to talk to her for a few minutes after arriving, and had then retired to the outer room. He had been sleeping ever since.

She liked Sam. The first time he took over for the night, he came in to introduce himself to her. He then waited until she introduced herself as well. She remembered their brief conversation had been accompanied by his avid scrutiny, and that afterward he had asked in a softened tone if he could do anything to make her more comfortable. She remembered thinking at that moment that although the only resemblance between this robust, white-haired Texan and her Grandfather's image was their age, something about him raised thoughts of a deeper similarity. It had occurred to her that although it might be wishful thinking on her part, she had the feeling that Sam believed her claims of innocence, but that he considered the time he spent guarding her as a trust he would not violate.

In any case, he had proved to be a dear old man who had checked on her comfort several times during the night. Yet however sincere he was in his concern, the thought of spending another day so confined was almost more than she could bear.

Meredith glanced again at her cell window. Trace should arrive soon. If he didn't . . .

The sudden appearance of Trace's face in the opening set Meredith's heart to pounding. Nodding, she waited a few minutes, and then moaned loudly. Sam's snoring continued. Meredith moaned more loudly, but the sound of Sam's even, rasping breaths continued unabated. She called out, her voice reflecting her anxiety. "Sam, please come in here. I don't feel well."

Sam's snoring halted with a few, gulping snorts.

She called out again, "Sam, please, I don't feel well."

The inner office door opened just as Meredith lay down on her cot. She saw the quizzical expression on the old man's face, and the way his full, white mustache quivered as he said with concern, "What's wrong, miss? Got a stomachache?"

"It's more than that, Sam," she groaned as she clutched her side. "I have such pain."

"Maybe I should call Doc Gibbs for you, miss." He shook his head. "I ain't taken care of a young lady since I married off my daughters more than ten years ago, and I—"

Meredith heard Sam gasp at the unexpected pressure of a gun to his back, simultaneous with the sound of Trace's voice as he said, "Don't move, Sam. I don't want to hurt you. I just want to get Meredith out of that cell, so do yourself a favor and do what I say."

"I ain't moving." Frowning, Sam looked back at the big man behind him and said, "To tell you the truth, I figure it's about time somebody did something about getting this young lady out of here. I've been around long enough to know a killer when I see one, and she ain't it. If it wasn't for that oath I took when I accepted this job from Sheriff Keller, I'd probably be standing in your spot right now."

"Step aside, then."

"You won't get no objection from me."

The old man stepped aside as Trace snatched the

keys from a hook on the wall, his gun held firmly as he unlocked Meredith's cell. He maneuvered Meredith behind him before he spoke again. "I'm going to tie you up so we can get out of here without a problem."

"I figured that." The old man held out his hands. "Get to it, then."

Trace's mouth twitched with what appeared to be amusement as he thrust the gun into Meredith's hands. "Hold this gun on him." He tied Sam's wrists obligingly, but Meredith was not amused by the unexpected weight of the revolver in her hand. "Don't tie him too tight."

Trace slanted Meredith a warning glance that briefly silenced her. She watched as he sat the old man on a nearby chair and tied his ankles as well. Unable to restrain herself, she said, "I'm sorry, Sam. You're not too uncomfortable, are you?"

"I'm fine, miss."

"Are you finished conversing?" Trace glared at Meredith as he paused with a gag in his hand. "I don't want to interrupt you."

Trace tied the gag around the old man's mouth and said to him, "You should be all right there until morning." Then taking back his gun with one hand and Meredith's arm with the other, he said flatly, "Let's get out of here."

Trace boosted Meredith up onto one of the horses he had secreted in a nearby alleyway. He mounted as well, and then nudged his horse forward onto a street where revelers from the saloon pursued the night's pleasure loudly, ignoring their progress as they maneuvered their way cautiously through the shadows. Finally on the road out of town, Trace nudged his mount to a faster pace, and then glanced again at Meredith as she did the same. In that split second of scrutiny as the silver moonlight lit their way, he noted that Meredith's expression was tight and uncertain. He remembered glancing down from the window into her stuffy, airless cell before their escape. She had rolled up the sleeves of his oversized shirt and had rolled the pants up to her knees. Her strange appearance only served to accent the unconsciously graceful movement of her arms as she lifted a shock of fiery hair from her neck for a moment's relief from the heat, and the long, slender length of her legs as she turned to pace the small cell. Her shirt clung to the womanly curves of her bosom, and as he had watched, a single drop of perspiration had trailed down between the firm, feminine mounds. Yet her expression—tense, desperate, vulnerable in a way she struggled to hide—had been even more devastating. It had torn at his heart. Her vulnerability remained, despite her stringent attempt to conceal it. He suddenly wished she truly believed he would protect her . . . that he would take care of her . . . that he would get her away from a town where her safety was in jeopardy because of an incident beyond her control, and that he would not allow anything to happen to her because . . . because . . .

Aware that his own feelings had begun exceeding the demands of his profession . . . that this puzzling woman had touched him in ways none other had, Trace frowned and kicked his mount to a faster pace. He needed to remember that Meredith was still the rich, spoiled, runaway daughter of a wealthy mother, and that despite everything that had happened since she had stepped down onto Texas soil, despite her temporary dependence on him, that fact had not changed. Yes, the sooner he completed this assignment, the better.

As for Deputy Cobb—it wasn't over yet. Cobb wouldn't be able to let Meredith escape him again. The only thing Cobb didn't realize was that Trace was just as determined as he.

After riding for an endless time, Trace pulled his mount to a halt when they emerged on a hidden path lit by silver moonlight. He turned as Meredith reined up beside him and scrutinized her in silence. Her face was pale. She was unaccustomed to such rough rides, and she was obviously exhausted.

He asked, "Do you need to rest?"

Meredith glanced nervously behind them. "I'm fine. I can make it if you can."

Sure.

His brow furrowed, Trace stared at the beautiful, brave, *exhausted* woman. She was tired, but she'd die before she'd admit it.

Making a sudden decision, Trace reached over and grasped the reins of Meredith's horse. He pulled the animal closer, then scooped Meredith from her saddle without warning, and placed her astride his saddle in front of him. Startled, she looked up at him with amber eyes wide and questioning, to which he responded, "We have a ways to go yet, and I can't afford to have you falling off your horse."

Meredith protested, "I told you, I can make it if you can."

Ignoring her response, Trace attached her horse's reins to his saddle and said, "Just lean back and rest. We'll be there soon."

"I told you—"

"Just do it."

Trace kicked his mount into a sudden leap forward that did not allow Meredith time for further protest. At first rigid with protest, she eventually relaxed back against him. Dozing, she was unconscious of the way her warm breasts pressed against his arm where he wrapped it securely around her waist, and of the way her rounded buttocks warmed the purely male part of him that suffered the contact with emotions just short of torment. Her spontaneous bravery had touched a spot down deep inside him. Her enigmatic appeal was relentless, but it was the softer part of her personality that he had glimpsed so briefly that aroused a need in him so intense that he was somehow helpless against it.

Conversely adjusting her position so that she sat closer still, Trace knew that she needed him now . . . temporarily . . . but his mind was at war with the part of him that refused to accept that logic.

And his original questions lingered. Why was she so determined to dissociate herself from her mother? Why had she gone off on her own? What did she hope to accomplish by defying all the rules of safety and convention so thoughtlessly?

Meredith's head nodded against his chest and Trace looked down at her. Her fiery hair brushed his neck as she slept; her fragile profile was etched against the nighttime shadows; her thick brush of lashes rested against the magnificent contours of her cheek as her lips touched the column of his throat.

And the truth was . . . he wanted her desperately.

* * *

"We're here."

Meredith awakened abruptly at the sound of Trace's announcement. It was still night and the moon was still shining brightly, illuminating a landscape that was eerily clear.

Momentarily disoriented, Meredith looked around her. She saw a cabin standing in the middle of a vacant area of ground. Beside it was a corral with a broken gate, and a distance away stood a building that appeared to be a barn. The buildings looked deserted.

She asked uncertainly, "Where is here?"

Not bothering to respond, Trace dismounted and then lifted her down from the saddle to stand beside him.

"You didn't answer my question. Where are we?"

"Does it matter?"

"Of course it matters! A posse is probably forming to chase us right at this moment."

"They'll never find us here."

A chill ran down Meredith spine. She had heard those words before, and she said sharply, "I want to know where we are." When Trace turned and began walking toward the cabin with his bedroll under his arm, she called after him, "Trace . . ."

"Come on, I'm tired." Turning back toward her, Trace said, "It's late, we've been traveling for hours over rough trails that a bumpkin like Deputy Cobb wouldn't be able to track us on in a million years. I need a few hours of sleep. We can talk later."

Meredith reluctantly followed him, aware that she was as tired as he. She halted just inside the cabin as Trace lit a lamp on the table. The cabin was starkly furnished in a common manner with a table and two chairs, a cot in the corner of the room, a dry sink with a pump all too similar to the faulty one she had seen only a few days previously, and a fireplace over which an iron pot hung. Yet the cabin was free of debris. She questioned, "Whose place is this?"

"Nobody's. This ranch is for sale, which is why it's relatively clean."

Meredith frowned. "Who would buy a place like this?"

Momentarily silent, Trace responded, "Somebody like me." He continued with a frown. "I ran into this place when I rode through the area a while back. Right now it's deserted and a good place for us to catch our breaths and decide where we go from here."

"A place for us to catch our breaths . . . which means we're both fugitives from the law now." Meredith's eyes filled with tears. They searched his as she whispered unexpectedly, "How did all this happen, Trace?"

There it was again, that tone to her voice . . . that appeal that tore at his innards. Without the protective mask of arrogance that she wore so convincingly, Meredith was young, honest, and totally defenseless against her situation.

His anger dispelling, Trace hugged Meredith briefly as he whispered, "I wish I had the answer, but we're both tired right now and we need sleep. We can face that question tomorrow."

Meredith felt unexpectedly at a loss when Trace released her. She turned to glance at the cot in the corner.

Trace responded to her glance, "I'll put my bedroll on the floor. You can take the cot."

"No. That isn't fair. I slept part of the way. You're more tired than I am."

"I'm also more accustomed to sleeping where I can."

Meredith shook her head. "No, we can both sleep on the cot. It's large enough, and we're adults."

Trace looked at her.

Meredith could feel her face suddenly flaming. "Don't look at me like that. Are you tired or not?" When he did not respond, she said, "Well, I'm tired, and I'm going to sleep on the cot. If you're afraid what people will say if they find out you slept there, too . . . well, that's your decision."

"It's not my reputation that would suffer, you know."

"You don't have to worry about that. I stopped caring what people think or say about me a long time ago." She shrugged. "Do what you want."

Climbing onto the cot without another word, Meredith kicked off her shoes and turned toward the wall. She felt the cot sag with Trace's weight moments later, and her heart pounded. She felt his warmth as he lay beside her and stretched his bedroll over them. His masculine scent filled her nostrils, and she breathed deeply of it. She remembered the strength of his arms as he had held her, and a tremor ran down her spine. She recalled the gentleness in his voice when he had spoken to her, and she ached to hear it again.

Meredith closed her eyes. They were adults and she needed to act like one. They could both handle the situation and she—

The sudden howl of a wolf penetrated the eerie stillness, and Meredith went rigid.

"What's wrong, Meredith?"

Trembling with fear as the howl sounded again, Meredith snapped back toward Trace where he lay beside her. His light eyes searched hers in the semi-light. She depended on him. No . . . she *cared* about him. The howling had always been a warning, but she couldn't lose him.

The howling sounded again, and Meredith closed her eyes. This couldn't be happening. She couldn't be hearing the howling now, not when she had finally found someone she could believe in.

Trace gripped her arms and repeated more urgently, "What's wrong?"

His hands were warm but his touch was unyielding. Meredith shivered as he demanded, "Talk to me. What's scaring you?"

Meredith rasped, "Did you hear that?"

"Did I hear what?"

"That wolf howling."

He hesitated. "Sure . . . I heard it."

Meredith blinked. "Wh . . . what? You heard it?"

Trace frowned. "You're in the Wild West now, Meredith. Wolves howl at the moon all the time out here. This may be the first, but it won't be the last time you'll hear them."

"Oh . . ." Struggling to smile at the sheer unexpectedness of his response, Meredith let out a ragged breath that emerged as a sob.

"Were you afraid? Is that it?" Trace's callused hand brushed her cheek. "You don't have to be afraid of anything when I'm here with you, Meredith. You know that, don't you?"

Meredith could not reply, and he whispered, "I asked you to trust me a while ago. I told you everything would be all right. I meant what I said and I still do. I promised I'd take care of you, and I keep my promises."

Trust . . . him.

Somehow still unwilling to accept his promise at face value, Meredith felt forced to repeat, "I have to be sure you understand, Trace. I have to be sure you believe me when I say I won't go back to New York with you, no matter how all this turns out . . . not now, not ever."

Trace's hand froze on her cheek.

She said again, "I need to be sure, Trace."

"All right. I understand."

It seemed somehow natural that Trace slid his arm around her and drew her against the crook of his shoulder—just as natural as the sweet taste of his breath as he whispered against her cheek, "Close your eyes and go to sleep, and don't be afraid. I won't let anything hurt you."

Meredith closed her eyes to the sound of Trace's whispered reassurance.

She had never felt safer.

She had never felt . . . less alone.

Letty awoke with a start as she lay in the darkness of her luxurious New York apartment. Alone in the nighttime stillness, she sat up in her bed and glanced around her. A great silver moon cast shadows that danced against the walls as her sheer curtains billowed in the night breeze. Everything was so quiet, but—

Letty's heart leapt to a sudden pounding as the eerie howling that had awakened her sounded again. She clamped her hands over her ears, ignoring the tears that sprang to her eyes as the sound reverberated on the silence.

No, she would not listen. She would not!

Through the watery haze of tears, she saw a familiar image materialize slowly before her. His gray hair lying in wild strands against his bared shoulders, his thin, wizened body erect, he looked at her intently with his penetrating gaze.

She called out to Grandfather, imploring him to stop the continuing howling. She begged him to speak to her. She beseeched him to explain why he was there, but he remained silent.

Gasping, she saw the image of a wolf running toward him in the distance. She tried to warn him, but her voice was suddenly frozen in her throat. Paralyzed with fear, she watched as the slavering animal neared dangerously close to Grandfather's resolute figure. Transfixed, she watched as the wolf reached his side, and then went suddenly still.

Grandfather's fingertips touched the wolf's head lightly, calming the animal. He then spoke a few words to her in his native tongue. Letty watched as Grandfather turned without warning and walked away, with the wolf a steadfast companion at his side.

Letty stared at them both until their images faded from her view. In the silence of her bedroom, the brief, enigmatic words Grandfather had uttered lingered in her mind.

He had said simply, *"It has begun."*

Chapter Five

"Who let you in here?"

Annoyed, Mason Little stood up behind his desk. He dismissed his clerk's frantic apology with a glance as he walked to the doorway and pushed the door closed behind Dobbs. He paused to scrutinize the fellow's unkempt appearance with a sneer and said tightly, "I hope no one saw you entering this office. Since you haven't bothered making any reports so far, I also hope you didn't come here expecting further payment from me for a service that I can't even be sure is being carried out."

Mason stood rigidly still in his elegantly furnished office as he waited for a reply. Trading on his relationship with his highly revered uncle, he had opened his law office a few years earlier. Wealthy clients, unaware that manipulation of the most devious type had allowed him to graduate from college and pass the bar, had flocked to its confines. In the time since, he had made it a practice to accept only affluent clients whose business would not interfere with his active social life—and whose affairs he could easily manipulate to his best advantage. He maintained his office simply and elegantly, with two clerks, William Sutter and Horace Lime. They were intimidated by him but well versed enough in the law to handle simple elements of his practice. They knew enough to turn their backs on his shadier practices, and they could be depended upon to be submissively diligent.

Keeping his raspy voice low enough not to be overheard by his hirelings in the outer office, Mason looked at Humphrey Dobbs and demanded sharply, "Damn you, answer me!"

"I wouldn't take that tone with me if I were you, Mr. Little." Dobbs smiled coldly. His oily, unwashed appearance seemed even more repugnant in the fashionable confines surrounding him. "As for your question, I didn't wait for anybody to let me into your office. I figure I've got as much right to be in here as any of your clients since I'm handling your dirty work for you." He pressed with unexpected sharpness, "Am I right or am I wrong?"

"I prefer that we keep our business between ourselves. In short, I don't want you here."

"That's too bad, ain't it?" Dobbs shrugged. "I wouldn't be here if you had kept your part of the bargain we made."

"What are you talking about? You're the one who didn't bother to meet me to make a report."

"I'm talking about the money you owe me and the fellas I sent out on the job you want them to do."

"I paid you!"

"No, you didn't. You gave me an *advance* that was supposed to be enough for me and for my fellas to travel wherever they had to go without a problem.

The only thing is, I got a telegram from one of my fellas this morning. It ain't as easy as you said it was going to be to follow them Pinkertons' trail. It's taking him longer than he expected and he needs more money."

"That's his problem."

"No, Mr. Little, it's yours, because if my fella has to come back home without being able to finish his job, you're going to pay him anyway."

"That isn't what we agreed upon."

"Ain't it?" Dobbs shrugged. "Maybe I forgot to mention that part of the deal."

"He's not going to get any more money from me!"

"Yes, he is."

"That's where you're wrong."

"No, I'm not." Dobbs' smile bared his yellowed teeth in a way that put Mason in mind of a rabid dog. It sent a chill down his spine as Dobbs continued, "I'm right because you don't have any alternative. Either my fella gets the money he needs, or Miss Letty gets a letter from an anonymous person telling her that you sent some fellas out to make sure her precious daughters don't get back alive."

Mason gasped. "You wouldn't do that!"

"Not if I get the money I want, I won't. You see . . ." Dobbs smiled, "My men are dedicated to their work. They're also looking forward to that big payday that's waiting at the end of the line, and they're working hard toward it."

"I told you what I expect."

"You expect my men to do their jobs. They expect to do it, too, but it's going to cost you more."

His chest beginning to heave with subdued anger, Mason said quietly, "How much more?"

"Double the advance you already gave will do."

"Double!"

Dobbs did not bother to reply.

Pausing, Mason asked, "When do you need it?"

"This afternoon. My fella doesn't like having money troubles when he's away from the city. I can wire a draft to a local bank and he can pick it up right off."

"As long as it is understood that I will subtract all advances from the final payment amount."

"That's fine with me. I ain't greedy."

"You may not be greedy, but you're not too smart, either!" Mason could not contain his mounting anger as he continued. "You made a mistake coming here. I'll bring you the money later this morning at the same place we met last time, but first—"

Dobbs' expression tightened as he snarled, "I ain't going to dicker with you about this."

Adamant, Mason continued. "But first, I want the reports that you've neglected to make so far. I need to know how your men are progressing on the jobs assigned to them."

"Some are progressing, and some ain't."

"Meaning?"

"One of my fellas is on the right trail. He should have the job handled pretty soon. The others will take care of things, too. It just might take a little longer."

"What do you mean by that?"

"I mean, my men do their jobs. Nothing stops them if they have what they need."

"All right, but I want to be kept apprised of the situations, do you understand? Send a messenger with your reports, and mark them personal. That will eliminate the need for you to come here. But remem-

YES! ☐

Sign me up for the **Historical Romance Book Club** and send my THREE FREE BOOKS! If I choose to stay in the club, I will pay only $13.50* each month, a savings of $6.47!

YES! ☐

Sign me up for the **Love Spell Book Club** and send my TWO FREE BOOKS! If I choose to stay in the club, I will pay only $8.50* each month, a savings of $5.48!

NAME: _____

ADDRESS: _____

_____

TELEPHONE: _____

E-MAIL: _____

☐ **I WANT TO PAY BY CREDIT CARD.**

☐  VISA   ☐ MasterCard   ☐ DISCOVER

ACCOUNT #: _____

EXPIRATION DATE: _____

SIGNATURE: _____

Send this card along with $2.00 shipping & handling for each club you wish to join, to:

**Romance Book Clubs
1 Mechanic Street
Norwalk, CT 06850-3431**

Or fax (must include credit card information!) to: 610.995.9274.
You can also sign up online at www.dorchesterpub.com.

*Plus $2.00 for shipping. Offer open to residents of the U.S. and Canada only.
Canadian residents please call 1.800.481.9191 for pricing information.
If under 18, a parent or guardian must sign. Terms, prices and conditions subject to change. Subscription subject to acceptance. Dorchester Publishing reserves the right to reject any order or cancel any subscription.

JOIN NOW!

ber, I want to know the minute each fellow finishes his job—the very minute!"

"You'll know as soon as I do."

"All right. It's settled, then. I'll take care of what you need after you leave, and I'll expect timely results." Frowning when Dobbs turned to leave, Mason repeated, "Don't come here again. And make sure you exit by the rear entrance of the building. I don't want anyone knowing you came to see me."

Dobbs' small eyes pinned Mason's as he said, "Your society friends might not like it, huh?"

"Just do what I said." Following Dobbs to the door, Mason said in a tone cultivated to be overheard by those in the outer office, "I'm sorry, sir. You'll have to find a lawyer from your side of town. Just wanting to sue a wealthy person doesn't make you suitable client material in this office."

Noting that his clerks frowned and avoided his eye as Dobbs made his exit, Mason said sharply, "Don't let that fellow in here again. He doesn't belong here."

Mason walked back into his office. He closed the door behind him and smiled. So, one of Letty's daughters would soon be taken care of. He didn't care which one of them it was. Any of them would do.

Dobbs smiled, pleased with himself as he headed for the back staircase of the *pretentious* building that housed Mason Little's *pretentious* office. It made no difference to him that he needed to exit unseen. He was actually more comfortable that way, and he had accomplished his purpose.

Dobbs withheld a chuckle. Little would get him the money that afternoon. He would then wire the draft immediately to his man, Elias Fink—and he would do it exactly as Fink had requested. Amused at Fink's cunning, he was only too happy to accommodate him. The clever fellow was covering his trail in the most ingenious way.

Yes, it seemed that Fink had thought of everything.

Deputy Cobb pulled the last of Sam Winston's bonds off his ankles. He watched as the older fellow drew himself stiffly to his feet near the small, empty cell where Meredith Moore had formerly been confined. Livid, he questioned incredulously, "How did you let this happen? You used to be Sheriff Keller's favorite deputy. You're supposed to know what you're doing. He trusted you, and I trusted you, too. Instead, you let the prisoner get away!"

"Well, all that trust didn't make me bulletproof, and that's what I would've had to be if I was going to ignore that gun in my back."

"Gun in your back . . ."

"That Stringer fella sneaked up behind me."

"How did he get behind you?"

"I didn't see him coming because I was more intent on what was ailing Miss Moore."

"Ailing her?"

Sam shrugged. "Whatever it was, it stopped the minute that Stringer fella showed up."

"And you just let them get away."

"I didn't have much choice."

The deputy stared at Sam contemptuously. "Well, that proves what I said anyways—that Meredith Moore and the Stringer fella were in this together."

"How do you figure that?"

"He wouldn't have broken her out of jail if they wasn't."

"I don't know. . . ." Sam shrugged his rounded shoulders and said, "You saw what that woman looks like. If I was twenty years younger, I might have tried anything so's she'd look at me the way she was looking at him."

"Real tight, were they?" Cobb sneered. "That proves my point."

Cobb turned to leave and Sam asked, "What are you going to do?"

Flushed with determination, Cobb turned back and said, "What do you think I'm going to do? I'm the law in this town now, and that's what I'm going to be until the town says otherwise, so I'm going to get me a posse and find them two. And when I do, the nearest tree—"

"Wait a minute!" Frowning, Sam protested, "Them two didn't do nothing that would cause you to talk like that!"

"Sheriff Keller might say otherwise."

"That woman didn't shoot Sheriff Keller!"

"She might as well have."

"We should get the Texas Rangers in here. They'll get to the bottom of things."

"Are you saying I ain't good enough to take care of things here?" When Sam did not respond, Cobb continued hotly. "I ain't calling in the Texas Rangers! This is my town now, and that's the way it's going to stay."

Sam took an involuntary backward step at the fervor of Cobb's reply. He said quietly, "You're making a mistake, Deputy."

"Maybe, but nobody's going to listen to you, old man, being's you're the one who let that woman get away."

Sam repeated, "You're making a mistake."

Dismissing Sam's comment with a sneer, Cobb walked away.

The sun peeked through the cracks in the window boards, sending its golden, morning rays down on the cot on which Trace and Meredith lay. Instantly awake, Trace touched the gun he had placed beside the cot. Relaxing when he determined there was no threat in the cabin, he looked down at Meredith where she lay curled up at his side. Her hair was a blaze of color against the dingy mattress. It contrasted sharply with her delicate coloring, especially where her pale cheek pressed against his bared shoulder. He acknowledged silently that although she was wearing disheveled men's clothing and looked nothing like the fashionably dressed city woman who had first come to Texas, she was still the most extravagantly lovely woman he had ever seen.

Trace's jaw tightened at the memory of the long, nighttime hours while Meredith had slept at his side. She had burrowed unconsciously closer to share his heat as the night cooled, and the fragrance of her hair had teased him; her sweet bodily scent had tormented him; and the occasional brush of her lips against the bared flesh of his chest was burned into his soul.

His heart began an accelerated pounding, forcing him to remind himself that Meredith Moore was now his responsibility, that she was totally alone in a foreign, threatening environment. She had struggled against depending on him, and he had asked her to trust him. With that trust came obligation. It was important to him that he did not allow emotion to interfere with that obligation.

The ache inside him expanded as he scrutinized

Meredith's sleeping countenance. Trace heard a voice in the back of his mind warn again that although Meredith lay so near, she was still far beyond his reach. The irony of the moment struck Trace forcefully. He recalled the young society women he had encountered in his assignments for Pinkerton who had made it known to him in ways that were not entirely subtle that his advances would be welcome. Despite their appeal, he had avoided them like the plague. He'd had too strong a sense of self to get involved with women when he knew he could only lose in the end. Yet although that reality had not changed, he had allowed Meredith Moore to get under his skin.

Common sense taunted that they would never have met if her wealthy mother hadn't hired the agency to find her. Yet that same common sense threatened to desert him when she lay so close beside him.

Suddenly conscious of the direction of his thoughts, Trace separated himself from Meredith's warmth and stood up beside the bed. He frowned darkly as he reached for the shirt he had shed the previous night and deliberately turned his back toward her. He silently cursed as he acknowledged a difficult but simple truth. He had wanted Meredith Moore from the first moment he saw her. Now that he had gotten to know her, he only wanted her more.

Meredith stirred. She reached out for the reassurance of the strong, male presence that had consoled her during the past night. She went rigid at the realization that Trace was not there.

Startled into wakefulness, Meredith looked up to see Trace standing with his back turned toward her as he reached for his shirt. Relief flushed hotly through her. A slow, unidentifiable fluttering gradually took its place as she scrutinized his turned back. His dark hair curled unfashionably at the back of his neck, yet it somehow tempted her touch. He was too tall, too muscular, and his shoulders were too broad to fit the stylish, city concept of the male physique, yet the smooth muscles rippling across his back were a symphony of movement unlike any she had ever seen. She found herself unable to withdraw her gaze as it slid down his tight rib cage to his narrow, male waist, flat hips, and the firm buttocks outlined in his trousers. She barely suppressed a protest when he slipped his arms into his shirt and pulled it closed in front, impeding her view.

Meredith recalled the moment the previous day when Trace recognized the exhaustion she had not allowed herself to voice. She remembered that a thrill had shot up her spine when he swept her from her mount with startling ease and placed her on his saddle in front of him. She recalled the moment when she finally leaned back to allow Trace to support her weight as their journey continued. In direct contrast to her previous experience with the malodorous bank robber, his scent was sweet and his arms were gentle in their strength. They became a refuge and comfort that stirred her in ways she was still unable to describe. She had felt the warmth of his breath against her hair. Her heartbeat had quickened at the occasional brush of his lips against her temple. She became acutely aware that with a subtle turn of her head, their lips might touch and she had chided herself for that thought—yet in a way, she now regretted the lost opportunity of that moment. She reminded herself that Trace's motive for helping her was purely professional; but she could not deny the nameless appeal that drew her so inexplicably to him.

She had eventually fallen asleep with Trace's arms providing a sense of safety and a sense of belonging and peace that had quenched a long-standing thirst inside her.

Unable to look away, Meredith watched as Trace continued dressing with his back turned to her, as he loosened the trouser buttons at his waist and tucked his shirt inside, then buttoned the closure up securely again over the purely male part of him that had been so close during the long night past. He turned toward her unexpectedly to reach for his boots and she felt the shock of the moment when his light-eyed gaze met hers. She took a quick breath at the heat that filled the brief distance between them, as all the long, empty years she had suffered became an aching void inside her. She held her breath tensely when Trace hesitated, and then released it with an expectant gasp when he closed that distance in a few, short steps.

The cot sank with his weight as Trace crouched beside her. She felt his strong body shudder, a trembling that shook her as well. He said hoarsely, "I didn't plan things to work out this way."

"I know."

Hesitating again, he said, "I'm not sure this is wise."

Meredith could not reply.

Trace whispered, "All I know, Meredith, is that I want you more than I've ever wanted any other woman." Caressing her cheek with a shaking hand, he continued. "But I need to be sure you feel the same. It can't be any other way for me."

Meredith was still unable to speak.

His hand falling slowly back to his side at her silence, his expression pained, Trace said, "All right, I suppose that's my answer."

Suddenly panicking when Trace began to withdraw from her, Meredith grasped his hand. As uncertain as she was of the driving emotion holding her in its grasp, as unsure of what the outcome of the moment would eventually be, she said instinctively, "No, don't, Trace! I'm not sure of very much at present, but there's one thing I do know. I wouldn't be able to bear it if you turned away from me right now."

Trace went still. She could feel his strong body quaking. She saw the tremor that touched his sober expression the moment before he abruptly snatched her up into his arms. Her lips parted in spontaneous acceptance as he lowered his mouth to hers. She was unaware of the moment when she reached out to touch the thick shock of dark hair that had fallen forward onto his forehead, or when it was that her hands slipped around his head to draw him closer. She knew only a sense of need and want, and of knowing it was right as the loving began.

Hardly conscious of his movements, Trace gathered Meredith into his arms. His lips touched hers, and a hunger for her stirred a subtle groan as his kiss sank deeper. Joy and an exuberant incredulity soared inside him—a sense of fulfillment that he had unknowingly craved his life long. She was sweet to his taste, fodder for the blaze that raged hotly inside him. He slid his hands into the fiery curls that had taunted him, kissed the fluttering lids that shielded her glorious eyes, smoothed the curve of her cheek with his lips, and paused to mutter endearments into her ear before finding his way to conquer her mouth once more.

His elation surging higher, Trace trembled with wonder at the delicate slope of her jaw, the white column of her throat, the graceful line of her shoulder. His joy exploded into wonderment when his mouth covered the crests of her breasts at last.

He heard her gasp as he caressed the pink nubs with his kisses. He felt her shuddering when he pushed aside her clothing so he might fully worship her delicate flesh. Her heard her gasp when he met the delicate mound between her thighs and tasted it gently. Shuddering, wanting, knowing a compelling need that could be abated in only one way, Trace slid his tongue into the warm crevice awaiting him. He felt her body jolt. He looked up to meet her startled gaze and mumbled a loving reassurance. Satisfied that he had calmed her trembling uncertainties, he then tasted her more deeply.

Knowing a need that would not cease, he kissed her moistness with tenderness. Constant in his fervor, he reveled in the glory of the moment. He felt the encompassing shudders that rapidly overwhelmed her. Aware that the moment was approaching, he slid his hands under her buttocks to elevate her fully to his attentions. He then heard her startled gasp the moment before she throbbed to sudden, passionate release.

Waiting only until her spasms had ceased, Trace slid himself back atop her. The flush of passion still colored her face as she lay silent and unmoving underneath him, and a rush of tenderness suffused him. He nudged her gently, and her eyelids flickered. He entered her with great restraint, gradually increasing the impetus of his deepening thrusts until Meredith met them fully with a gasping need that matched his own.

The ache inside him was too powerful to contain any longer. He thrust himself deeply within her, rejoicing when Meredith's soft cry echoed his own as they met with sudden, mutual fulfillment.

Trace breathed deeply in the silence that followed. He felt suddenly overwhelmed. He slid his arms under Meredith, hardly able to believe the past moments of complete possession. But her eyes were still closed, and suddenly wary, he prompted, "Meredith, are you all right?"

She did not open her eyes and panic touched his mind. He urged, "Look at me, Meredith."

"I don't want to."

Trace went still. A slow dread pervaded his senses. "Open your eyes, Meredith."

Her eyes still closed, she whispered, "No."

"Meredith . . ."

"Please, Trace . . ."

He should have known.

Despising his weakness, Trace drew Meredith instinctively closer even as a resounding regret registered in his mind. He had taken advantage of her. In his desire for her, he had misread what she had said. He had believed what he had wanted to believe. She had been more innocent than she chose to reveal, and he had overwhelmed her in a moment of uncertainty. She had trusted him, and he had proved unworthy of her trust.

Still clutching her close, Trace whispered, "Meredith, I—"

"Don't talk, Trace, please. Not yet. I don't want this moment to end."

Stunned at her unexpected whisper, Trace did not immediately reply. Meredith opened her eyes when he responded hoarsely, "I thought—"

"I don't want to think right now, Trace." Her gaze warm honey, Meredith whispered, "I've done so much thinking all my life, and planning, and waiting, but the past few days have proved to me that some things just . . . happen. I'm not exactly sure what that means, but right now, at this time and place in your arms, I know this is right."

A touch of tentativeness entered her gaze. Meredith whispered, "I just wish this moment could go on forever."

Trace stared silently at the beautiful woman lying breathlessly close. At first haughtily distant, then conversely turning herself over completely to his guidance, and finally so painfully honest that she tore him inside out with her intimate logic, Meredith was a paradox unlike any he had known before. He was certain that there were still many surprises to come. "You know I can't make you any guarantees right now, Meredith. But I can tell you that I'll never desert you. Not now, not ever. I promise you that, and I always keep my promises."

Never meaning his words more, Trace did not wait for her reply before lowering his mouth again to hers.

"Aunt Letty, are you all right? You don't look well."

"Mason, dear, I'm fine." Letty took a deep breath and pushed back a straying lock of dark hair as she struggled to maintain her smile. She had not been sleeping well. The howlings had been constant. Something was happening, something she was unable to control.

Her *life* was out of control.

Letty scrutinized Mason's expression. No, Mason could not possibly understand. He had come to see her that morning about some legal papers she was supposed to show him. In truth, she hardly remembered mentioning them to him, so stunned was she by the image she had seen the previous night.

Grandfather, with a formerly vicious wolf at his side.

With no logical explanation for the haunting vision, Letty knew only that Grandfather would not have appeared without a reason.

"Aunt Letty, to be honest, paperwork isn't the true reason for my visit this afternoon." His expression softened. Mason took Letty's hand. "My servant told me that he heard you haven't been present at your salon the past two evenings. I was worried that you were ill."

"No," Removing her hand from Mason's grip, Letty took a step in retreat as she said, "I've been . . . been busy with other matters."

"Surely you're not allowing this business with the Pinkertons to concern you. Your lawyers must have been advising you of any progress that's been made."

"No, I haven't heard from them since I commissioned the work."

"Perhaps it's time you should inquire, then."

"I have complete trust in the law firm, Mason. Mr. Pittman will do his best for me."

"I suppose." Mason placed the paperwork on the

table beside them. "If this contract is an example of their work, I'd say it is sufficient."

"Sufficient?"

"Adequate . . . good . . . but Wallace, Pittman, and O'Brien doesn't have the personal interest I would have in your legal affairs, Aunt Letty. If you turned them over to me, I could guarantee you that I would handle them more than just adequately."

"Mason." Letty looked at him with her great eyes sympathetic. The royal blue of her gown cast an ivory glow on her almost translucent skin. "I appreciate your offer, but Wallace, Pittman, and O'Brien have been loyal to me, and I've learned the hard way that loyalty is difficult to come by. I can't afford to sacrifice it in any quarter."

"Of course, Aunt Letty." Mason offered a sincere smile. "Just remember, I'm always here to help you if you need me."

"Mason, you are a dear."

Leaning toward him unexpectedly, Letty kissed Mason's smooth cheek. She then said, "If you'll excuse me, I intend attending the salon this evening. My presence has obviously been missed, and I've missed the salon, too."

"Yes, business is business."

"My salon is more than business for me, Mason," Letty corrected softly. "It has become a way of life for me, a way of gaining an acceptance that was formerly denied me. Unfortunately, somewhere along the way it also became my obsession. That is an error I'm hoping to correct."

"Of course, Aunt Letty. I understand."

Doubting that he did, but grateful for his concern,

Letty felt somehow compelled to cut Mason's visit short. She could not understand her impatience with him of late, nor the way his concern seemed to gnaw at her peace of mind. She said conversely, "I hope you will visit me again, Mason. You visits are always a pleasure for me."

"Of course, Aunt Letty."

Barely waiting until Mason had exited the room, Letty headed for her bedroom with Mason dismissed from her mind. She would make an entrance at the salon that evening. She needed the distraction of hearing the gasps that were sure to sound when she entered with her exquisite red gown glittering under the lights of the chandeliers.

Yes, she needed the distraction, and she could hear the gasps now.

Mason pulled Letty's apartment door closed behind him and started down the hallway, barely able to maintain a civil expression. Paperwork be damned! He had gone there after a meeting with Dobbs to give him the additional advance he needed to send to his "fella." The sum had almost emptied his waning bank account. He had gone to Letty's with the hope that he might be able to convince her to turn over her legal affairs to him, but he had failed again. She had not even been able to give him some news about her daughters that might lift his spirits.

Mason's lips twitched with subdued anger. He had wasted his time, and the memory of his dear aunt Letty's platonic kiss on the cheek almost made him gag.

Wallace, Pittman, and O'Brien were so loyal to her, were they? Alexander Pittman would do his best for her, would he? She had failed to mention that young Alexander Pittman was infatuated with her, and that she used his infatuation to her advantage, just as she had used so many men before him. His uncle Archibald was a prime example of her ability to use men susceptible to her charms.

Mason strove to control the fury that a visit with Letty always stirred. But he wasn't one of Letty's fools, and he would win out over her in the end. And if anyone were to be used this time, it would be Aunt Letty herself. He would make sure of that.

Elias Fink walked slowly into the Winsome Bank as the afternoon began to wane. Tall and thin, his clean-shaven face lined by dissolute years and his dark eyes cold, he approached the teller and said abruptly, "I hear this bank was robbed a few days ago."

"That's right." The teller eyed him warily and said, "Two thieves got off with most of the bank's money. We're waiting for a shipment of cash from the main branch. It should get here any day now."

Fink nodded and then said, "I hear a red-haired, citified woman was one of the bank robbers."

"That's right. Deputy Cobb put her in jail, but she escaped."

"A red-haired woman named Meredith Moore."

The teller's eyes widened at his obvious familiarity with her name. He glanced at the nearby desk where Howard Larson worked laboriously over a column of numbers. He said, "That's the bank manager right over there. Maybe you should talk to him. He has more information about that woman than I do."

"Yes, maybe I should. I came here to pick up

money from a bank draft that was just wired here. He's probably the best man to talk to about that, too."

Fink waited as the teller left his cage, tapped a stout, round-faced fellow on the shoulder, and whispered to the man when he looked up.

Responding to the bank manager's smile as the fellow stood up, Fink approached the desk and accepted his hand.

Fink said solemnly, "I see from the sign on your desk that you're Howard Larson, the bank manager. I need to introduce myself to you. My name is Trace Stringer. I'm a Pinkerton detective. A private party whose name I can't divulge hired my agency to bring Miss Meredith Moore back to New York City."

Fink added with continued solemnity, "Miss Moore is wanted for murder."

Trace slid his arms around Meredith's waist as she packed the last item into Trace's saddlebag. They had dozed until the sun had reached its summit in the sky, so involved in each other that they had not taken time to consider the future that was rapidly closing in around them.

Aware of the danger in that omission, Trace had finally dressed, determined to correct it. He had forced himself to ignore the yearning that came to life each time he neared Meredith and had retrieved the foodstuffs he had carefully purchased. He had begun preparing a meal with Meredith's gaze following him every step of the way. Finally looking back at her, he had seen her face flush, and his determination was forgotten in a flood of emotion that found them again in each other's arms. It was now hours later. Their stomachs had been sated, but another part of him was urging him on with a deeper hunger.

Tucking his head down into the warm hollow of Meredith's neck, Trace brushed his lips against the delicate skin there. He was rewarded with the spontaneous shudder that rocked Meredith's frame. Aware of where that moment could lead, he stepped back, frowning as Meredith turned toward him.

"All right, I'll say it." Trace took a breath as he fought to restrain the hunger rising anew inside him. "I can't get enough of you, and that's dangerous. We should be on our way out of here by now. This place won't stay safe if we stay here too long."

His explanation cut short as Meredith pressed her mouth unexpectedly to his, Trace indulged the taste of her for brief moments before drawing back reluctantly to whisper, "I'm a professional, Meredith, and this isn't the way a professional is supposed to act."

Meredith whispered in response, "This isn't the way I'm supposed to act, either." Pressing herself tight against him, she continued hesitantly. "I've always been the sensible one, Trace. I'm the oldest of my sisters. I was the one who held us together, who looked out for us, and who found the way for us to keep in touch when things got bad. I think that's why Grandfather came to me and I—"

Trace came instantly alert. "You have relatives? That's not what your dossier says. Do they live around here?"

"I think . . . I'm not sure. . . ." Pausing, Meredith started again. "That's the reason I came west, to find out more about the family my mother would never talk about, and about my father."

"He died before you were born." Trace smoothed a straying wisp of hair back from her cheek as he continued softly, "But you look like him. You have his coloring and his determination."

"My mother loved my father, that's the only thing I'm sure of. My mother's eyes filled on the few occasions when she mentioned him. It was the only time I can recall that she showed any real emotion. Everything else was for show, emotion she used for the moment, like the parade of 'uncles' my sisters and I became accustomed to seeing in the years before my mother sent us to private school. I promised myself I wouldn't let anything get in the way of solving the mystery of my past. I need to know more about myself, Trace." Emotion thickening her throat, Meredith said softly, "I need to know why I should be the one to be hearing all these mysterious rumblings connected to days before my sisters and I were born, and to be seeing things that I can't explain."

Trace waited for her to continue. When she did not, he pressed, "What rumblings are you talking about?"

Meredith shrugged. "It's hard to explain. I suppose I need to know that I can trust myself to follow through about them, and that my sisters can trust me to continue on for their sakes as well as mine. I thought it would be easy, but everything went wrong as soon as I arrived in Winsome. Now I'm wanted by the law, and I've even managed to make the man sent to protect me a wanted man, too."

"We need to set something straight, Meredith." Trace began hesitantly. "Your mother didn't hire the Pinkerton Agency to protect you. Your mother hired the agency to find you and present you with an ultimatum so you'd come home."

Meredith paled before responding with an emotionless laugh. "Funny, isn't it, that after all that's happened in the past, I should still believe my mother was concerned enough about me that she would hire someone to follow and protect me? Instead, she's just concerned about how this will look for her when everyone realizes her daughters left her. She still thinks an ultimatum is the answer."

"She wants you back, Meredith."

"On her terms."

"Whichever way you want to take it, she says she'll disinherit you if you don't return before her fortieth birthday."

"As if I care about being disinherited!"

"Your mother is wealthy, and only someone who's been raised with wealth thinks money isn't important. In reality, it's more important than you think."

"Is that why you took this assignment, for the money?"

"If you mean because I was hired to find you, yes."

Momentarily silent, Meredith responded, "Well, you found me and I'm refusing to come home. Your job is completed. You can go back to New York and I'll take care of myself from here on."

"Like you're taking care of yourself now?"

Meredith took a backward step. Trace steeled himself against the deprivation of her warmth as she said, "So you're telling me that I'm depending on my mother's help after all, because I'm depending on you."

"No, I'm telling you that everything isn't as black and white as you seem to think it is—a matter of wanting to do something, and then doing it. Life gets in the way."

"You mean like bank robberies, missing money, and dead sheriffs."

"Right."

"And a Pinkerton who was sent to bring me back, but who found momentary diversion in my stupidity."

"No."

"Maybe I'm more like my mother than I wanted to believe."

"Don't say that unless you mean it in a positive way." Trace took a step closer. "I've never seen your mother, but I hear she's a beautiful woman. You're beautiful, too, Meredith."

"Beauty doesn't mean anything. My sisters and I are beautiful and our mother is rich, but we still led a deprived childhood."

"Deprived?"

"Deprived of parents, of family, of any kind of a history that we could look back on. All we had was each other, and my mother even tried to take that away from us."

"And now your sisters and you have separated of your own accord."

"Only for a little while so we can find out who we really are, so we can find out if I . . . if we . . ." A single tear trailed down Meredith's cheek, but she brushed it away. "Instead, my life is a bigger mess than it was before."

"That's what I'm here to fix, Meredith."

Meredith looked up at him. She was about to reply when the door snapped open unexpectedly, startling her as a familiar voice commented, "You ain't doing too good a job of that, either."

His hand snapping to his gun belt at the same moment that he pushed Meredith behind him, Trace turned to see Sam Winston standing solemnly in the doorway. His great white mustache twitching, Sam said, "My gun's in my gun belt where it belongs, big fella, so you can put yours back, too. That is, if you're the man I think you are."

Trace's gaze jumped to the copse visible through the open doorway and Sam responded, "I came alone. I didn't want no gun-happy posse trailing behind me like Deputy Cobb has in mind."

Motioning Sam forward, Trace walked cautiously to the doorway and peered outside with his gun still drawn as Sam nodded politely to Meredith. Satisfied that Sam was telling the truth, he holstered his gun and said gruffly, "What's this all about? How did you find us?"

"I followed your trail."

"That couldn't have been easy."

"Sheriff Keller didn't get the reputation for being a good tracker all by himself. It's a sad truth, though, that his present deputy couldn't track an elephant in a barnyard if his life depended on it."

"I had the feeling that we fooled you too easily with that ruse Meredith and I used to get her out of jail," Trace confessed.

"Yeah, well, I was sort of glad you came up with something. I figured if you didn't get her out, I'd have to find a way to do something."

Trace remained silent as Sam glanced at Meredith's pale countenance and continued. "Look here, I'm an old hand at this kind of thing. Sheriff Keller and me worked together for years. Like I said, one look at Miss Moore and I knew she wasn't guilty of the crimes that the deputy charged her with. Unlike Deputy Cobb, I figure I owe it to Sheriff Keller to make sure the right person pays for his death. Deputy Cobb—he's just out to get somebody hanged for it so he can satisfy the town, and he doesn't care whether the person is guilty or not as long as he comes out ahead. Needless to say, that rubs me the wrong way. Besides," Sam added, "this lady is too pretty to decorate the end of a noose."

Trace saw the shudder that shook Meredith and slid his arm around her. "What is your name anyway, fella?" Sam asked him suddenly. "It sure as hell ain't Trace Stringer, because Trace Stringer just arrived in Winsome."

"What?"

Momentarily stunned, Trace waited as Sam replied, "Stringer introduced himself as a Pinkerton detective. It seems he's out to find Miss Moore. He says she's wanted back East . . . for murder."

"Murder!"

Trace tightened his arm around Meredith as she gasped. He said flatly, "I'm Trace Stringer, and I've got the Pinkerton identification to prove it. I was sent out here to find Meredith, but not because she's wanted for murder—because her mother wants her to come back to New York."

"This other Trace Stringer has Pinkerton identification, too."

"It's fake."

"It looked good to me."

"It's . . . fake." Trace's voice dropped a note lower as he took an aggressive step.

Lifting the flat of his hand toward him, Sam said, "Hold on. There's no cause to get angry. I'm just telling you like it is. The whole town thinks that fella's Trace Stringer and you're the imposter. Howard Larson just cashed a draft wired to Trace Stringer for him, so Howard seems to have been satisfied with his identification, too. I know Deputy Cobb is real impressed with him. He's taken Stringer under his wing—Lord help him. They were starting out to track you when I left Winsome." He shrugged as he added, "They should be good and lost by now."

"You're sure of that."

"I told you, that deputy couldn't track an elephant—"

"In a barnyard, I know." Trace paused. "But you managed to track us here."

Sam looked at Trace solemnly. "You don't give yourself enough credit, fella. You did a real good job of covering up your trail. If I wasn't the tracker that I am, I never could've found you. And believe me, there ain't another tracker like me in that whole town of Winsome."

Trace glanced at Meredith. Her color was gray as she bit her lip to stop its trembling. "You may as well come the rest of the way in, Sam." Trace relented. "It looks like we're not going anywhere until we figure out what's going on here."

Speaking up for the first time, Meredith said, "You believed me, Sam, that I was innocent?"

Sam nodded.

"Why? Because I don't look like a murderer?"

"Ma'am, I had me two daughters that I raised on my own after my wife died. They're married and gone out to live with their husbands now, but as much trouble as they gave me, they always had a look in their eyes that said they was good girls. You've got that same look in your eye, and there's nobody who is going to tell me any different."

With a few quick steps, Meredith threw her arms unexpectedly around the old man's neck and kissed his cheek. She said softly, "Thank you. Thank you so much, Sam."

Her face was flushed when she drew back. She looked up at Trace and said with an echo of the old Meredith in her tone, "All right, what do we do now?"

Elias Fink sat his horse impatiently in the midst of the silent posse. He watched as Deputy Cobb dismounted and examined the area more closely, searching vainly for the trail he still refused to admit that he had lost over an hour earlier. It hadn't taken Fink long to realize that that the deputy was a fool, and that his tracking skills were poor. He got the feeling that the rest of the posse felt the same way when a few of the men dismounted from their horses and studied the ground beside the deputy.

Fink's mouth twitched with annoyance. He didn't like this hitch in his plans. He had figured that the forged Pinkerton papers he'd had made up before leaving New York would make up for his lack of western savvy once he presented them to the local law and declared that Meredith Moore was wanted for murder. He had used Trace Stringer's name so that if anyone chose to check with the agency, Pinkerton would confirm that an agent named Stringer worked for him. He had figured that the local law would then lead the way. It was just a stroke of luck that Meredith Moore managed to get herself involved in a bank robbery, and that Stringer broke her out of jail without telling anyone he was a Pinkerton. As far as the dead sheriff was concerned, he couldn't care less who killed him as long as Meredith Moore never made it back to New York City.

Fink watched as Deputy Cobb straightened up his scrawny form and said, "I guess we lost him, fellas, but that don't mean I'm going to give up. I'm going to get them both, or I'll die tryin'."

Fink nodded. That sounded pretty good to him right now. He looked at Cobb as the fellow turned toward him and said, "I figure you've got something in mind about finding that woman and her boyfriend, Stringer, so I figure we can talk about it back in town while we eat. With the two of us on her trail, neither one of them is going to get away, that's one thing that's for sure."

Fink turned his mount back in the direction of town with the rest of the posse, never more aware that he was on his own.

"You're sure?" Rita stared at Howard as he stood a few feet away in her kitchen. He had come home a few minutes earlier. She had prepared his supper haphazardly and left it on the table. It had cooled, but she didn't really care. She could not afford to allow her husband to get accustomed to knowing she had slaved over a hot stove. The situation was only temporary. She would rehire the cook as soon as the auditors cleared Howard. She needed her life to be progressing normally when she became a *widow*. It would not work any other way.

Rita stared at her husband as he maintained his silence. She pressed, "Howard, answer me!"

Howard replied stiffly, "Yes, I'm sure. A Pinkerton named Trace Stringer came into town today. I don't know who the other fellow was, but this was the real Trace Stringer. I saw his Pinkerton identification, and he also knew all the details about the draft that was wired in Stringer's name to the bank. He said he was hired to find Meredith Moore because she's wanted for murder back East."

Rita could hardly contain her jubilation. "That couldn't be better! Meredith Moore hooks up with a bank robber who shoots the sheriff. She manages to hide the bulk of the money stolen from the bank and only returns a small portion with the thought that her honesty will prove she's innocent. Her plan backfires and her boyfriend who claims he's Trace Stringer has to break her out of jail—and now the real Trace Stringer arrives in Winsome to declare that he's a Pinkerton who's after Meredith Moore because she's wanted for murder!"

"But she escaped! She's on the loose with her boyfriend and nobody can find them."

"What does that matter, you fool? The fact that Meredith Moore is a wanted woman will make the auditors believe that story."

"But—"

"But what, Howard?" Her temper short, Rita repeated with disgust, "But what?"

"What if Meredith Moore is caught and she makes the Pinkerton believe that she doesn't have the money, and there was never more money in the vault in the first place?"

"That isn't plausible."

"What if the auditors become suspicious of me, and they decide to overlook Miss Moore and go straight into my finances?"

"Howard . . ."

"What if they discover my embezzlement and decide that I'm partially to blame for Sheriff Keller's death?"

"If . . . if . . . if . . . !" Rita took a threatening step toward her husband. "I'm tired of hearing that word when the truth is that Pinkerton will never find Meredith Moore and her boyfriend if he follows the deputy's advice!" Pausing to draw herself under control, Rita continued. "You are fortunate that you have me, Howard, because you're too stupid to realize things are going our way. But don't worry, I'll take care of things." Her expression tight, she ordered, "Now sit down and eat. Your food is getting cold."

Sitting without a response, Howard picked up his fork. Rita watched her husband, a deep revulsion registering in her mind. She sat in her chair across from him, the thought of becoming a grieving widow ever more appealing.

"Rita Larson's pendant watch in Doc Gibbs' yard?" Sam shook his head as if negating that thought. "Rita Larson ain't my favorite person, but thinking that she might have had something to do with Sheriff Keller's death . . ."

Trace stared at Sam's uncertain expression as his statement trailed away. After Sam's unexpected arrival a few hours earlier, they had talked and eaten. Sam was preparing to leave, but parts of their conversation seemed to have stuck in his craw.

Trace responded, "I could be wrong. You know Rita Larson better than I do, but something Doc said about the way he found Sheriff Keller's body didn't sound right to me. Doc said the whole scene looked peaceful, too peaceful, if I read Doc's expression correctly.

Sheriff Keller's bed was perfectly arranged with the coverlet tucked in and his hands folded, almost like a woman would set the scene. I get the feeling that isn't the way Doc is accustomed to seeing people die."

"As far as this pendant watch is concerned . . ." Sam took the shiny timepiece out of his pocket and looked at it again. "I'll take it to town and find out for sure if it belongs to Rita, but that doesn't really prove anything. She might have lost that pendant watch a week earlier when she was visiting a lady from her church at Doc's house."

"The watch was as clean as a new penny. It couldn't have been in the yard that long."

"There could be a hundred other explanations for why it was there, even if it does belong to Rita."

"Name one."

Sam's full white mustache twitched. He went silent, and then shrugged. "All right, you've got me there, but what possible reason would she have for killing Sheriff Keller?"

"Her husband claimed that thousands were missing from the bank money bag we brought back to town, but Meredith says she didn't feel any appreciable difference in the money bag's weight when we returned it. Maybe that money wasn't there in the first place."

"Howard was the only person who could have taken that money, not Rita."

"Agreed."

Sam continued. "But the sad truth is that Rita is the only one with guts in that family. Howard knows his numbers, but he's jelly inside."

Meredith interjected with surprise, "Sam! That's a terrible thing to say."

"It may be a terrible thing to say, but it's the truth." Sam's brows drew together in a rare frown as he shoved the pendant watch back into his pocket and said, "I'll find out for sure if this is Rita's watch, all right. That shouldn't be hard to do. I'll also send that wire to the Pinkerton Agency for you."

"I appreciate that, Sam. It would be hard for me to get back into town right now, but if that watch does belong to Rita Larson, I'll take it from there."

Sam stilled and then said, "Don't go off half-cocked, boy. There's no telling who that fella is who's impersonating you or why he's doing it. You may be biting off more than you can chew."

"Don't worry. I'm accustomed to handling situations like this."

Her expression stiff, Meredith interjected, "What about me? Am I supposed to wait here and do nothing?"

"That's right!"

Sam and Trace spoke in unexpected unison, but it was Trace who continued. "For some unknown reason, that impersonator is going out of his way to make you appear to be a murderer, which doesn't make it safe for you to get involved."

"It's not safe for you, either."

"That's my job, Meredith."

Meredith returned hotly, "It was your job to deliver my mother's ultimatum to me and to bring either me or a signed refusal back—that's what you said."

"Yes, well . . ." Trace's gaze dropped briefly to Meredith's lips as he said, "The circumstances have changed."

Meredith's face colored. Sam's eyebrows rose briefly as he said, "I suppose I should be going now, but you both might as well stay here for the time being. You're as safe as you'd be anywheres else. Come hell or high water, I'll be back tomorrow with what I find out. You can depend on it. It won't take me any longer than that to make certain if this is really Rita Larson's watch and to send the telegram. As for the response to your wire, that might take a little time."

Stepping toward Sam unexpectedly, Meredith said, "I can't thank you enough for doing this, Sam, and for believing in me."

"Don't thank me, darlin'." Taking her hand, Sam smiled. "Sheriff Keller was my friend. I may be old, but there's a streak of lawman still in me, and I ain't about to let a jackass like Deputy Cobb use my friend's death to his advantage. Besides, if I was thirty years younger, this big fella here wouldn't stand a chance with you, no matter what he thinks, and that's the truth."

Sam drew Meredith's hand to his lips and Meredith's eyes filled with tears.

Dropping Meredith's hand, Sam looked Trace in the eye and said, "You're a lucky man, Trace Stringer."

Trace tightened his arm around Meredith as Sam walked out the doorway. He watched as the old man mounted and tipped his hat before riding off.

Looking back at Meredith when Sam disappeared into the brush, Trace said with conviction, "Sam's a fine old fella, but I want you to know just in case you were wondering—thirty years younger or not, I would never have let anyone take you away from me."

Chapter Six

Elias Fink leaned casually against the upright in front of Winsome's mercantile store, casually scrutinizing Winsome's daily routine as the sun slipped rapidly toward the horizon. He barely resisted frowning at the unfamiliarity of the small town. He had been on his own since he was twelve when his father left him with his mother, a woman who drank herself into unconsciousness every night. He had been relieved of his mother's constant demands on him when she was discovered dead in an alleyway shortly after his father disappeared. Actually, she had done him a favor because he had survived well afterward with a cunning that came naturally to him. He had lied easily and distorted facts to suit the situation. He had inwardly mocked those he deceived and had prided himself on his ability to do so. His confidence had grown with every encounter. The dark alleyways and mean streets of the city became his home; and as he grew, he had darkened them with blood whenever the situation suited.

Without a single pang of conscience, he had never looked back. And if he had not made many friends along the way, he was satisfied to be respected by a certain element for his abilities, and to be feared by most who came up against him.

Yes, life had been good, until . . .

Fink's lips twitched with discomfort. His present situation was different from any he had run up against, and that irritated him. A job that he could easily have taken care of in the city had become difficult through no fault of his own. He had planned well to compensate for his shortcomings in this unnatural environment, yet the time spent with Deputy Cobb earlier had confirmed that the man was a fool who could not be depended upon.

Fink eyed the small town cautiously. He had questioned the witnesses to the bank robbery with the thought that he might learn more about Meredith Moore's circumstances, but the effort had been a complete waste of time. He was only too aware that he was a fish out of water and that the real Trace Stringer was western born, giving him the clear advantage. The fact that Stringer and Meredith appeared to have joined forces made his job even harder.

Fink ground his teeth with frustration. He needed to shift the balance in his favor. He was not certain how to accomplish that fact, but the few hours he had spent traveling with the posse had taught him that he needed to study the residents of the town a little longer before he would be able to right the situation.

The sight of a familiar figure riding onto the street stopped Fink's thoughts cold. It was Sam Winston, the old man with the white mustache who had been guarding Meredith's cell when she escaped. He had learned from Deputy Cobb that Sam had been Sheriff Keller's deputy until Sam decided he was too old to do the job on a regular basis. Sheriff Keller had reportedly valued Sam and had been sorry to lose the old fellow. For that reason, it seemed somehow strange to him that Sam had been as easily tricked as he said he was when Meredith escaped. It had seemed strange to the men in the posse, too, especially since Sam had claimed he was too old to lend his tracking talents to the chase.

His eyes narrowed as Sam rode up to the hitching post in front of the bank and dismounted easily. Fink suddenly recalled the comment made by the well-meaning reverend of the local church and his wife that they had gone to Sam's house at the edge of town to afford him solace, but that they had been unable to find him anywhere.

Fink studied Sam more closely as the fellow stepped up onto the board sidewalk. There was nothing old or feeble about the fellow when he strode toward the bank with a true sense of purpose. Sam pushed open the bank's door and walked inside, seeming not to give a second thought to the fact that the bank had extended its hours due to the anxiety of depositors after the robbery. Nor did he appear to allow the death of a friend to interfere with the business he needed to conduct there.

Obeying instinct, Fink pushed himself away from the upright and started walking toward the bank. He reached it just as Sam approached the bank manager's desk and addressed Howard Larson with a smile.

But Fink wasn't fooled by that smile. Walking up

to the teller's window where several persons stood in line in front of him, he listened intently to the conversation between Sam and Larson as he waited his turn.

Sam had taken a direct route back from the cabin, cutting in half the time it had taken him to track Trace and Meredith there. The pendant watch that Trace had given him had burned a hole in his pocket every step of the way. He was anxious to ascertain, once and for all, whether the watch belonged to Rita Larson. He still found Trace's suspicions difficult to believe. He had never really liked Rita. There was something about her, a subtle kind of superiority that was ingrained in her. He had the feeling that there was ice behind Rita's smile, almost as if she considered herself too good for the town. Howard obviously idolized her, but the truth was, Sam had a feeling that Rita inwardly despised her husband.

Yet to think that Rita had killed the sheriff—

Sam stopped at Howard's desk. Seeing him, Howard stood up with a half smile and straightened his jacket over his portly frame before extending his hand in greeting. Sam felt a tug of remorse for the deception he intended.

"Good evening, Sam." Appearing to choose his words, Howard said, "I heard what happened at the jail. I . . . I'm sorry that you were placed in such a difficult position."

"I'm sorry, too." Sam shrugged. "But that fella claiming to be Stringer took me by surprise. I couldn't do nothing once he had his gun on me."

"It must have been difficult having them get away, especially since Sheriff Keller was your good friend.

The men in the posse were surprised that you didn't ride out with them."

"I guess my age is catching up with me, because the truth is that I wasn't up to it. I think Sheriff Keller would understand. Anyways, what happened don't make me any less law-abiding. I don't want nothing that don't belong to me." Reaching into his pocket, Sam withdrew the pendant watch and said, "I found this watch on the street a little while back. Willard Dread said he thought it probably belonged to your wife since you got one that looked just like it in the mail. I figured your wife was probably feeling real bad about losing it if it's hers, and I wanted to return it."

Sam held his breath as Howard took the watch from his palm. Howard surprised him by pressing a hidden catch that flicked the back of the watch open. He read along with Howard the inscription: TO RITA, WITH LOVE FROM HOWARD.

Howard blinked. Looking back up at him, Howard said, "It's Rita's watch, all right. It's strange that she didn't mention she had lost it."

Sam managed to maintain an expressionless demeanor as Howard said politely, "Thank you for returning it, Sam. Rita will be happy to get it back, I'm sure."

Obviously disturbed when he put the watch into his drawer, Howard said unexpectedly, "Is there anything else I can do for you, Sam? I'm sorry to be abrupt but we'll be closing in a little while and I still have some work to do."

"No, that's what I came here for." Sam took a backward step. "I'm glad the watch is going back to its owner. It didn't suit me nohow."

His hand feeling scorched from Howard's parting handshake, Sam headed for the door. On the boardwalk out of sight of the bank, Sam stopped abruptly to catch his breath. He hadn't really wanted to believe that the watch belonged to Rita, but it did. He didn't want to think what that implied. Nor could he understand why a man had come to town impersonating Trace. The circumstances appeared linked in some way, but for the life of him, he could not fathom how.

Sam took a deep breath as he started for his horse. He needed to talk to Trace. He would send the telegram to Pinkerton as Trace had asked. It would probably take a few days to get an answer, but he'd start out for the cabin at first light. Together they'd decide where to go from there—but he was sure of one thing. He'd find out who was truly responsible for Sheriff Keller's death if it was the last thing he ever did.

The shadows of dusk were fading into evening as Meredith stood beside the cabin fireplace and looked at the roast dripping its juices onto the flaring flames. She had never felt more helpless in her life. She pushed back a stray lock of hair that had fallen forward on her forehead and looked up anxiously at Trace as he stood beside the table. His back was turned toward her, and memory suddenly returned to passionate minutes that had begun in that same way. She recalled that Trace's broad shoulders had blocked out the world as his naked length had lain stretched out upon hers, leaving only the two of them in the glory of the moment. She remembered the power of his arms as he had crushed her tight against him, the sound of his hoarse whisper in her ear as his body began quaking, and she recalled that when they had soared to gasping ecstasy they had—

Suddenly aware where her thoughts were leading her, Meredith swallowed and took a breath. Trace had said he couldn't get enough of her, and she was beginning to believe that she was no different than he. But she was new to the feelings running rampant inside her. She had never experienced the warmth of knowing that someone whom she respected, trusted, and who had proved himself to her, also brought her to life in a way she had never anticipated.

Trace looked up unexpectedly and Meredith snapped her attention back to the roast. Trace had gone hunting after Sam left. He had returned within minutes with the proceeds of his hunt hanging from his hand. She was still embarrassed by her reaction to the sight of their dinner in the raw and the instinctive convulsing of her stomach that she had been unable to hide. Without saying a word, Trace had walked back out the doorway. He had returned with a roast ready to be cooked that bore no resemblance to its original state.

Trace had then lit a fire in the fireplace, put the roast on a spit, and begun preparing the rest of the meal from their limited supplies. He had asked only that she baste the meat occasionally with a mixture from the juices that he had prepared. Simple enough, except that he hadn't told her how to ascertain when the meat was cooked.

The roast sputtered and darkened before her eyes, and Meredith despaired. She was unprepared for Trace's voice behind her when he said, "I guess it's time to eat."

Meredith gave a short nod as she looked back up at him, aware that their lips were only inches apart. She breathed a sigh of relief when Trace lifted the spit and carried the roast to the table, then sliced the meat with the knife from the sheath at his waist. He had made biscuits from flour and water and whatever other incidentals he carried in his saddlebags. He had cooked rice from the sack that Sam had brought, and he had opened a can of peaches that Sam had also left for them.

Yes, it was a meal fit for a king.

Trace's smile faltered when he turned toward Meredith to see her glorious eyes filled with tears. "What's wrong, Meredith? Don't you feel well?"

"I'm sorry."

"Sorry?"

"You've been working so hard to feed us, and I haven't done a thing to help you."

"Meredith . . ."

"I'm out of my element here, Trace. I'm helpless, worthless, unable to function. I'm totally reliant on you. I don't like that feeling. I've always thought of myself as self-sufficient, but now I can see that was only vain ignorance on my part."

"That's not true."

"It is. I'm spoiled by the life I've led! I've made a mess of things ever since I left New York."

"That's not true, either."

"It isn't?" Deep into her self-derision, Meredith exclaimed, "Tell me just one thing that I've done right since I came to Texas."

"Meredith." Trace's gaze was intent and his strong features were sober. The broad expanse of his shoulders blocked out all but his sincerity as he whispered, "You've done one thing right—the most important thing."

"One thing?"

Mesmerized, Meredith could not seem to move as Trace lowered his mouth to hers. She felt the caress of his lips, the heat as his kiss strained deeper, as his arms snapped closed round her, and his fingers wrapped tightly in her hair. She felt his heart pounding against hers as his mouth slid to her ear to whisper soft endearments that set her trembling. She pressed herself closer as his body strained against hers. She felt the rise of his passion, and she exalted at the power of the force that rose so heatedly between them. She separated her lips, allowing him access to the inner reaches of her mouth as her heart accelerated and her body ached for his.

On the cot with Trace's weight upon her at last, she gasped with joy as his lips explored her sweet flesh. She clasped him tighter, impatient for the intimacy that would make them complete. She held her breath as he paused at the warm delta of her passion and then thrust himself inside her. She was uncertain exactly when she joined his thrusts, meeting them with equal emphasis, indulging the sweet hunger that rose inside her.

She felt the moment approaching. She saw Trace look down at her, the green sparks in his eyes glowing with an emotion that stole her breath. She could hear herself gasp the moment before her elation burst into mutual culmination that sent them soaring.

Still and breathless in his arms minutes later, Meredith felt the weight of Trace's gaze upon her and she opened her eyes. He repeated in a whisper, "You've done one thing right since you came to Texas, darlin', the most important thing."

A single tear escaped Meredith's eye. It slid down onto the cot underneath them as she clasped him tight against her. Her emotions too tenuous, she could not say the words that filled her heart as she raised her mouth again to his.

"I have your watch, Rita."

"What?"

Rita looked up from the sink to see Howard standing in the doorway. She swallowed a gasp when she saw the pendant watch dangling from his hand. She approached him with an effort at calm and took it from his hand. "Where did you find it?"

Studying her closely, his full face beaded with perspiration, Howard replied, "I didn't. Sam Winston found it on the street. Why didn't you tell me you lost it?"

"He found it on the street? Where? Did he say?" Rita took a breath, and said with a shaky smile, "I'm just curious. I retraced my steps the day I realized I had lost it, but I couldn't find it anywhere."

Howard paused and then blurted, "What's going on, Rita? Sam didn't look right when he came in to see me. I have the feeling he didn't want me to tell him that the watch was yours."

"Why did you, then? I mean, if the poor fellow wanted to keep it that much—"

"He didn't want it, Rita! He just didn't want me to confirm that it was yours!"

"You're imagining things. It's a beautiful watch and valuable, too. I was horrified that I had lost it, and Sam was probably hoping that he'd never find its owner."

"Rita . . ."

"You're looking for hidden meanings that don't exist, Howard. This whole thing with the auditors is playing on your mind." Rita moved closer to Howard, despising the step she was being forced to take. She gently stroked his cheek. "I'm worried about you. I don't want this debacle to get you down. It's almost over, and this watch has nothing to do with it. I lost it and didn't want to tell you, that's all. You have my word for that."

"Rita . . ."

"Howard, let me relax you." Realizing that nothing else would distract him from his suspicions, Rita said in a purring tone, "You're hungry, but your supper is cold and we have better things to do right now than to eat. We're not expecting anyone and you know I can make you forget all your troubles in the privacy of our room. You'd like that, wouldn't you, Howard?"

"I want an answer, Rita."

Howard's response was adamant, but Rita felt the trembling that had begun shaking his ample frame. She knew success was within her grasp when she slid her hand down to caress the swelling bulge below his belt. "We have the rest of the night. When we're done, you'll see how foolish your concerns were. I'll prove to you that they were foolish, just like I'm proving to you now how much I want this time for us to be together."

"Rita . . ."

His control appearing to snap, Howard grasped her suddenly close. Silently suffering the intrusion of his tongue and the indignity of his seeking hands as he kissed her with voracious passion, Rita shoved the pendant watch into her pocket and slid her arms around him. She heard him grunt pathetically when he kissed her again. She allowed him to draw her toward their room and the bed awaiting him.

Rita bit her lips against her disgust as Howard scrambled to loosen her clothes. She closed her eyes at her distaste when his naked bulk fell upon her at last. She told herself that it would soon be over and she would resume complete control of him again.

Determined to exploit her power to the fullest extent, Rita clamped her arms around Howard as her thoughts raged in rhythm with his thrusts.

Yes, it would soon be over.

Yes, she would wear him out.

Yes, he would then fall asleep.

And when that crisis had been taken care of, it would be time to figure out what she needed to do about Sam.

Mounted on a rented mare, Elias Fink followed Sam at a distance as the old man rode slowly toward his cabin at the edge of town. Fink had listened intently to the conversation between Howard Larson and Sam at the bank. He had not understood the significance of the watch that Sam had returned to Howard or the import of the exchange between the two men, but he had seen the reaction Sam had striven to hide as he had stopped on the board sidewalk out of sight of the bank. His suspicion that the watch had something to do with Trace Stringer and Meredith Moore was confirmed when Sam went directly to the telegraph office to send a wire to the New York office of the Pinkerton Detective Agency. He knew because the telegram had requested that Pinkerton forward proof of Stringer's identity directly to Sam, and because Sam had signed the wire *with Stringer's name.*

It had not been difficult for him to arrange for that wire not to be sent. He had simply flashed his bogus Pinkerton identification and told the clerk that Sam was interfering with his investigation. When the telegram was destroyed, he had obtained a promise from the clerk to keep the matter quiet. He had then left the office just in time to see Sam mount back up on his horse and ride slowly out of town.

Fink had known instinctively that he could not afford to allow Sam out of his sight, and that Sam would report the result of his conversation with Howard to Stringer as soon as he could. He had hoped to follow Sam directly to Stringer's and Meredith's location. He had not expected Sam to head home to spend the night in his own bed, thereby forcing him to pass the night in discomfort as he waited for Sam to make his next move.

Halting his mount when Sam turned toward his cabin, Fink watched from a copse as Sam dismounted and pushed the door open. He saw the flicker of light as Sam lit a lamp inside. He waited until Sam had settled his mount for the night and had lowered the light to sleep before approaching the cabin at last.

Satisfied that the cabin was silent, Fink made his way to a window to peer inside. He allowed a few moments for his eyes to adjust to the dim interior before searching the cabin with his gaze. Gratified, he saw the uneven lump on the cot in the corner of the primitive dwelling and smiled. Sam had already fallen asleep. The old man would probably stay asleep until the next morning when he would—

Startled by the unexpected pressure of a gun in his back, Fink heard Sam's gravelly voice rasp coldly, "Make a move and you're a dead man."

Sam held his gun steady as Fink took a breath and responded tensely, "You're making a mistake, Sam."

"No, I ain't." Sam stared at the fellow with contempt. He had dealt with this fellow's type before, smooth as oil and just as slippery. He continued. "You figured you was so smart by keeping your distance while you followed me from town, but I saw you. I know your name ain't Trace Stringer like you claim. I know you've got a reason for pretending to be him and for following me, too, so I figure it's time for you to spit it out."

"I *am* Trace Stringer." Halting Fink as he attempted to turn toward him, Sam jammed the gun into his back more tightly, forcing Fink to continue cautiously. "I know that other fella convinced you that he's Stringer, but he isn't. If you give me a chance to reach into my pocket, I'll show you proof of who I am."

"Don't try it." Aware that Fink was attempting a ruse, Sam snapped, "I know your identification is fake. What I want to know is exactly who you are and why you came to Winsome."

"I'm Trace Stringer, I tell you. The family of the fellow Meredith Moore killed hired me to find her and bring her back."

"You're lying."

"No, I'm telling the truth."

Sam squinted at the sheer audacity of the man. Fink

actually believed he could lie himself out of it. He didn't have a chance, but experience had taught Sam that if he let the fella talk long enough, he was bound to say something that he could hang his hat on.

Sam listened intently as Fink continued more smoothly. "The deputy had it figured out right from the beginning. I don't know how that other fella pretending to be me found out my name or why he's using it, but he's obviously in league with Meredith Moore and the dead man who robbed the bank."

"You're lying."

"No, I only followed you because you sent that telegram and used Stringer's name. I figured that you—"

Sam was unprepared when Fink turned toward him unexpectedly, simultaneously knocking the gun out of his hand and delivering a stunning blow to his stomach. Sam doubled over with pain. Gasping, he saw Fink reach the gun he had dropped, and fury flashed white hot inside him. Straightening up despite his breathlessness, Sam fought to wrest the gun from Fink's hand, sensing Fink's surprise as they staggered to the ground in the heat of their struggle.

They rolled, twisting and turning as dominance fluctuated violently from minute to minute. Sam felt victory within his grasp when Fink suddenly shoved him with a last burst of strength, freeing himself from Sam's grasp. Fink scrambled for the fallen gun and turned it toward Sam at the same moment that Sam's hand closed around it.

The sound of a single gunshot reverberated on the night air, halting the struggle abruptly.

Strangely, Sam felt no pain from the bullet that struck his chest. Wavering unsteadily on his feet, he felt only a sense of anger that the exchange between them had gone so poorly.

Unaware that he had fallen, Sam suddenly felt the hard ground underneath his back. He struggled to breathe. The sound gurgled in his throat as Fink's shadow loomed over him.

His vision paled.

Sound faded.

Sam's final thought was a silent, lingering protest. He hadn't wanted it to end this way.

Looking down at Sam coldly, Fink scrutinized the bloody wound that had widened on the old man's chest. He had recognized the distinctive rattle in the fellow's throat. He had heard it before, and knew what it meant even before the fellow stopped breathing.

The old man was dead, damn it!

Muttering a string of curses, Fink continued to stare at Sam's motionless figure. He hadn't wanted him to die yet! He had hoped that by following Sam to Trace's and Meredith's location, he could finish his job quickly. Now he had to wait. He had no doubt that Trace Stringer would eventually come to town to find out what happened to Sam—but he couldn't be certain when that would be.

He hated waiting.

He hated Winsome.

But he hated failing even more.

Making a quick decision, Fink left Sam outside and entered the cabin silently. He pushed the table and chairs over on their sides, knocked shelves from the wall, thrust Sam's belongings helter-skelter, and uncovering the bed, slit the mattress and pulled out the contents in an effort to make it appear that Sam had been killed in a robbery. He was relatively certain that his effort wouldn't fool anyone, but he needed time, a distraction, so he could get his job done.

Satisfied that he had accomplished his purpose, Fink left the cabin and strode back to the copse where he had concealed his horse. Mounting up with another mumbled curse, he left Sam where he had fallen without sparing him a second thought as he headed back to Winsome.

Meredith awoke with a start in the darkness of the isolated cabin. Disoriented and uncertain why a sense of disaster was suddenly so strong, she turned toward Trace where he lay asleep beside her. The warmth of his flesh pressing against hers calmed her. The sound of his even breathing consoled her. She stared at his strong features relaxed in sleep, the dark brows and thick, stubby eyelashes covering his light eyes. His presence reassured her—until the howl of a wolf sounded anew.

Meredith went still. Chills ran down her spine when the howl sounded again, then again and again until the echoing bays overlapped each other in a maddening din. Shuddering, she was hardly able to breathe when she saw *his* image approaching her in the darkness.

Grandfather drew nearer as the howling contin-ued. The expression on his lined face was sober. His bared chest rose and fell in even breaths that did not disturb the gray hair lying against his shoulders. He remained silent until a shadowed wolf loped to his side and the howling suddenly ceased.

Meredith's trepidation mounted until Grandfather spoke at last in low, guttural tones filled with anxiety. She waited fearfully as their meaning filtered through the language barrier between them.

Danger stalks you. Caution.

Hardly able to control her shaking, Meredith whispered in reply, "I don't understand. Please explain, Grandfather."

Loss . . . pain . . . uncertainty will come. Caution.

Meredith reached out tentatively toward the shadowed figure. A single tear trailed down her cheek as she responded, "Please, tell me what you mean."

Danger is near.

Meredith glanced at Trace where he slept beside her. He had not seemed to hear the howling. He did not appear to hear the exchange between Grandfather and her. Uncertain if she should wake him, she looked back at Grandfather to see with dismay that he had already turned away.

She called out to him, "Grandfather, please, I need to know more."

But it was too late.

Watching as Grandfather disappeared into the shadows with the wolf at his side, Meredith heard the howling begin anew. It gained in volume and she closed her eyes. It stopped abruptly at the sound of Trace's voice as he whispered, "Meredith, are you all right?"

Meredith opened her eyes and responded hoarsely, "Did you hear it, Trace?"

"Did I hear what?"

"The wolf howling. It woke me up."

"I didn't hear anything, darlin'."

"The sound was incessant. I couldn't bear it."

Hesitating, he then said, "I'll look outside to see if there're any animals nearby."

Scooping up his six-gun as he stood beside the bed, Trace walked to the window in the darkness. He paused there with the moonlight glinting on his naked flesh, and Meredith took a breath at the pure male power he so effortlessly exuded. He opened the door cautiously and peered into the darkness outside. After a few minutes, he closed the door and slid the lock before turning back toward her.

Meredith shivered as Trace slid back into bed beside her and said, "If there was something out there before, it's gone now, but it was probably just a dream."

Trace drew her close as she whispered, "You didn't hear anything? You didn't see—"

When she halted abruptly, Trace asked, "I didn't see what, darlin'?"

"Nothing. I guess it was just a dream."

Meredith moved closer to Trace and forced her eyes closed.

Danger stalks you. Caution.

The warning lingered.

Rita walked with a measured step along Winsome's boardwalk. She greeted passersby with a smile and a nod as she approached the bank, but her mood was far from jovial. The previous night had been a horrendous experience. She had expected that Howard would be easily exhausted by the intimacy she had instigated in order to calm his fears—but she was wrong. Almost as if he were deliberately punishing her for the long periods she had insisted upon between intimacies of that sort "for her health's sake," Howard had been insatiable. He had demanded more and more until it was she who was exhausted. She had tried to distract him with the supper that still lay on the table awaiting him, but he'd had no mind for food. Yet seeming to flaunt his obesity, he had taken the time to stand naked to relieve himself *three times* before he was finally done with her.

She had smiled through it all, but her humiliation was complete when he finally fell asleep. She had sworn at that moment that she would avenge herself for the intimate assaults that she had pretended to enjoy. She had promised herself that she would make him suffer just as she had suffered.

Satisfied at that thought, she had then turned her mind to the problem of Sam. She knew exactly when she had lost her pendant watch, and she knew it had not been while she was walking on the street. Sam had lied about that for a reason she could not yet define, but the simple fact that he had lied made him a threat to the future she had so carefully planned. She could not afford to allow that threat to continue.

Having made that decision, Rita knew she would have to handle the situation quickly, in the same way that she had once before. Her trip to town that morning was intended to ascertain Sam's usual itinerary. Armed with that knowledge, she intended to proceed with what must be done.

Rita looked up at the greeting of a local woman. She smiled but did not stop when the woman paused to talk. The woman was as common as her attire. Rita was keenly aware that the simple lavender gown she wore was more expensive than that woman's entire wardrobe, that the woman had never in her life owned shoes like those she'd had designed to match the dress, and that the exclusivity of the small, feathered *chapeau* that sat perkily on her elaborately coiffed head—a creation of one of New York's most popular milliners—was entirely lost on the woman's ordinary sensibilities.

Rita increased her pace. She did not belong in a small Texas town that did not recognize fashion, and she had nothing in common with that dreary housewife. She was wasted there.

The thought reinforcing the decision she had reached in the darkness of the previous night, Rita raised her chin and stepped through the doorway of the Winsome Bank. She started toward Howard's desk, but her step slowed at the sight of Howard's darkening frown as a clerk spoke to him softly. She glanced around her to see that the bank was unnaturally silent, and her step came to a halt. Something was seriously wrong.

Howard looked up unexpectedly and saw her. His round face flushed and Rita barely concealed her distaste. Did he actually think she had come to see him because she couldn't bear to be separated from him after the previous night? It occurred to her in a flash that he was actually fool enough to believe she had!

Starting toward Howard when he dismissed his clerk and stood up to greet her, Rita forced a smile. His expression was troubled as she neared. He took her hand and said softly, "As you have probably already noticed, we are all staggering under a serious blow here this morning—the death of a good friend."

Rita frowned. "A friend? Who?"

"Sam Winston. He was found dead outside his cabin this morning when Reverend and Mrs. Bates visited with the thought of providing him comfort at the death of Sheriff Keller."

"He's dead?" Incredulous, Rita asked, "How did he die?"

"He was murdered."

"Murdered!" Rita gasped. "Who? Why?"

"I don't know." Howard drew her to the chair beside his desk. "Sit down, Rita. I can see you're as shocked as we all are at the news."

"Yes, I'm shocked."

"My dear."

"Who did it?"

"No one knows. It looked like a robbery or an act of savage scavengers."

Rita did not reply.

"Would you like some water, dear?"

Rita looked up at Howard's flushed face. Idiot! The difference between sorrow and relief obviously escaped him.

"You look angry, dear, but you shouldn't be. Deputy Cobb has already been notified. He seems to think Sam's death is related to the bank robbery, and that Meredith Moore and her boyfriend, the imposter who called himself Trace Stringer, are responsible for the killing. He thinks it was just made to look like a robbery."

"Why does he think that? I mean, does the deputy have a theory why either of those two wanted to kill Sam?"

"The deputy said that Sam was probably on their trail and they decided to put an end to him."

"Oh, that can't be right, because Sam—"

Rita checked her response and Howard said sympathetically, "Are you all right, dear? I'm so sorry to give you such terrible news, but I thought it would be better if you heard it from me now that you're here."

"Of course." Rita stood up abruptly. Unable to suffer her husband's nauseating concern any longer, she said, "I'm going home."

"I'm sorry you're so disturbed. Do you need to have someone accompany you, Rita?" Howard offered a tentative smile. "I could take you home if you need me."

The innuendo in Howard's question almost was more than she could bear. Rita snapped, "No, I'm fine."

"Rita . . ."

Altering her expression, Rita offered more sweetly, "I'm fine, really, Howard. I'm shocked at the news, but I'll recover."

"You're sure?"

The bastard.

Rita gritted her teeth. "I'm sure."

Taking her handkerchief from her reticule to blot an imaginary tear, Rita said, "I'll be home if you have any further news to tell me."

"Of course, dear."

Aware that she was the focus of attention in the bank as she walked toward the door, Rita blotted her eyes again and turned out onto the board sidewalk. Outside, she barely restrained her smile. She turned back in the direction of her house, wishing with all her heart that she knew who had killed Sam Winston.

She would really like to thank him.

* * *

Meredith could feel the tension building. The sun was beginning to set as she glanced at Trace where he stood a few feet away from her in the cabin. They had awakened in each other's arms that morning, and the joy of it had been overwhelming. It occurred to Meredith that she had never felt safer or more loved than when Trace had raised himself on his elbow to look down at her while they had lain so intimately close. His light-eyed gaze had stirred emotions so deep that they had stolen her breath. His touch had been gentle as he had stroked a straying wisp from her forehead, and his kiss . . . his kiss had spoken a silent promise that her heart had heard more clearly than any words he could have uttered.

The terror of the previous night faded, and the golden afterglow of their lovemaking lingered as they had eaten a sparing breakfast. Trace had then gone hunting for food for their afternoon meal. He had since returned. He had tended to the horses, they had eaten again, and she had cleaned up as he did other miscellaneous chores—but unspoken tension had increased with the passing hours.

As he had done countless times during the long afternoon, Trace glanced again toward the overgrown trail that Sam had taken back to town a day earlier, and her stomach clenched tight.

Loss . . . pain . . . uncertainty.

Aware that the sun was quickly dropping toward the horizon, Meredith looked at the hard set of Trace's jaw. The events of the previous night were heavy on her mind when she spoke aloud the concern that neither of them had previously dared to voice.

"Sam should be back by now. It shouldn't have taken him that long to find out if the pendant watch really belongs to Rita Larson."

Trace's frame was taut as he turned back toward her. "He said he'd come back as soon as he discovered for sure whether it was hers. Sam's an old-fashioned kind of fella, a man of his word. He'd be here by now if something hadn't gone wrong."

Taking an anxious step toward Trace as the previous night's fears surged anew, Meredith said softly, "What's that supposed to mean?"

"It means that something has happened, and I'll be damned if I'm going to wait here to find out what it is."

"Trace . . ."

Closing the distance between them, Trace gripped Meredith's shoulders and said, "I have to go to Winsome, Meredith. Sam took a chance coming here. He relied on an instinct that told him you were innocent and we could be trusted. It's time for me to rely on my instinct, too."

"Meaning?"

"Meaning, instinct tells me that Sam ran into trouble because of us. He could be waiting for me to show up to help him right now."

"Waiting for *us* to show up to help him."

"No. I'm going back to Winsome alone. It'll be dark by the time I get there and I'll be able to move around with relative safety."

"You're joking, aren't you, Trace?" Meredith shook herself free of his grip. "I'm not going to stay here waiting and wondering when you'll return, just like we've been waiting and wondering about Sam. I won't do it."

"You don't have a choice."

"Yes, I do. I'm going with you."

"It's too dangerous."

"It's no more dangerous than it would be for me to stay here alone."

"Yes, it is. If I shouldn't come back—" Gripping her shoulders again as a jolt shook her at his words, Trace continued. "Meredith, listen to me. I don't expect anything to happen to me, but if it should, if I should be delayed any more than two days, you can follow the trail that leads northward from here. It will take you to Caldwell, the next town. You can get on the train traveling north and you can go home."

"I don't have a home right now."

"That's not true. Your mother—"

"My mother doesn't care about me, don't you understand? She would expect me to kowtow to her wishes if I return. Besides, I haven't accomplished what I came out here to do yet. I don't intend to leave before I find out who I really am, or before I solve the mysteries in my past. I'm not going to let anyone or anything force me to abandon that goal."

"I don't want to change anything about you, but I'm done talking about this. I'm going to Winsome and you're staying here."

"No."

"Yes."

"You're wasting your breath and precious time. I'm going with you."

"Meredith . . ."

"I'm going with you."

Her gaze locking with his, Meredith stared at Trace. She saw the flicker that moved across his expression when he searched her face a moment longer before relenting. "All right, but you had damned well better do exactly what I say or we're both going to suffer for it."

"You can depend on me, Trace. I wouldn't risk your safety for any reason."

His gaze momentarily softening, Trace said, "Because you're grateful to me, because you're out of your element here, and you need me."

"No. Because you make me feel . . . *real*, Trace. I don't want to risk that."

"I don't want to risk it, either." He continued hoarsely. "Let's go. It's getting dark, but there'll be a full moon, so we shouldn't have any trouble finding our way back to Winsome. We won't be as easily recognized at night, either, especially the way you're dressed. You just have to remember to keep your hair hidden under your hat and to avert your face if we run into anybody on the trail."

"All right."

"Meredith . . ."

"I said, all right. You're giving the orders—for the time being, anyway."

The shadow of a smile moved across Trace's lips as he said, "That's all I needed to hear."

Meredith realized abruptly that Trace was right. Of all the things she had done wrong since she had stepped down on Texas soil, she had done one thing right.

That truth was never clearer, because she suddenly knew that she had found the man she loved.

"I want you to stay here, at the cabin."

Meredith looked up at Trace as he spoke. They had traveled directly to Sam's empty cabin at the far edge of town and had arrived under the light of the full moon. She knew Trace had not really expected to find Sam there, but neither had they expected to find the cabin ransacked. Shelves had been ripped from their brackets, table and chairs were turned on their sides, Sam's mattress was slit and the stuffing was pulled apart as if someone had expected to find something hidden there. Just about everything of any value appeared to have been stolen, broken, or tossed aside, as if the scavengers who had made the mess knew Sam would not be returning.

A chill ran down Meredith's spine. "I already told you, I won't let you leave me behind, Trace."

"Look at this place!" His expression tight, Trace said, "I let you come with me this far, but you know what this means as well as I do. I need to find out what happened here, and why. You'll only be in the way."

"You think something happened to Sam because of that pendant watch you gave him, but you're telling me I'll be safer waiting here than if I'm with you."

"That's right. Nobody will come back to this place now, especially at this time of night. You'll be safe here while I'm in town. I'll come back for you as soon as I can."

"Trace . . ."

"Please, Meredith, do this for me." His expression tense, Trace said, "With any luck, I'll be just another cowpoke on his way to town for some fun on a Saturday night, but nobody with any sense will believe you're just another cowpoke for very long."

"How do you expect to find out what happened to Sam without revealing who you are?"

"There's one person I think I can trust to tell me the truth about what happened to Sam."

"And if you find out you can't trust him?"

"Then I'll handle it, and I'll handle it better knowing you're safe. I'll be back as soon as I can be. I promise."

Loss . . . pain . . . uncertainty. Danger stalks you.

Her throat tight, Meredith looked up into Trace's intense expression. If danger stalked her, she could not allow it to fall on Trace as well. He was right again. He was better off alone. "All right. I'll stay here."

Momentarily silent at her sudden agreement, Trace then turned toward the saddlebag he had carried inside and removed a revolver. He thrust it into Meredith's hand. "I want you to keep this with you while I'm gone."

The revolver felt cold and foreign against her palm and Meredith shook her head. "No, I don't want it."

"Take it. You don't have to be an experienced shot to use it. All you have to do is point and pull the trigger."

"No."

"Take it, Meredith. I won't go unless you do."

"Trace—"

Trace interrupted softly. "If I thought you'd have any real need for that gun, I wouldn't leave you here, but knowing you have some protection will give me peace of mind while I'm gone. Take it, please."

Swallowing tightly, Meredith nodded. She was unprepared when Trace grasped her close and kissed her hard. Separating himself from her with a tight expression, he then said simply, "I'll be back."

She locked the door behind Trace, waiting solemnly until the sound of his mount's hoofbeats faded into the distance. Meredith then turned, righted the chair behind her, and sat down stiffly. It was going to be a long night.

Elias Fink could hardly contain his glee.

Secreted in the same copse where he had hidden his mount the previous night, he watched Trace Stringer's mounted figure gallop toward Winsome with the full moon lighting his way. The fool had left Meredith Moore alone!

Stringer rode out of sight and Fink recalled the comment someone had made about him having the intuition of a hunter. He was now sure that was true. Intuition had kept him on an impatient watch outside Sam's cabin since early morning. Intuition had told him that no matter how uncomfortable and long a wait he would have, it would pay off with a clear opportunity to accomplish the task he had been hired for. Intuition had kept him in place when the sun had set and darkness had fallen, and he had known instinctively who the two riders were when Trace Stringer and Meredith rode up to the cabin at last.

That same intuition had warned, however, that it would not be wise to face off against Trace Stringer. It cautioned that he would do well to wait for a better opportunity to eliminate Letty Wolf's eldest daughter than was first presented to him, and his intuition had been right again.

Fink was elated. Meredith was in clear view of his rifle sights as she sat on a chair near the window, but he needed to wait a little longer. He had already become accustomed to the peculiarities of the flat Texas landscape. He knew sound carried for miles in the nighttime stillness. He also knew that although Stringer seemed determined to reach Winsome as quickly as possible, he would turn back to the cabin without delay at the sound of a rifle shot. The odds against him were poor at best in the Texas wilds, where Stringer had the distinct advantage over him. He needed only to wait a little longer, until Stringer was far enough away not to hear his rifle's report. He could then accomplish his purpose without interference, could return to Winsome, and be on his way the following day before Stringer had any chance of figuring out what happened.

Fink smiled at that thought. He had done a considerable amount of work for Humphrey Dobbs in the past. His success in this venture would ensure that his reputation remained untarnished.

Yes, he just needed to be patient a little longer.

Meredith's heart was pounding, and she was uncertain why as she sat stiffly by the locked door of Sam's cabin. She glanced at the chaos of tumbled furniture around her. She had not moved since Trace had left, and she was uncertain if she would move until he returned. The condition of the cabin depressed her. It lent a sense of finality to her thoughts of Sam. She knew Trace felt responsible for anything that might have happened to Sam, but he could not feel more responsible than she. She could only hope that Trace would discover that Sam was all right, and he—

Meredith's thoughts halted abruptly as a feral howl rent the silence. She rose to her feet with a sense of panic when it sounded again. She remembered that Trace had said wolves often bayed at a Texas moon, but that thought somehow did not eliminate the slow horror that the sound induced.

Unable to bear her uncertainty as the forlorn cries grew more constant, Meredith walked slowly toward the door. She unlocked it and pulled it open abruptly, her breathing coming in quick rasps as she scrutinized the horizon with the hope of seeing the outline of an animal baying tribute to the moonlit sky.

But she did not.

The howling sounded again, and Meredith gasped. She raised her hands to her ears to block out the sound, refusing to listen as the air grew heavy with its reverberations, refusing to allow the forlorn wails to drive her imagination wild. Suddenly slamming the door closed, she locked it behind her and returned to her chair. Trembling, she picked up the revolver she had dropped onto the floor, placed it on her lap, and closed her eyes.

Elias Fink steadied his rifle and fixed the scope on Meredith as she sat unmoving on the chair inside Sam's cabin. The moonlight cast a silver glow on the darkened Texas landscape as he studied her perfect features in magnification. The interior of the cabin was well lit, allowing him a clear view of the brilliant red curls that spilled down onto her shoulders, and the womanly curves only partially hidden by the baggy shirt and trousers she wore. He hesitated, considering the pleasure of peeling away that shabby shirt to reveal the ripe femininity underneath. He wondered if it would be worth his while to leave his position of safety to take advantage of what she had to offer before she met her demise.

Fink considered that thought a moment longer, then shook his head. Stringer had traveled out of range by now. He would not be able to hear his rifle shot, but Fink couldn't afford unnecessary chances. His reputation and the further use of his talents in the city depended on his success in this venture. Humphrey Dobbs was a hard taskmaster, but Dobbs would see to it that his future was secure if he knew he could count on him.

Too bad. Fink's finger tightened on the trigger. He could have made Meredith Moore's last moments truly memorable.

But what was that—the snap of a twig in the shadows and a rustling of leaves behind him?

Fink turned back toward the sounds, his eyes widening with shock at the sight of small, yellow eyes glowing in the darkness. Freezing into stillness, he saw the outline of a massive, slavering animal crouched to attack. In a moment of stark terror he heard a low growl.

Reacting instinctively, he pointed his rifle at the animal and fired.

Misfire! Fear turned into horror as the animal leapt toward him, knocking the firearm from his hands with the weight of his muscular body. He tried to scream as the animal locked his jaws around his throat, but no sound emerged. He struggled, punching the animal with his fists in an attempt to dislodge its grip, but he was no match for the feral strength of the jaws squeezing off his breath.

The acrid taste of his own blood filled his mouth as Fink's flailing arms began losing their strength. He choked, unable to breathe. He stared up at the sky, his arms going limp as the animal shook his increasingly listless form with new fury. Yellow eyes glared savagely down into his as the animal tightened its grip on his throat.

The stars faded from his sight. The night grew dark.

Fink's last, conscious thought was that he had killed efficiently and without regret, but he was no match for the wrath of destiny that he had glimpsed in those yellow eyes.

Letty walked through the elaborately decorated room as the gaiety of her thrice-weekly soirees continued around her. Music overflowed, bright lights twinkled, and the finest liquor glistened in crystal glasses—liquor that flowed freely to revelers fortunate enough to have received a sought-after invitation to become a member of her "society." Only the best, the most respected, the *wealthiest* members of the social set attended, ensuring that the charge for membership—already outrageous by any standard—would certainly grow.

Struck with a sudden dizziness, Letty faltered in her step and gripped a nearby post for support. Panicking when she heard the plaintiff echo of a wolf's howl, the same that had interrupted her sleep throughout the long nights past, she wiped the perspiration from her brow and attempted to steady herself. Her presence at the soiree had been sorely missed for the past few nights while she had been haunted by the sound. She knew everyone present, and everyone knew her. She had become famous in the city, a lovely, gracious, and entertaining fixture that guaranteed success at her parties. Her beauty was legendary, and her reputation teased, drawing men to her side with the hope of experiencing her favor. She had been on the way to the podium that had been set up especially for her so that she might speak to her guests, but the words she had intended to say slipped from her thoughts.

The light briefly dimmed as the howl sounded again in her mind, and Letty gripped the post more tightly. She looked up at the touch of a strong hand on her arm to see James looking at her with concern.

"Are you all right, Letty?"

"I'm fine." Letty forced a smile. Tall, virile, and handsome despite the sprinkling of gray in his light hair, James was a man of the world who was at an age where he had experienced life's trials fully and had come to terms with them. She wondered absentmindedly how he had done that, and why he would bother to suffer through them again after she had already dismissed him from her bed.

Sparing no time for that quandary, Letty said sharply, "Let go of my arm, James, please. I'm fine, I tell you."

"You don't look fine. You look pale and disoriented."

"Thank you. I always enjoy a compliment."

"I'm concerned about you, Letty."

She responded coldly, "I thought we had already settled that matter, but in the event you don't remember, I'll repeat that you have no right to your concern, James. We enjoyed each other's company for a while, but that time is past. It's over . . . done."

"Is it?"

Letty ignored his response. "As far as my little spell is concerned, I'm tired. I've been working too hard. I was intending to leave early tonight and I suppose the time has come sooner than I thought it would. But don't let me interfere with your evening." Glancing at the sultry brunette who watched them jealously, she continued. "Melissa Hartley would welcome your attentions any time you chose to favor her. She's a lovely woman and a very wealthy widow. You should take advantage of the opportunity she affords you."

"Letty . . ."

Unable to bear the concern in his gaze, Letty said more softly, "I don't want your help, James! I don't need it. Take my advice and find yourself a good woman to come home to at night, instead of coming here where there is no future for you."

James smiled. "I don't want a good woman, Letty. I want you."

Raising her chin, Letty replied, "Then you are doomed to be disappointed."

Dismissing James with a glance, Letty whispered a few orders to her maitre d', and then started for the door. The howls were growing louder. Something was wrong.

Letty paused briefly at the doorway of the suite as uncertainty overwhelmed her. She needed to set her life right again. She needed to see her daughters. She needed to talk to them, to explain things that she'd not had the time or the inclination to talk about in the past. She hoped desperately it was not too late.

Letty glanced back for a last look at the high-spirited scene, only to note that James' concerned gaze followed her. She had known many men in the course of the past few years, but she had been determined that she would never allow herself to love again. James would not be the exception.

Raising her chin a notch higher, Letty dispensed with her former plans. She walked out through the doorway to the disappointed protests of her guests and gave her driver his instructions. Alone at last, she attempted to dismiss the feral wails echoing in her mind as they pulled away, as well as the fear that she could not seem to overcome.

Trace reined his mount to a more modest pace as the lights of Winsome became clearly visible. Just as he had reckoned, the weekend drew cowpokes from the surrounding ranches to the Winsome Saloon, making his entrance into town almost unnoticeable. Slowing his pace, he tipped his hat down farther on his forehead and rounded his shoulders as he joined the group of cowpokes riding in for a night on the town.

Grateful for the anonymity the pleasure seekers granted him, Trace followed them to the hitching post in front of the saloon. He dismounted and fastened his reins to the rail without looking up, aware that his mount was unrecognizable among the others secured there. Adjusting the brim of his hat even lower, he headed for the swinging doors. He sidestepped the doors at the last minute as if intending to strike up a conversation with the brightly painted saloon woman who stood in the shadows nearby, but he then walked past her. He waited only until he was fairly certain he was hidden by the shadows before crossing the street and making his way back toward the house on the opposite side.

Trace pushed open the front door of the house, certain it would not be locked, and walked into the parlor. He looked at the clock on the wall. It was fifteen minutes past nine o'clock.

Trace pulled a chair up beside the door and sat

down. Doc kept a strict schedule. Trace would not have long to wait.

Within minutes Trace heard the sound of a step at the front door. He stood up and drew back into the shadows as the door opened, and Doc entered. Trace stepped out into the light as Doc closed the door behind him and asked with a start, "What are you doing here?"

"I came to talk to you, Doc."

Doc stared at him, frowning as he said, "You're the real Trace Stringer, aren't you? That other damned fella is the imposter." When Trace did not reply he shook his head. "I sensed it all along, and I knew I was right when that other fella let a damned fool like Deputy Cobb take him under his wing."

Trace said simply, "I need your help, Doc."

Doc's frown darkened. "Sheriff Keller was a friend of mine, so what can I do for you?"

"About Sam Winston . . ."

"It's too late for either of us to help old Sam." Trace went still as Doc continued. "He's lying in the undertaker's parlor right now. He was murdered, and it's my thought that it's all related to Sheriff Keller's death somehow."

"Sam was murdered?"

"Nobody can figure out why anybody would rob Sam's cabin. Everybody in these parts knows Sam didn't have much. That isn't what his life was about, but I figure that isn't what his death was about, either."

Trace said hoarsely, "You don't think somebody killed Sam because he caught them robbing his place."

"No. That don't make sense."

Trace asked bluntly, "What does make sense to you about all this, Doc?"

Appearing to consider that thought for a silent moment, Doc replied, "First of all, I never did think that woman, Meredith Moore, was a bank robber. I don't care what Deputy Cobb says, no woman who looks like her would tie up with a dirty, no-good bum like that fella who robbed the bank. Second, she'd have to be a fool to come back to Winsome with you once she was out and on her way, if she wasn't innocent, that is."

"Deputy Cobb seems to think that because she's a tenderfoot, she figured the law would catch up with her somewhere along the line, and that she figured if she cleared herself by bringing back part of the money, she'd be free to spend the rest at her leisure."

"Poppycock! If she was guilty, she would've taken it all and would've run off as fast as she could, especially if she had a man like you to share the money with."

"What about the fella that showed up and told everybody he was me?"

Doc shook his head. "I'm stumped there. That fella didn't come to Winsome to bring Meredith back for murder. I'm sure of that."

"What I can't figure is how he found out my name and that Meredith's mother had hired the Pinkerton Agency to find her daughters."

Doc's eyes narrowed. "Meredith has sisters?"

"Two of them. Two other Pinkerton agents are out looking for them right now."

"Which probably means they're in as much trouble as this poor young woman is." Doc paused, and then said, "Everything seems to lead back to that, don't it?"

Trace's frown deepened. "Where is that fella who claims to be me right now?"

"I don't know." Doc shrugged. "Deputy Cobb and him were closer than two peas in a pod for a while, but the deputy was real upset today because he was looking for him all day long, and wasn't able to find him."

"What do you mean?"

"The fella claiming to be you disappeared. He left his things back at the hotel room, so he didn't leave town for good, but he bought enough supplies for the day at the mercantile, rode off on a rented mare, and he hasn't come back yet."

"He didn't come back tonight?"

"Hell, no! Deputy Cobb was complaining about it when I saw him on the street a while ago. He says the fellow's an ingrate for not taking him along if he was following up on a clue."

"Is that what he thought?"

"Somebody told Deputy Cobb he saw that fella and it looked like he was heading toward Sam's place. I can't figure that but he—"

Halting abruptly when Trace's eyes widened and he turned suddenly toward the door, Doc said, "Where're you going?"

Trace did not respond as he raced out onto the street.

Meredith sat on the chair in Sam's ransacked cabin, the gun Trace had given her still lying on her lap. The howling had stopped briefly, and she had been relieved. She had jumped with a start when it resumed abruptly a little while later. She clamped her hands over her ears, but gradually lowered them back to her sides when she noted a new tone to the baying when it started again.

No longer plaintiff and forlorn, the howling had a new intensity, as if strengthened by the brief lull, as if renewed. Somehow soothed by that thought, by a feeling that Grandfather was watching over her, Meredith felt fear slip away.

Uncertain how long she had sat motionless in that spot, Meredith heard the sound of racing hoofbeats in the yard. She dashed to the door and unlocked it just as Trace arrived on the step. She did not say a word when he grasped her in his arms and crushed her tight against him. She felt the power of the myriad emotions racing through him as his lips met hers, and she indulged the wonder.

Chapter Seven

A warm morning sun streamed through the canopy of trees, warming Trace's shoulders as he walked out of Sam's cabin with a frown. He glanced back into the interior where Meredith still slept on the tattered mattress that they had shared while making love the previous evening.

The short ride to Sam's cabin had been the longest of his life while he had rebuked himself for the stupidity of leaving Meredith alone and in possible danger. He recalled that he had jumped down from the saddle at the same moment that his mount reached the yard, and that he had run to the door, only to have Meredith meet him there, safe and sound, but somehow as desperate as he was to see her.

Damn, he loved her.

That realization had never been more profound than in the moment when he had pulled her into his arms and crushed her close. He had known then that she had become a part of him, and that without her, he would never be fully whole again.

He had kissed her and made love to her with a passion driven by the specter of loss and the joy of finding her again. And when he was done, when Meredith lay naked and replete in his arms in the darkness of the cabin, he had made love to her again. But he had taken her slowly then, with a loving tenderness that only she could raise inside him.

Wakeful while she slept through the night, however, he had perused her sleeping face and had begun to question the desperation with which Meredith had greeted him. She had not yet known that Sam had been murdered at that cabin. She had not known that the imposter could have been somewhere out there stalking her, possibly nearby. She had not been overwhelmed by the fear of being alone, and he knew she had enough confidence in him to believe he would come back to her. Instead, there was something else, something Meredith seemed to keep hidden from him in unfinished sentences and unspoken moments when her great amber eyes widened and then filled mysteriously while she avoided his questions.

His uncertainty during those moments had led him to admit that he had deliberately encouraged her to trust him and feel safe with him. He did not like admitting to himself that he had come close to failing her.

Unable to get past that thought, he had then slid his arms around Meredith and clutched her close. She had whimpered in her sleep, and he had kissed her lips. He had never loved her more.

But it was now morning and the bright sunlight raised those questions anew. Still frowning, he looked back toward the cabin to see that Meredith had come to the door. Somewhere during the long night, he had told her about Sam's death, and she had been unable to control her grief. That sorrow mixed with a strange uncertainty was visible in her expression when she glanced at him. He knew he had the ability to dismiss her uncertainty, if only briefly, but her focus seemed to have shifted suddenly. She was staring upward at the sky, and Trace turned to follow the direction of her gaze.

Vultures.

Trace went still. They were close to the cabin . . . too close.

He walked back silently into the cabin and strapped his gun around his hips. He saw Meredith's complexion blanch when he said, "Stay here. I need to check on something."

"Where are you going?"

"Stay here."

Leaving the cabin without another word, Trace climbed slowly toward the rise near a copse. It had not missed his notice that on a surrounding terrain that was mainly flat, the rise was a perfect spot from which to view the cabin and its interior without being visible to those inside.

Trace drew his gun from his holster as he climbed closer to the rise. He halted abruptly as vultures preparing to feast scattered at his approach with wings flapping. Two more steps, and his jaw locked tight. The almost unrecognizable body of the imposter lay mangled in the great pool of blood that had drained from the ragged wound in his throat. The fellow's eyes were open and stretched wide with terror, and signs of a violent struggle were visible.

His throat had been ripped wide open.

Trace could remember seeing carnage that vicious only once before.

Trace took a few steps closer. He looked up when the imposter's horse whinnied from the place where it was tied up a distance away. Another step, and he saw a rifle cocked and lying a few feet from the dead man's hand, as if he might have been ready to fire when he was attacked.

Trace turned to look back at the cabin in clear view behind him, then at the bloodied body. His chest heaving, he stared down at the dead man and cursed. He knew where the sights of that bastard's rifle had been focused!

Turning at the sound of a step behind him, Trace heard Meredith gasp when she stepped into view of the camp. He grasped her arm to steady her when she swayed. He heard the tremor in her voice that she sought to hide when she said, "Wh . . . what happened to him?"

"It looks to me like an animal attacked him." Trace shook his head. "That's strange, because his horse was tethered nearby and unable to run. It was an easy target that the average animal should have preferred to an armed man. This fella must've done something to frighten the animal."

Her color draining, Meredith said weakly, "What kind of an animal are you talking about?"

"I don't know. Does it matter?"

"Yes."

Trace stared at Meredith's adamant expression and responded, "I don't see any signs that a bear was in the camp. This fella's food is intact, and he doesn't appear to have been mauled except for the wound in his throat."

"Trace, tell me."

"It looks to me like a comparatively smaller animal managed to do this. Probably a wolf."

Grasping Meredith with both hands when her body shuddered convulsively, Trace frowned and said, "You shouldn't be here, Meredith. Let's go."

"You can't leave him here, Trace." Her voice trembling, Meredith rasped, "This man was an imposter and he was up to something, but the vultures won't leave his body alone."

Trace interjected harshly, "He was up to something all right. Do you see that rifle over there? He was going to use it on you."

Her eyes widening, Meredith muttered, "How do you know it was me he was after? We were both in that cabin."

"Because Doc said he was out here all day. He couldn't have been after me because he didn't try to take a shot when we arrived. He didn't try to use his gun when I mounted up and rode off, either. He was obviously waiting until I couldn't hear the shot so he could make a clear getaway."

"How do you know that? Maybe he was killed before we got here."

"He was in a perfect vantage point to see into the cabin, and he was obviously crouching with the rifle in his hands—ready to fire—when he was attacked. He had no reason to do that unless he expected to use that rifle . . . on you."

"But why would he want to kill me?"

"That's what I want to know, and that's what I'm going to find out."

"How? Sam's dead. He can't help us now, and we can't go into Winsome."

"We can't go into Winsome, but *he* can."

Trace motioned toward the bloodied body lying nearby, and Meredith gulped.

Aware that Meredith had taken about all she could stand, Trace slid his arm around her and muttered, "This fella is dead, Meredith, but I want you to remember something. He was out to kill you, and he may be the fella who killed Sam, too."

"No!"

Meredith took another gulping breath as Trace continued. "But like it or not, he's going to help *us* now."

"He's dead, Trace."

"Right, and I'm going to make sure everybody in Winsome knows about it, too."

Taking Meredith's arm, Trace turned her back toward the cabin. He had work to do.

Light-headed, her breathing clipped, Meredith watched as Trace guided the imposter's chestnut mare down from the copse where it had been hobbled during the night. Trace had ushered her firmly back to the cabin after she saw the imposter's body, and she had not protested. The bloody sight had been horrific, a nightmare that was only too real.

Despite herself, Meredith recalled the steady howling that had continued during Trace's absence the previous night. She remembered Grandfather's warning. She recalled tremulously that the baying had suddenly stopped, only to begin again a short time later with renewed vigor.

Her shuddering increasing, she shook her head. No, it was just a coincidence. It had to be.

Trace drew the mare behind him as he stepped down onto level ground, and Meredith gripped the door frame for support. Tied to the saddle was the imposter's bloodied body.

Meredith glanced at Trace's face to see that it was pale underneath his sun-darkened skin, and she said shakily, "What are you going to do now?"

"I'm going to send this horse back to town."

Stunned, Meredith gasped, "How do you expect to do that?"

"This mare came from the livery stable in town. She's hungry and thirsty, and I fixed the bit in her mouth to make sure she can't stop along the way to graze. She'll go right back to the stable to eat."

"You're sure."

"I'm sure."

"What will that accomplish?"

Trace responded darkly, "This bastard isn't a pretty sight, and you can be sure somebody at that livery stable will call the deputy real quick. Things should start happening then."

"I don't understand."

"The town won't let the deputy dismiss this. They all still think he's Trace Stringer, a Pinkerton. They'll want to know what happened, why it happened, and who did it—for their own safety. All we have to do is watch and listen."

"But how are we supposed to do that, Trace? We can't go into town."

"Doc will let us know what's happening."

"Doc Gibbs?"

"Sheriff Keller was his friend, and he has no love for Deputy Cobb, but this first step is up to us."

Turning, Trace gave the mare a hearty slap on the

rump that sent it galloping off. Looking back at Meredith, he said abruptly, "Now it's time for us to get out of here."

Still stunned by the passage of events, Meredith followed Trace without a reply.

"I'm telling you, Deputy, I ain't going to let that body stay in my barn any longer. I want you to get it out of here!"

Shaken, Barney King was still breathing heavily from his headlong dash to the sheriff's office and back. The portly proprietor of the livery stable continued shakily, "I ain't never seen nothing like it before. That fella's body is draped over my mare like a sack of potatoes, and his head is barely attached to his neck. It ain't no human who killed him, but it was a human who put him on that horse and sent him back to town, that's for sure."

Deputy Cobb's narrow shoulders twitched. He didn't like this, and he hadn't been expecting it. He had been angry when this Pinkerton fella left town without telling him. He had figured that the fella was secretly following a lead and wanted to get all the glory for himself when he found the Moore woman, but it looked like that Pinkerton wasn't as smart as he thought he was.

"What are you going to do, Deputy? I want him out of here."

"I heard you the first time!" Cobb looked around him. A crowd was already beginning to gather at the stable doorway. He heard the mumblings, and he knew somebody was going to start asking questions soon, like what he was going to do next.

Almost as if he had spoken his thoughts aloud,

Cobb heard Joe Rankin's voice grow louder. He turned toward the stocky rancher when the fellow demanded, "What are you going to do about this, Deputy? My family is out there on my ranch. I need to be sure they're safe when I'm not with them. It don't look to me like they're safe at all the way things stand, what with a murderer running wild and dead bodies showing up here like this."

Taking the mare's reins firmly in his hand, Cobb responded tightly, "The first thing I'm going to do is to take this fella to the undertaker."

Rankin pressed, "What then? How are you going to find the fella who put him on that horse and sent him back here?"

Cobb pulled the mare behind him, ignoring the animal's lifeless burden as he said, "I'll get to that, but before I do, I need to wire that Pinkerton Agency and tell them that they ain't going to be hearing from their agent no more."

Rankin protested, "That doesn't make my family any safer."

Deputy Cobb glared as he snapped, "I ain't going to be announcing to you or anybody else what I'm going to do then. Just remember, we have a killer out there that sent this fella's body back for a reason. Well, I'm going to find out that reason, and when I do, I'll take it from there."

Gratified that his response had stopped Rankin in his tracks, Cobb pulled the mare behind him as he stepped out onto the street.

"This looks like a good enough place for us to stay."

Meredith halted her mount behind Trace, frowning as she looked around her. She saw nothing—no shelter of any kind—just a thick stand of trees surrounding them. Trace and she had packed up and left Sam's cabin almost immediately after Trace had sent the mare carrying the imposter's body back to Winsome. She had not protested, knowing that Trace knew better than she how to handle the situation. Trace had taken a trail away from the cabin, carefully covering their tracks every step of the way. She could not be sure how far they had traveled; yet she was stunned that he seemed content to stop at a place that she considered nothing more than a heavily wooded wilderness.

As if responding to her silent quandary, Trace dismounted and lifted her down from her horse. He smiled as he said, "I figure this is a good place to camp."

"Camp."

His smile fading, Trace said, "We need to stay as close as possible to Winsome if we expect to learn anything there. Sam's cabin wasn't safe anymore. It would be the first place the deputy would look for us now, and he's bound to know the location of any unoccupied cabins in the area."

"But—"

"We'll be safe here. It's secluded, and we'll be able to see if anyone is coming our way." Pausing, he said, "I know you're accustomed to better accommodations, but we don't have a choice right now. I need to find out who that fella impersonating me really was, and why he was using my name."

"Yes, but—"

"Come on." Curling his arm around her, Trace urged her forward. They had only gone a short way when she heard the sound of running water and saw a place where the terrain dipped down and a stream fed into a shaded pool. Responding to her silent question when she looked up at him, Trace said, "The runoff from this little water hole is making its way down to the Brazos." He smiled. "Hell, every little stream in Texas makes its way to the Brazos River sooner or later. It's good water, Meredith. Good for drinking, and good for washing off the grime of the trail, too."

"You seem familiar with this area, Trace."

"I've traveled around here for Pinkerton a few times and I've camped out more often than not. I found this place when I was passing through. All of Texas is home to me. I like it here."

"All of which makes it important for you to clear your name with the law."

"That, too."

"Too?"

Trace's expression grew grim. "The sun's shining, the air is warm, and we're safe for a while, but the fact that you're also a wanted woman hasn't changed, Meredith. I need to see that it does, to make sure the truth is known, especially if you still want to find out more about your beginnings."

Her expression suddenly adamant, Meredith said, "I won't leave until I do, Trace. I can't. I need to discover what . . . how . . ."

Meredith halted abruptly, and Trace waited for her to continue. His light eyes searched hers. When she glanced away, he said, "I think it's time that you finished what you were about to say."

"What do you mean?"

"There's more to what you told me about the reason you were so determined to come to Texas."

"Maybe."

"Meredith . . ."

Meredith began hesitantly. "My mother never talked to my sisters and me about the past. I need to find out who I am."

"What else, Meredith?" Trace faced her soberly. "I need to know how and why two men who threatened you were killed so savagely."

"I didn't do it!"

"I know that, but I also know you're hiding something."

"No, I'm not."

"Meredith . . ."

The scrutiny of Trace's gaze was suddenly more than she could bear. "You won't believe me. You'll think I'm crazy, and I wouldn't blame you. I think I'm crazy sometimes, too."

"I'd never think that."

Meredith could feel the wall she had built around the secret part of her slowly crumbling. "Is that true, Trace? Will you believe in me no matter what I tell you?"

"Try me."

"I've never told anyone before, not even my sisters."

Remaining silent, Trace waited for her to begin.

Deputy Cobb walked into Winsome's telegraph office with a swagger he did not feel. He didn't like the way things were going. He had been the focus of attention in town since Barney King's mare came galloping back home with its gory burden. He had managed to put off Joe Rankin with some nonsense about keeping his plans secret, but he didn't actually know what to do next.

Cobb silently groaned. He never thought he'd see the day he'd wish that Sheriff Keller were there. The sheriff had been a bee in his bonnet, never leaving him alone. He had remained at his job as deputy because he had liked wearing a badge and the respect due him, but he would have chucked it all if he'd had sufficient funds to leave town in style.

After the sheriff was shot, though, things changed for the better for him. It had looked for a while like he would be the town hero, especially when it seemed like the sheriff might not recover and he'd had Meredith Moore in custody. It didn't matter much to him whether she was guilty. She wasn't a Texas kind of woman and it was easy to convince the townsfolk that she'd had a hidden agenda when she came to Winsome.

Then Sam let him down by allowing the Moore woman to escape, and his trouble had started. Uncertain what to do when he lost her trail, he had been at a loss until the Pinkerton showed up in town. He had figured a fella with Stringer's experience would lead him in the right direction. Unfortunately, he was wrong.

Silently frustrated, Deputy Cobb approached the telegrapher's desk. Things just weren't going the way he had expected. Sheriff Keller had made everything look so easy. The only thing he could think to do now was to wire the Pinkerton Agency about Stringer's death and hope that the agency would stir things up a bit and turn things around.

Actually, he was depending on it.

The telegraph clerk turned toward him, and Cobb said with false bravado, "I need to send a wire to the Pinkerton Detective Agency in New York City."

"I know the address." The clerk paused and then added, "Sam gave it to me when he asked me to send the agency a telegram."

Surprised, Cobb responded, "Sam sent a telegram to the Pinkerton Agency?"

"No."

"You just said—"

"I said Sam wanted to send the agency a telegram. He wrote one out, but I didn't get a chance to send it. That Stringer fella came in before I could. He showed me his identification, and said Sam was trying to interfere with his investigation. He took the sheet right out of my hand and made me promise not to tell anybody about it."

"Stringer did that?"

"I wasn't sure about it all at first, but it didn't make any difference to Sam anyhow because he was killed right afterward. Now Stringer is dead, too, so I figure there's no need to keep quiet about it anymore."

Cobb pressed, "What did Sam's wire say?"

"I don't know. That Stringer fella took it before I got a chance to read what Sam wrote."

Frustrated, Cobb said tightly, "I don't want nobody stopping this telegram from getting to the Pinkerton Agency, do you hear? They need to know what happened to their man."

"Yes, sir."

Snatching up a telegraph blank, Cobb scribbled a brief message. He handed it to the clerk and said, "Send it now, while I'm watching."

"Yes, sir."

Waiting until the telegrapher's key finally stopped and the clerk looked back up at him, Cobb nodded. He did not bother to pay for the service as he walked out the door. After all, he was the law in Winsome. He didn't have to.

The wooded glade was silent when Meredith finally finished speaking. Her eyes were trained on Trace and her face was pale. Trace knew she had not shared her secret lightly and she was waiting for him to respond. Knowing he needed to reply honestly, he recapped her tale in his mind:

She had heard a wolf howling warnings in the night since childhood. The howl was sometimes accompanied by a vision of an old, gray-haired fellow that she came to call Grandfather. Grandfather had warned her when she came to Texas that she was in danger. When the bank robber kidnapped her and prepared to attack her, the unexpected appearance of a wolf allowed her to escape. She heard a wolf howling as she rode away, but she'd had no idea that the bank robber was dead. She had heard a wolf howling the previous night when the imposter was killed in the same savage manner.

You won't believe me. You'll think I'm crazy.

Birds chirped loudly in the branches overhead as Trace's silence lengthened. Meredith's explanation was not what he had expected to hear, yet he had known from the first moment he met Meredith that there was nothing commonplace about her.

Trace said cautiously, "I know it was hard for you to tell me that, Meredith."

"You don't believe me." Meredith raised a hand to her brow and shook her head. "You think I'm insane. I guess I wouldn't believe me, either."

"I believe you."

Her hand freezing in midmotion, Meredith stared at him as Trace continued. "I believe you told me the truth as you know it. I know you didn't have anything to do with the deaths of those two men, and I know they deserved what happened to them."

Meredith said slowly, "You believe I told you what I think is true, but you don't believe that it *is* the truth."

Trace nodded.

Meredith's eyes filled with tears as she said with sudden candor, "The truth is, I don't know if everything I told you is real, either, Trace. That's why I came to Texas. But now two men are dead, and finding out what's real and what isn't is more urgent than before. I can't leave until I know once and for all why all this is happening."

Conscious of her trembling, Trace held her close as he whispered, "We both have things we need to settle here, Meredith, and I promise you this—we'll settle those questions once and for all together."

Promises.

Trace said he never broke them.

And . . . she believed him.

The modest office of the Pinkerton Detective Agency was silent as Robert Pinkerton stood up rigidly at his rolltop desk and stared at the telegram he had received only a few minutes previously. He had thought the wire would be from Trace Stringer, saying he had finished the job and was on his way home, but it was not.

Robert read the telegram again:

THIS IS OFFICIAL NOTICE STOP PINKERTON
AGENT TRACE STRINGER IS DEAD STOP THE MAN-
NER OF HIS DEATH IS UNCERTAIN AND THE
WOMAN HE WAS SEEKING HAS NOT BEEN APPRE-
HENDED STOP PLEASE WIRE PREFERENCE FOR BUR-
IAL AS SOON AS POSSIBLE STOP DEPUTY WILLIAM
COBB, WINSOME, TEXAS SHERIFF'S OFFICE

Robert stared at the sheet in his hand. Trace was dead?

No, that couldn't be.

Making a snap decision, Robert folded the telegram carefully, shoved it into the pocket of his suit, and started toward the door.

"Millie, where are you?"

Letty called her maid impatiently when the doorbell of her Park Avenue apartment rang for the third time and her maid did not respond. It was approaching noon, but she had awakened only a short time earlier from a fitful night's sleep. Countless images had haunted her. In her dreams, she had slipped back in time. The intensity of Wes' lovemaking had been vividly real, as real as the image of her newborn, fatherless daughter lying beside her as tears rolled down her cheeks. She had heard again the sweet urgency in John's voice when he spoke of his dreams of the future for her and her fatherless child, and she had relived the tears she had shed all too soon. She had viewed the gentle consolation of Archibald's gaze, and she had suffered again the loss of loving security when he was taken from her. She had seen flashes of her daughters as they grew, and she had felt her despair stir anew.

The faces and voices that followed had swirled in a whirlpool of days, months, and years that had left her dizzy and disoriented. Strangely, her only clear memories were of the howling that had persisted through that endless period, and of Grandfather's pale image as he had appeared in silent reminder of things she had struggled to forget.

She did not remember when she first realized that she was alone again. Her daughters had left her months earlier, and she had hardened her heart against them as she had pursued a lifestyle that cast out all trace of her past. She was not sure what had brought her to that realization, whether it was the unrelenting howling that gave her no rest, if it was Grandfather's unyielding presence, or if it was the look in James' eyes during intimate moments that said he wanted more than she was prepared to give. She only knew—

The doorbell rang again, interrupting her thoughts, and Letty stood up impatiently. She was not prepared to meet visitors. She was still wearing a simple morning gown, with her undressed hair against her shoulders, and her face washed clean of the artifices she normally assumed to enhance her beauty. Annoyed, she made a note to speak to Millie about her lapse. She started toward the door, unaware that her natural beauty shone gloriously through, illuminating an appearance that denied the passage of years. She pulled the door open to see Alexander Pittman standing solemnly there.

"Alexander." Momentarily at a loss, she said uncertainly, "I apologize for greeting you in dishabille, but I wasn't expecting visitors."

"No, it is I who apologize, Letty." His youthful

face flushed, the barrister continued nervously. "But I have some startling news to impart and I knew you would want to be informed immediately."

Letty took a backward step. The look on Alexander's face was all too familiar. She started trembling as she said hoarsely, "Come inside, please."

Her step unsteady, Letty turned as they reached the sitting room. "What happened?" she asked, her face pale.

"Please, sit. I didn't mean to frighten you, but as your legal adviser and the man in charge of the special project you assigned to me, I felt you needed to hear what I've just learned."

Following his suggestion out of sheer desperation, Letty demanded shakily, "Tell me what happened, Alexander."

Alexander drew his chair closer and took her hand. "I did as you asked. I hired Pinkerton agents to find and contact your daughters with specific instructions as to how to approach them when they did. I've received a report about the fellow who was sent to find Meredith." Alexander paused. "He's dead, Letty. Robert Pinkerton received a telegram from a local law officer in Texas where your daughter appears to have gone, telling him that his agent was killed under mysterious circumstances. The telegram made specific reference to your daughter, saying she had not been 'apprehended.'"

"Apprehended! My daughter is not a criminal! She couldn't have been responsible for his death, if that's what they're thinking. I hope you specified when you hired the agency to find them that my daughters haven't done anything illegal."

"I did, and Robert Pinkerton himself assured me

that he is confused by the telegram. He obviously considered the fellow he sent to be one of his best agents, and he was noticeably upset by the news of his demise."

"What does he intend to do about it?" Letty's heart pounded and a familiar tightness began squeezing at her head. "I need to know that no harm will come to my daughter and that she isn't being hunted like . . . like a wild animal."

"I'm sure she isn't, but I felt I needed to be honest with you, Letty, to prepare you for the complications that have developed." His expression anxious, Alexander said earnestly, "You know I will always do my best to make sure your wishes are carried out exactly as you expressed them. You are a special woman who deserves special treatment, and I am bound by my profession and by my deep affection for you to do all I can to answer your concerns."

Letty retorted breathlessly, "My daughters are special, too. I need to know they are safe and that I haven't caused a complication that may somehow endanger them."

"I won't let that happen." Squeezing her hand more tightly, Alexander said, "Robert Pinkerton is already on his way to Texas to talk in person to the law officer who sent him the message, and to arrange for his agent's remains."

"His remains."

"I promise you that I'll take care of this, Letty. There is nothing that I consider more important than seeing to it that you are satisfied with my services." His fair skin coloring expressively, Alexander said, "You trust me to do this for you, don't you?"

Letty struggled to retain control of her emotions.

"I trust you, Alexander. I know you'll do all that can be done. I only ask that you tell me whatever you find out as soon as you learn it."

"Of course."

"About my other daughters . . ."

"I'm sorry. I have no news to report about them yet."

Standing up abruptly, her head as tight as a vise, Letty said, "I need to lie down now."

"Of course."

Letty turned when Millie entered the room with an anxious expression and said, "Ma'am, you called me?"

"Yes, I did. Please show Mr. Pittman out and then bring me one of my headache remedies."

Letty turned abruptly toward her room as Alexander stood silent behind her. Her knees wobbling as she neared her bed, she lay down and waited patiently for Millie to bring her medicine. She was pressing her temples tightly when the young maid put her pills on the night table beside her and said apologetically, "I'm sorry, ma'am. I was in the storage room. I didn't hear the doorbell. I didn't know anyone was here until I heard Mr. Pittman's voice."

Ignoring Millie's apology, Letty swallowed her pills without hesitation, and then said softly, "I want you to send a messenger for Mason. Tell him to come here. He is family and he is as concerned about my daughters as I am. He will need to know what happened."

"Yes, ma'am."

"I can talk to him."

"Yes, ma'am."

"Hurry, please."

Brushing away an unwanted tear when Millie pulled the door shut behind her, Letty closed her eyes. A single plea drummed over and over in her mind.

No, please, not again.

Meredith glanced at the stand of trees around her and shook her head with incredulity. Trace was intending to camp on the ground, without a roof over their heads. How her life had changed. Until this surreal Texas experience, she did not remember ever having slept without a comfortable mattress and clean white sheets underneath her. She had been too young at the time to recall arriving at Uncle Archibald's house, but she did remember that the bed was clean and warm, and that her sister lay nearby in her crib. From that day forward, even while her sisters and she were eventually separated, her sleeping accommodations were beyond reproach. Her mother had seen to it that she could never be criticized for neglecting her children in that way.

Her present situation was so different. As she traveled, she had slept with little comfort under conditions that had seemed barbaric; yet she had told herself that the situation would improve when she reached her destination. Contrarily, in the time since, she had spent nighttime hours escaping on horseback through unfamiliar darkness, and had ended up sleeping in a cabin that was dank and unclean. She had spent another night lying on a mattress that probably had a life span longer than her own. She had also slept on a torn mattress on a cabin floor in the midst of virtual chaos. Yet on those occasions, she had slept more soundly than she had ever slept in her life. She supposed the reason for that was simple. On two of those occasions, she had slept in the arms of the man she loved.

A warm flush covered Meredith's face as she glanced back toward the campsite to see that Trace was tending to the horses. It had been difficult to tell him the secrets that she had kept to herself for a lifetime. She knew she would never forget the look on his face when he spoke his carefully weighed response with an honesty clearly written in his gaze. She had known in that moment that whatever the future held, he would stand by her, and for that reason she had loved him even more.

Their afternoon meal had been delayed because the emotion of the moment had raised even deeper emotions between them that neither of them had been able to deny. They had later eaten the meal that Trace prepared. Her hunger was sated, but she was ill at ease with the realization that in these unfamiliar environs, she was still totally reliant on him. She disliked that thought. She preferred to pull her own weight. She needed Trace to see that she was not really as helpless as she appeared to be, even though she knew Trace accepted her deficiency without conscious thought. She supposed she should consider herself fortunate that Trace—tender, considerate, determined, and all man in a way that had stolen her heart—had been assigned to her case. In the back of her mind, however, she could not help but wonder if fate had had a hand.

Trust . . . him.

Meredith glanced again at Trace. She felt her heart give a little leap at his innate, masculine appeal. She realized belatedly that despite her initial reaction to this secluded copse, their present isolation fostered a sense of peace inside her. The danger of their circumstances seemed so far away.

Crouching down, Meredith trailed her fingers in the cool pool water nearby. She sighed. The air was warm, the wooded grove was silent, and the water was inviting. There would never be a better time.

Standing up, Meredith began removing her clothes. She felt a cool breeze brush her skin as she allowed her borrowed trousers to drop to the ground, and then unbuttoned the oversized shirt she wore. Strangely, she had almost become accustomed to the freedom of the unusual garments she had been forced to wear. Worn and practically threadbare, they were comfortable in a way that the close-fitting garments she was accustomed to were not. The pleasure of the soft cotton against her skin was unexpected, not unlike the pleasure she derived from the feel of Trace's hard body moving against hers.

Meredith shook her head at the flush that thought raised. Dropping the shirt beside the pants, she decided against stripping away the sheer undergarment she wore. She knew it would dry easily and she hoped it would be as refreshed as she when she was done.

Meredith waded into the stream and caught her breath when the cold water hit her heated skin. She stood knee deep for long moments, then walked out to the deepest point, where it touched her waist, before setting out with long strokes that carried her to the opposite shore and back.

Heavenly!

She was bobbing and dipping, allowing the water

to cover her completely when she saw Trace standing beside the pool with a tense expression and a blanket in his hand. One look at his frown and she stroked back to the bank. She couldn't help but tremble when she stepped out into his arms and he wrapped the blanket around her with a signal for silence. She moved to the edge of the glade, concealed with Trace as he drew his six-gun and they watched a posse approach on the trail a distance away.

"They're so close." Meredith spoke in a shaken whisper as the posse with Deputy Cobb at its head came almost abreast of them.

"Deputy Cobb hasn't the slightest idea we're here." Trace did not take his eyes from the mounted group. "He's riding blind. His posse all but announced itself as it approached. I saw it when it was more than a mile away."

Breathing heavily, Meredith replied, "But responsible ranchers are riding with him. Surely they can read a trail better than he can."

"He wears the only badge in town, Meredith, and he was Sheriff Keller's choice as a deputy. That gives him credibility in their minds and they're not about to go against him."

"Where are they going?"

"They're on the way toward an abandoned shack a little ways from here. I knew that would be one of the first places they would head for."

"What will they do when they don't find us there, Trace? They'll be coming back this way."

"Maybe not. If I don't miss my guess, Cobb will probably try to impress the men in the posse by taking another trail back, by covering more country so it won't look like he wasted their time. Besides, it'll be dark by the time they head home and they won't be expecting to see anything even if they come back in this direction."

"Trace . . ."

"Don't worry, Meredith. You'll be safe. I won't let things finish up any other way."

Attempting a smile, Meredith said, "Is that a guarantee?"

"Damned right."

Standing up after the posse disappeared from sight, Trace drew Meredith to her feet and curled his arm around her. Suddenly aware that the blanket covering her was soaked through, Meredith turned back to the pool's bank for her clothes. Trace did not follow her. Instead, he strode back to the campsite and began packing up their supplies.

Caution.

Meredith dropped the blanket and reached for her clothing. Despite Trace's loving reassurances, the peace she had formerly felt was shattered, and she could not help wondering how it would all end.

Chapter Eight

Mason struggled to present a sympathetic facade as he viewed Aunt Letty's troubled countenance—but it was more difficult than he had ever imagined it could be. He had responded to her urgent summons, and had found her appearing unusually disheveled and upset, still dressed in a morning gown although the morning hour was well past. Her face was pale, and her eyes were red and deeply ringed. He remembered hearing some of the infatuated males in her retinue whisper that her beauty was faultless, that her eyes were dark and brooding, fathomless, somehow mysterious and stirring. It amused him to wonder what they'd say if they could see her now.

Forcing his gaze to remain sober and intent, Mason listened as Letty continued with barely maintained composure. "Alexander said the Pinkerton he hired to find Meredith was killed under uncertain circumstances. He's dead, Mason, and the telegram said that Meredith hadn't been 'apprehended' yet. I can only think that means the law believes Meredith is responsible for his death."

"I doubt that, Aunt Letty. Certainly no one could look at Meredith and think she could kill anyone."

"I don't know about that. As far as anyone in Texas knows, Meredith is a 'Yankee.' I've had experience with the prejudice that a young woman can suffer. I know how it distorts things."

"You're worrying yourself unnecessarily."

"Alexander said Robert Pinkerton was personally on his way down to Texas to find out what happened. He said he'd keep me informed, but . . ." Letty's composure twitched before she continued more softly. "I haven't been the mother I should have been to any of my daughters. I don't have an adequate excuse for the way I treated them except that I was too involved with my own affairs to pay much attention to their needs. And now it's beginning to look as if I've come to that realization too late."

"You're too hard on yourself, Aunt Letty." His smooth-shaven face composed in a deceiving mask of concern, Mason said softly, "You were good to your girls. You saw to it that they were taken care of and well educated."

"Yes, I did that."

Mason smiled. "That's what a parent does."

Letty did not immediately reply. Mason watched as her expression twitched again and she said, "I hope you don't mind that I summoned you here. I've become aware of the importance of family of late. I know we aren't actually related, but you've always been truly dear. Archibald was very fond of you."

"And I of him," Mason said smoothly.

"That's why he mentioned you in his will."

"He was a good man."

Letty said hesitantly, "I . . . I did love him, you know, for his kindness and gentleness."

"You don't need to explain, Aunt Letty, and I'm sure you don't need to be concerned about Meredith. Whatever happened to that Pinkerton, I'm sure it's not connected to her. Meredith is a strong young woman. She'll find her way, and she'll find her way back to you, I'm sure."

Letty was not able to reply.

"Don't worry." Mason's flesh crawled as he patted Meredith's hand. "Robert Pinkerton will probably clear everything up for you."

Unable to bear the farce of his concern another moment, Mason stood up abruptly. "I'm sorry, but I have to leave, Aunt Letty. I have an appointment that I can't break. I hope you understand."

"Of course, Mason."

He added purposefully, "But you will keep me informed of what you learn about Meredith, won't you? She will be on my mind."

"Of course." Standing up as well, Letty pushed a stray lock of her unbound hair back from her face as she said, "You are a dear fellow, Mason."

Steeling himself, Mason leaned forward and kissed his *aunt* on the cheek. Barely able to mumble an adequate farewell, he pulled the door of the suite closed behind him. Careful to glance around the hallway to make certain he was not observed, he smiled broadly.

So, the Pinkerton who had been sent to find Meredith was dead. It appeared that Dobbs' man did his work well. This probably meant dear Aunt Letty's eldest daughter was dead, too.

As for dear Uncle Archibald, if the old man really

did have a true affection for him, as his aging mistress said, he wouldn't have left him a mere pittance while giving the majority of his fortune to charity.

His mind snapping back to Letty, Mason smiled again. Meredith's body would undoubtedly be discovered soon, probably somewhere in the wilderness not very far from the site of the Pinkerton's demise. His dear aunt would most likely summon him the minute she received the news. He would be properly shocked and saddened, of course; and despite the actions of his damned uncle who was *so fond of him*, he would then be one-third of the way to becoming a very rich man.

Robert Pinkerton stared down for silent moments at the body so carefully arranged in the coffin in front of him. He had arrived in Winsome less than an hour earlier. He was tired. The past two days had been a nightmare. He had gone immediately to report the telegram's contents to Alexander Pittman, who had been openly shocked by the news. Pittman had barely been able to speak after reading the wire. He'd had little reaction when Robert said he would go to Texas immediately to verify the telegram.

Robert had then gone directly to the train station, and had arrived just in time to take a train connecting to his destination. Ill-prepared for the journey he had undertaken, he had faced a morass of last-minute travel decisions and finally a long ride on horseback that eliminated the delay of transportation schedules. He had arrived in town less than an hour earlier and had gone directly to the sheriff's office.

Deputy Cobb hadn't blinked an eye when he had requested to see Trace's body. Robert had the feeling that the fellow was waiting to see what he would do. When he finally saw the body, there was only one thing he could say.

"Who is this man?"

Standing beside him in Winsome's dimly lit undertaker's parlor with the bearded mortician watching from a distance, Deputy Cobb appeared too stunned by Robert's reaction to respond. Yet Cobb was no more stunned than he.

Robert waited impatiently for the deputy's reply. He had felt a nudge of discomfort at the deputy's reaction upon first meeting him. Experience had taught him that a lawman did not usually appreciate the interference of a privately engaged detective, no matter what agency he came from.

When Cobb did not reply, Robert repeated, "Who is this man? He isn't Trace Stringer. I've never seen him before."

The deputy stammered, "He had identification that proved who he was."

"He identified himself to you?"

"He did."

"Stringer wouldn't have done that."

"Well, if this ain't Trace Stringer, who is it?"

"That's what I'd like to know. Stringer's assignment was to find Miss Meredith Moore."

"I know. She's wanted for murder up North."

"Who told you that? Meredith Moore is a respectable young woman who simply left New York City without telling her mother where she was headed. Her mother hired our agency to find her. Trace Stringer's assignment was to follow through."

"Why did she run off?"

"That's of little consequence."

"She's not wanted for murder up North?"

"No."

Appearing to recover his bluster, the deputy said gruffly, "Well, she's wanted for murder down here! She and another fella robbed the Winsome Bank only minutes after she got here."

"That's ridiculous. Miss Moore's mother is a very wealthy woman."

"She and her partner shot the sheriff, too. He died later. It looks like Moore and that boyfriend of hers killed Sam Winston, too."

"What boyfriend? Trace didn't report that Miss Moore was traveling with a boyfriend."

"She sure enough was. That fella broke her out of jail as smooth as silk."

"You put Miss Moore behind bars?" His expression reflecting his disbelief, Robert asked abruptly, "What does her boyfriend look like?"

"He's a big fella with dark hair and kinda strange eyes that look like he could see right through a man."

"Bigger than the average fellow, rangy, soft-spoken, and polite, but with a look about him that said he couldn't be pushed. Those eyes . . . hazel."

"Hazel?"

"Light, a cross between brown and green, piercing."

"That's him, all right."

"That's Trace Stringer."

The deputy went still. Robert could almost see his mind working. Everything was backward. Stringer wasn't Stringer, and the real Stringer wasn't Meredith's boyfriend. Instead, he was the Pinkerton who had been sent out to find the Meredith Moore who had a wealthy mother and who wasn't wanted for murder at all.

The deputy asked abruptly, "So, who is this fella in the coffin?"

"That's what I'd like to know."

His chest heaving with obvious frustration, Deputy Cobb took a backward step. "Well, if he ain't Trace Stringer, at least we've now got a name for the fella who helped get Meredith Moore out of jail. Come to think of it, we've got a name for the fella who helped her kill Sam, too."

Robert snapped, "Whoever that Sam fellow is, I sincerely doubt Stringer was responsible for his death." Increasingly aware that he could expect no help from the confused lawman, he said abruptly, "I'm going to get a room at the hotel. I need some sleep. I'll be in town until this is all settled, so if you learn anything, I'd appreciate it if you'd let me know."

Robert turned toward the door when he did not receive a response. He was almost over the threshold when the deputy called out behind him, "You ain't going to pay to bury this fella, then?"

Robert's deadening glance was all the response required.

"I'm going with you, Trace." Trace glanced back at Meredith sharply, and she said more adamantly, "I'm not going to let you go back into town to see Doc alone!"

"I don't think whether I should go to Winsome alone or not is the real question here."

Trace scrutinized the area again briefly. So far, they had been safe in the wooded copse. They had spent the previous day traveling to Sam's cabin to look it over again, hoping to discover a clue as to who had killed him and why. He had found a pool of dried blood outside by the rear window of his cabin. The ground had borne the tracks of countless footprints, indicating Sam's body had been discovered there and then transported back to town. Meredith had appeared confused by it all, but Trace was not. Considering that the fellow impersonating him had seemed intent on killing her, he could only surmise that Sam had given away his connection to them somehow while attempting to verify the owner of the pendant watch. Sam must have been killed purely for the purpose of forcing Meredith and Trace to show up looking for the poor old man.

Guilt nagged. Sam was dead because he had wanted to help them. If Trace's suspicions were correct, the fellow who had killed him was now dead, too, and since Meredith refused to leave the area until she had accomplished her purpose in coming there, Trace knew instinctively that wasn't the last of it.

Questions plagued him. Who had sent that nameless fellow after Meredith, and why? How did that fellow know Pinkerton had sent him to find Meredith, and why did that fellow choose to impersonate him?

With those questions remaining, Trace was certain of only one thing. Meredith was in danger on two counts—from the law, and for the reason he could not yet define.

"All right, so what is the real problem, then?"

Brought back sharply to the present by Meredith's question, Trace noted that she waited impatiently for his response. His stomach twisted tight. Meredith had no idea how stunning she was, staring at him adamantly. She could not see how the bright Texas sun had tinted her fair skin a golden hue, how her unbound, fiery hair seemed to sizzle in the sun's rays, how her great amber eyes appeared to glow in startling contrast to her sun-kissed appearance—and she had no realization that the way she looked at him made him ache with wanting. He did not want to sever the closeness that the past few days had fostered, but he knew he must. He needed to discover the source of the danger that stalked her. He needed to because it was his job, and because he loved her.

"Trace . . ."

Shrugging off his temporary lapse, he said, "The problem is that I can't take you with me when I go to town to see Doc tonight, and I can't leave you here unprotected, either."

Meredith went still. "Why would I need protection here?"

"Meredith, something killed that bank robber and the fella who was stalking you, something vicious and deadly."

She took a breath. "You said it was a wolf."

"Or something like a wolf." Unwilling to cater to her fantasies, he countered, "A wolverine could have done that much damage."

"But a wolverine doesn't howl at the moon."

"Meredith . . ."

Meredith took another breath. "It doesn't matter, anyway, because I'm going with you." When Trace didn't reply, she said, "You left me behind before. That didn't work out too well."

Faced with the memory, Trace relented. "All right. We'll go into Winsome together, but not until twilight. It'll be safer then."

"I'll be ready whenever you are."

"Good."

Silence.

Speaking softly into the breach, Meredith asked, "But that's hours from now. What should we do until then?"

Trace stared at her. She couldn't possibly mean . . .

Aware that whether she did or not, there was only one response he wanted to make, Trace took her into his arms.

Howard Larson sat frozen in the empty bank office. The sun was setting, all his employees had gone home for the day, the door was closed to further customers, and he had only to shut off the lights and lock the doors behind him, yet he was reluctant to leave. Somehow, his home held little appeal.

Howard remembered the night that Rita and he had spent together in endless passion, and he sighed. When he had gone home the following day, it was as if that previous night had never happened. Rita had avoided him and had all but grimaced at his touch. She had filled the time they spent together with inane conversation meant to tire him, and she had accomplished her purpose. He had gone to bed alone, and he had done her the favor of pretending to be asleep when she followed later.

It occurred to him in sad afterthought that Rita's unexpected passion had been conveniently summoned to make him forget his questions about her pendant watch, questions that she had carefully sidestepped before lying with him. Those questions still went unanswered.

News of Robert Pinkerton's arrival had circulated

in town with the speed of light, as had the news that the fellow who had said he was a Pinkerton was not a Pinkerton after all.

Howard shuddered. The man would be buried in a grave that did not even bear a marker, as if he had never existed. Howard shuddered again, wondering how Rita would react to his own demise should he go first. He hated to think that she would be relieved. But that wasn't the worst of it.

Howard stood up abruptly and reached for his keys. Within minutes, he was on the outside boardwalk, walking toward his home. As expected, Rita was waiting for him at the door. She wasn't smiling.

"Is it true? Did Robert Pinkerton arrive in town this morning and tell the sheriff that the fellow lying dead in the undertaker's parlor wasn't his agent?"

Howard replied candidly, "I'm surprised that you need to ask me that question. You're usually so well informed."

"I heard the gossip. I just want to be sure it's true."

"Yes, it is." Howard looked at the kitchen table. "Where's my supper?"

"You're late and it got cold. I threw it out."

"You did what?"

Her face reddening, Rita seemed to swell with anger as she said, "Food doesn't concern me now. Do you know what Robert Pinkerton's presence in this town means? He's a famous detective. He's here to find out where his agent is. If the fellow with Meredith Moore is really Trace Stringer, and if his agent was sent out here to find her by her wealthy mother as the gossip indicates, that means her claim that she brought back the money bag safe and sound will gain some credibility. That also means *you* will be investigated, Howard. That means your accounts will be scrutinized with a fine-toothed comb, and your embezzlement will probably be discovered!"

"Which will be what I deserve, Rita."

"But *not* what I deserve!"

His round face reddening as frustration and guilt assumed control, Howard replied, "Isn't it? I didn't embezzle those funds for myself."

"You would have had no need to embezzle if you'd been the person you represented yourself to be when you married me."

Howard responded sadly, "Somehow you fail to realize, Rita, that although I didn't turn out to be the person you expected me to be, you aren't the person that you pretended to be when I proposed, either."

Shocked at his reply, Rita was momentarily unable to respond, allowing Howard to continue. "I tried to please you. I knew you were disappointed in me from the early days of our marriage. You made that plain enough. I was too timid to succeed. I was too lazy, too involved with inconsequentials, unwilling to put myself forward enough socially. I was too easily satisfied with common goals. The list of your complaints goes on and on."

"And they're true, every one of them!"

"Are they?"

"You know they are!"

"No, I don't." Surprising himself, Howard continued softly despite the growing shrillness in Rita's tone. "I really am talented with figures, you know. I could have succeeded in my first position if you hadn't pressed me to perform beyond my capabilities."

"Before we were married, you led me to believe that there were no capabilities that were beyond you!"

"That was bravado, my attempt to impress you so that you would possibly love me the way I loved you. I realize now that effort was wasted, that you were incapable of loving me no matter what I did. But make no mistake about it, Rita. My bravado had a heavy touch of truth in it that could so easily have been developed if you had—"

"So, your failures are all my fault, then! Is that what you're trying to tell me?"

"Surely not *all* your fault."

"I say it is all *your* fault, every failure, every move we were forced to make, as well as our financial difficulties. You are an embarrassment to me, Howard! You have turned me into a woman that I never dreamed I could ever become, and you've done it systematically, with your lack of drive and gumption, and with your cowardice! Now you've taken the final step and have become a criminal—a thief. Do you really believe I'll take this ultimate betrayal lying down? I tell you, I will not!"

Somehow debilitated by his wife's wrath, Howard replied, "At this point in time, I don't see how either of us has a choice."

"Don't you?" Her full face flaming, Rita said, "I warned you that I'm not a coward like you, Howard. I'm not afraid to act decisively."

"I'm still hoping you don't mean by that that you—"

"I mean that I do not deserve the mantle you have forced upon me. I will not sit placidly by and accept it."

"Rita," Howard said with sudden clarity, "did it ever occur to you that *you* may have forced a mantle on me that *I* did not deserve?"

"Oh, really? The truth is that you are weak, Howard. Your weakness is the only reason for the situation we find ourselves in right now. You have always been weak, and although it pains me to admit how great a mistake I made when I married you, you will always *be* weak."

"But weakness is not one of your problems."

Rita did not reply.

Howard stared at his once lovely wife. He *had* been weak, too weak to face the thought that there was no way to amend the missteps of the past. All that was left for him now in order to prove his manhood was to take the last, irrevocable step.

"Don't consider it for a moment, Howard!"

Howard stared at Rita, unable to believe she had read his thoughts so clearly. She ordered, "It's too late to confess to the authorities, because a confession at this time would only lead the auditors and the sheriff to believe that you were the one who killed Sheriff Keller and Sam."

"Sheriff Keller died a natural death, and as for Sam, no one would believe I'm capable of murder!"

"Are you sure of that? Are you willing to risk your future and mine on that possibility?" Rita took a threatening step forward, eyes blazing. "Idiot! Even if you are willing to risk the direction of our lives, I am not! You owe me a decent outlook for the future, Howard, especially since you failed to keep any of your other promises to me."

"Rita . . ."

"Tell me you will say nothing to the authorities. Tell me you will not leave me totally naked in front of this town by taking away my pride just as you've taken everything else from me."

The deadening ache inside Howard rapidly expanded. He looked at the woman who awaited his response. Had he really done everything to her that she claimed? Had he changed the woman he loved into this grasping shrew who . . . who *despised* him? He couldn't be sure.

Confused, unable to think anymore, too weary to face more of his wife's harangue, Howard said flatly, "I'm going to bed."

"What?"

"Good night."

"You haven't answered me, Howard!"

Howard turned his back on Rita without replying, leaving his wife shocked and livid behind him. The sound of her gasping breaths followed him, but Howard derived no satisfaction from it. Perhaps she was right. Perhaps he was solely to blame for all their problems—and perhaps he was not.

Howard closed the bedroom door behind him. Intensely grateful for the silence surrounding him, he knew only one thing for sure. He had not been able to bear the sound of Rita's voice any longer.

The sun had set, elongating the shadows on Winsome's main street. In the brief twilight before dark, Meredith made her way toward the Last Chance Saloon, following the informal procession of cowpokes in search of an evening's pleasure.

Hardly raising her head, Meredith watched Trace's distinctive figure as he dismounted from his horse a distance ahead of her, and then slipped into the shadows to approach Doc's house so circuitously that he was all but unseen. She had made sure to lag far behind while following him into Winsome so that no one would realize they were together. Her blazing hair tucked up under a wide-brimmed hat that shielded her face, and her shoulders casually slumped, she attempted to appear as just another young cowpoke out for a night of frivolity. She knew her disguise depended on the semidarkness. Trace's deceivingly careless scrutiny as he had glanced behind him several times was proof of his concern.

Meredith knew instinctively that Trace's discomfort with the situation ran deep, and that his feelings for her were intensely personal. She was not truly certain how intimate feelings had developed so rapidly between them, or how permanent his feelings were. Trace's experience was far greater than hers, but she did not fault him for that. Her only fear was that his emotions were stimulated by the danger of their situation, while she knew that her love for him was based solely on the man she had discovered him to be.

Prior to coming to Texas, Meredith would have resented the protective attitude Trace had naturally assumed toward her. In the face of her own mother's disregard for her daughters, Meredith had just as naturally stepped into the role of caretaker for her siblings. It had been the world against the sisters, with only her willpower and determination keeping them unified and strong. Everything had worked out according to her plans, and she had unconsciously begun believing that with thorough planning, she was invincible.

After coming to Texas, however, she had realized how very fragile invincibility could be. And her experiences here had only seemed to deepen the longstanding mysteries she had come west to solve.

The first and most difficult lesson she had learned

was that her invincibility was merely a dream that had turned into a nightmare.

Her second lesson—learning the hard way that her "perfect planning" was not so perfect after all—had been almost as hard.

Trace stood momentarily illuminated by the light of Doc's open doorway, and Meredith's heart did a sudden flip-flop. Her third lesson was most lovingly learned. It had not been difficult at all.

Meredith recalled her reaction when seeing Trace for the first time. He was too tall, too brawny, and too masculine. She remembered unconsciously feeling that he wore those attributes as a deliberate challenge to her, and she had responded predictably. She had not considered that he could possibly be as truly *male* as he seemed to be. She had felt that the spontaneous conflicts between them made it impossible for him to be as sincerely understanding and dedicated to her welfare as he "pretended." In the space of a few short days, however, when she was in the most dire of circumstances, he changed the conceptions she had drawn over a lifetime. He did that simply by teaching her the meaning of *trust*—a word stressed so emphatically by the shadowy, gray-haired figure she lovingly called Grandfather—a meaning she now realized she had never fully comprehended.

Despite it all, she was still uncertain exactly when Trace had moved fully into her heart. She supposed she had finally acknowledged his presence there when he accepted without question her vague and difficult explanations about Grandfather, about the howlings, and about the related uncertainties in her past. His gaze unflinching, he had responded truthfully and logically that he believed her to be sincere in everything she had told him. He had then added quietly, in a way all his own, that emotion had a way of distorting reality, making the impossible appear credible.

She knew what that meant. Trace didn't believe any of it, although he did believe in her. She supposed she couldn't ask for more.

Trace slipped out of sight in Doc's house, interrupting her introspection just as Meredith drew up in front of the Last Chance Saloon. Remembering Trace's instructions, she dismounted and followed his surreptitious path until she slipped through Doc's doorway at last.

Trace pushed the door closed behind her as Meredith turned toward the unfamiliar, middle-aged fellow nearby who could only be Doc Gibbs. She noted the fellow's speculative glance as he addressed her, saying, "I was expecting Trace, but I admit to being surprised by the company he brought with him. I can only assume by your obvious beauty that you are the infamous Meredith Moore." Extending his hand, the fellow said simply, "If so, I'm pleased to meet you. Everyone calls me Doc."

Meredith accepted Doc's hand soberly. She maintained her silence as Trace said, "I didn't come here tonight to introduce you to Meredith, Doc. I need to know what's going on. Deputy Cobb has been searching for us nonstop. I have the feeling that the situation with him is worsening."

"The deputy figures you had to be the person who sent that imposter's body into town, and he's angry. He hasn't changed his mind about bringing the Texas Rangers in on this, if that's what you thought he'd be forced to do. He doesn't like them and he's still determined not to miss out on the opportunity to become a hero in Winsome. To do that he has to pin blame for the deaths of Sheriff Keller and Sam on someone, and you and Meredith suit his purpose."

"That imposter fella tried to kill Meredith. I'm not certain *what* killed him."

Momentarily silenced by Trace's comment, Doc continued. "He's dead and buried now, and especially since he was officially declared a pretender—"

"Officially? What do you mean?"

"Robert Pinkerton took one look at the fellow's body and said he never saw him before. The deputy was stunned, but he still refused to change his opinion that you and Meredith are responsible for Sam's death."

"Wait a minute."

Meredith watched the distinctive tightening of Trace's expression as he continued. "Robert Pinkerton is here, in Winsome?"

"I thought you knew." Doc shook his head. "I figured you and him were working together now."

"Where is he?"

"He took a room at the hotel. It's my thought that it was as great a shock to Pinkerton as it was to the deputy that the fellow calling himself Trace Stringer wasn't who he claimed to be." Doc added, "I suspect it was a relief to him also, if I'm to judge by the talk circulating in town."

"I need to talk to him, Doc."

"I'd say that's a good idea. I don't have anything else to tell you right now—except I need to warn you." Doc added with frowning hesitation, "Don't make the mistake of underestimating the deputy. Cobb may not be the brightest fellow, but he has an uncertain past, and he's resolute. He's determined that you and Meredith will pay for everything bad that's happened in Winsome since Sheriff Keller's death."

"I have to talk to Robert."

Doc repeated warningly, "Trace—"

"I heard what you said, Doc, and I'll keep it in mind. If there's one thing I've learned, it's not always the smartest fellas who are the most dangerous." He added, "Don't worry about getting in touch with me if anything comes up. I'll make sure to check back with you."

He said in parting, "Thanks, Doc," then left with a brief salute as he drew Meredith out into the darkness.

"So this is Meredith Moore. . . ." Robert Pinkerton glanced at Trace as he stated flatly, "I admit to being surprised that you brought her here. I can't say I think it was the wisest thing to do."

His gaze narrowing in the barely adequate confines of Robert's hotel room, Trace responded, "Since I'm more familiar with the situation than you are, Robert, I think I'm the best judge of that."

"Maybe." Turning his attention back to Meredith, Robert said politely, "I'm pleased to meet you at last, Miss Moore, but I can't say that these circumstances are what I expected."

Speaking up as boldly as he, Meredith said, "Did you expect me to come running back to New York City when my mother threatened to cut me out of her will, Mr. Pinkerton? If so, you were wrong. Despite the present threats hanging over me, I don't intend going back to New York City until I finish what I came here for." She added, "And when I do return—if I do—I won't be going back to my mother."

"That's up to you, of course. Trace knows how to take it from there." Robert added, "What neither he nor I expected, however, was that this assignment would become a threat to both your lives."

"I didn't expect it, either," was Meredith's frigid response.

"Why did you come here?" Trace asked, unable to keep an edge of sharpness from his tone.

"Why? Isn't that obvious?" Appearing surprised by the question, Robert responded, "I received a wire from Deputy Cobb saying Trace Stringer had been killed. He wanted to know how I wanted to bury you. My only stop was to inform Alexander Pittman of the contents of the telegram before I locked my office door and boarded a train to Texas."

"Alexander Pittman, my mother's attorney?" Meredith interjected stiffly. "You told him that the Pinkerton agent my mother hired to follow me had been killed?"

"I also told him that Deputy Cobb mentioned that you—Meredith Moore—hadn't been apprehended yet."

"Apprehended?"

"That was the word the deputy used."

She questioned tightly, "The telegram made no mention of the fictional Trace Stringer's claim that I was wanted for murder up North?"

"I didn't know about that prevarication until I arrived."

Meredith nodded. "So my mother thinks her plan to make me return has somehow gone awry."

"If that's the way you want to look at it."

Meredith frowned at Robert's response. She was about to reply when Trace spoke up. "We don't have time for this. If you want an official report from me now that you know I'm alive, Robert, this is it. I've made contact with Letty Wolf's daughter, but I've encountered complications in the case that were unanticipated. Miss Moore refuses to return to New York City at this time and she—"

Meredith interrupted. "I want my mother to understand clearly that I came to Texas to accomplish a specific purpose, and I will not return to New York City under the conditions she stipulated."

"And your purpose is?"

Meredith's response was unhesitant. "That's none of your business, nor my mother's, Mr. Pinkerton."

Surprising her, Robert replied simply, "Please call me Robert, Miss Moore."

Meredith was unwilling to reply with equal courtesy as Trace said flatly, "You need to go back to New York City, Robert."

"I just got here."

"You can't do this assignment any good in Texas." His dark brows tight, Trace continued. "Something was wrong from the beginning. Some questions need to be answered. Who sent that fellow to kill Meredith, and why? How did that fellow know that a Pinkerton had been hired to find Meredith? How did he know that you had assigned Meredith's case to me, and why did he choose to let everyone believe he was the real Trace Stringer? Somebody doesn't want Letty's daughters to come home for any reason, and I don't like being used to suit someone's purpose. You need to find out who that person is, and you can't do it from here."

"What about the charges the deputy is trying to bring against you and Miss Moore?"

"I'll take care of them."

Meredith interrupted tensely. "My sisters—if someone sent a killer to prevent me from returning to my mother, that same someone probably did the same for my sisters. My sisters are in danger, too."

"That could be." Robert continued slowly, "Which means the agents I assigned to your sisters are probably working under the same difficult circumstances as Trace is."

Meredith was suddenly breathless as she replied, "I need to know that my sisters are safe."

Responding in Robert's stead, Trace said solemnly, "Pinkertons are competent and dedicated, Meredith. Your sisters are safe if the Pinkerton agents sent after them have managed to find them."

"How can you be sure of that?"

"Because they have to be." Trace placed a steadying hand on Meredith's shoulder. "They'll do their job."

Silently assessing them, Robert seemed to make up his mind. "I suppose you're right, Trace. You know the situation here better than I do. I need to go back to the city where I can find out the information you need. I'll leave as soon as I can—tomorrow."

"I'd appreciate that." Trace paused a moment and then added, "You can send information to me by wiring Doc Gibbs. Just don't mention my name."

"So you've already set up a contact here."

Trace did not reply.

"Like I said, I'll leave tomorrow." Turning back to face Meredith, Robert said, "I'm pleased to have met you, Miss Moore. I can see why your mother doesn't want to lose you."

"My mother doesn't even know me."

"But Trace does."

No reply.

"I suppose that says it all." Extending his hand toward Trace, Robert said succinctly, "You'll hear from me."

The silence between them heavy after their covert departure from Robert's hotel room, Trace turned toward Meredith as she stumbled in the dark alleyway. It was not until he gripped her arm to steady her that he felt her trembling, and the reason for her tense silence became abruptly clear. Unable to stop himself, Trace slipped his arms around her and held her close. His heart ached at the sobs she fought to control as she whispered, "My sisters, Trace. They're helpless, and they're in danger."

"Robert sent his best men out to find them. He'll determine what's going on when he gets back to New York and he'll find a way to warn them." Trace added encouragingly, "One thing is sure. No one will find either of your sisters before the Pinkerton assigned to her does, and that means your sisters will be safe."

"I want to believe you, Trace."

"Believe me, then, because it's true."

Still struggling for control as Trace's hoarse whisper lingered in the brief silence, Meredith finally said simply, "I do . . . I do believe you."

Trace tightened his arms around her. She believed him, and *in* him. Her acknowledgment touched his heart. He loved her more with every passing minute, yet his love for her kept him from saying the words that could pressure her in the most vulnerable moment.

Instead, Trace held her tight, wishing that she had said . . . more.

* * *

The emptiness of a long evening stretched before Howard Larson as he traversed the board sidewalk of Winsome's brightly lit main street. He had been walking aimlessly for the past hour. His attempt to sleep after Rita's malevolent harangue earlier had proved useless, and his respite was brief when Rita joined him in bed to continue where she had left off in her vituperative tirade.

With no recourse, he had gotten up, dressed, and then stunned Rita for the second time that night by walking out the front door without a word. In the time since, he had examined his conscience more thoroughly, but he had not come to any definitive decisions. He had been at a total loss as to what course to take when he reached the alleyway beside the Red Willow Hotel.

Hardly able to believe his eyes, Howard halted abruptly. He drew back into the shadows of the overhang so he might focus his gaze more intently into the alleyway darkness without being seen, so he might be certain of what he saw.

Yes, it was the real Trace Stringer and Meredith Moore. Whatever their reason for taking the chance of coming to town when they were being sought by the law, they had halted boldly in the dank corridor. Appearing unmindful of their danger, they were wrapped in each other's arms!

Howard could not help staring. There was no mistaking anyone the size of Trace Stringer; and despite her unusual dress, there was no mistaking Meredith Moore when their intimate posture caused a few fiery strands of hair to cascade onto her shoulders from underneath her wide-brimmed hat.

Their embrace lingered, and the knot inside Howard tightened. It had never been like that between Rita and him—the intimate heat of physical contact, the spontaneous touching that meant so much, the simple satisfaction of being in each other's arms. Unless it suited her purpose, Rita had not even bothered pretending to enjoy being close to him for the past few years, although he had tried to please her in every way.

Had she truly changed, or had he simply deluded himself from the beginning that she was something she was not?

Doubts continued to assault his mind, leaving Howard with only one certainty. Rita was not the woman he had believed her to be, but what was worse, he couldn't *trust* her anymore.

Silent and unseen as Trace and Meredith's embrace lingered, Howard turned abruptly back toward his house with a frown. He was tired of walking. If Rita was awake when he returned, he would ignore her harangue, just as she appeared to ignore reason. He would go home with only one firm decision made— that he had confided in his wife for the last time.

As for Trace Stringer and Meredith Moore, whatever their reason for returning to Winsome, he would conveniently forget having seen them. That was the only rational way to handle a situation where he had become sincerely confused as to what was truly the right or wrong thing to do.

Howard was walking briskly back toward his house when the thought struck him. Poor Rita. She had picked the worst of all times to reveal her true colors.

Strangely enough, that thought prompted him to smile.

Chapter Nine

"You're pale, Letty."

Letty looked up at the sound of the familiar voice that carried clearly over the din surrounding her. Several days had passed since Alexander Pittman had stunned her with the announcement that the Pinkerton who had been dispatched to follow Meredith, had been killed; that her daughter had not been *apprehended;* and that Robert Pinkerton had taken the first train to Texas so he might discover exactly what happened.

Her life came to a halt in that moment. At first she ignored the frivolity of her thrice-weekly soirees and remained confined in her room. She hoped desperately for Grandfather's appearance and the consolation that often resulted from his visits, but he did not come. Instead, the howlings had been constant—dire warnings that she did not fully comprehend. When she finally admitted to herself that her own shortcomings, and not the phenomenal success of her soirees was the reason her daughters had left her, she finally summoned the strength to tend to the business that she had spent her life building.

Letty stared back coldly into James' assessing gaze. She did not appreciate his observation.

"Don't listen to him, Letty." Standing close beside her, Arthur Steeple defended her heatedly. "He's just jealous because you're spending most of your time with me tonight."

Half her age, light-haired, and slender in a way that was almost boyish, Arthur Steeple was enamored of her. He looked at her with worshipful, puppy-dog eyes and rushed to do her bidding. Under other circumstances, she might have been silently amused that the young man didn't seem to know or care that she was old enough to be his mother. She might have played with him for a while before dismissing him in a gentle way that added to his confidence and made him a lifelong friend—but at the moment those games were far from her mind.

Letty silently acknowledged that James was correct. She was pale, but she also knew that her pallor complemented the moonlight satin of the gown she wore. She had been told that the miniscule stars studding the neckline reflected with a silver hue in her eyes, and that the same decoration around the hem of her gown gave her the appearance of floating across the floor—when the truth that night was simply that she was tired, and every step was an effort.

"Perhaps I am jealous of the attention Letty is showing you, Arthur." James's response was surprisingly generous considering the anger that had flashed in his eyes at the young man's response. He continued. "But I am concerned, especially since Letty has spent less and less time at her soirees recently."

"She's fine, and she's more beautiful tonight than ever."

Aware that Arthur was beginning to take offense at James' statements, Letty said with a flicker of darkened lashes, "Oh dear, Arthur, my glass is empty! Do you suppose you could arrange to have one of my attendants fill it from my special stock?" She added softly, "I'd be pleased if you'd have him fill your glass, too."

"Of course, Letty, but—"

"Don't worry about me, Arthur." Aware that Arthur hesitated to leave because of him, James said easily, "I don't intend remaining in this crowded room much longer. I've had just about enough *fun* tonight."

Arthur paused, and then turned obediently to make his way back toward the buffet table. Letty waited only until Arthur was out of earshot before she replied with a smile, "If you were hoping to gain my attention with your comment, you may rest assured that you did, James. I agree with you, though. I am pale tonight, but that doesn't seem to have affected my appeal."

"I didn't say that it had."

Letty's smile gradually faded. Her enthusiasm for her soirees throughout the years had never waned, and her attendance there, her natural ability to draw men to her, and her outstanding beauty became the highlights of many members' evening. She had achieved a place in society that was solely her own, and she had enjoyed the ever-changing circle of admirers surrounding her.

She had since been written up with reviews in society columns where she had previously been ignored, a heady compliment indeed; and although the reviews were inconsistent, she was pleased to be formally acknowledged. Like Arthur, men half her age commonly mooned about her, plying her with compliments in the hope of entering her inner circle and solving the mystery about her that she had managed to perpetuate through the years.

Considered a step above a demimonde by a few unyielding aristocrats, yet revered by others, she had laughed at criticisms while making sure her inner circle was ever changing, and that the mystery remained.

She was well aware, however, that there was a downside to the popularity that sustained her unusual position. Although she had acquired a dependable staff that worked tirelessly in her behalf, and despite the fact that her soirees were merry, musical, and fraught with surprises whether she was able to attend them or not, her absences—however uncommon—were noted with whispers and rumors that spread with amazing rapidity.

She had heard them all before:

Letty has an undiagnosed illness.

Letty is on a sojourn with her latest lover.

Letty is . . . pregnant!

She had dismissed the rumors in the past, but lately they were more difficult to ignore.

Perspiration dotted Letty's brow. Everything changed after her daughters disappeared. She pretended she didn't care that they had separated themselves from her without a word, but a sense of urgency began governing her days. Howlings that had been infrequent began keeping her wakeful through long, nighttime hours. Grandfather's visits began assuming a disturbing quality that bore none of the consolation of his previous visits. It had been more than she could bear, and she was unable to avoid the truth any longer. She had known she needed to act quickly or she would lose her daughters forever.

Having accepted that belated realization in the middle of a tormented night, she had taken what she believed was the only path remaining to her when she contacted Alexander Pittman. But Alexander's last visit had left her reeling.

Letty looked back up at James where he stood tall and robust in his evening dress. Her rejection of him did not seem to have affected his confidence in any way. Brown hair only touched with gray, his features warmly reflecting the passage of years, and his physique carefully maintained, James wore his maturity like a badge of honor. She could not understand how he had still managed to remain a bachelor after the death of his wife years earlier. That was as great a mystery to her as why he could possibly want her.

Letty considered that thought with a shrug. *More the fool, he.*

"Letty . . ."

Snapping her back to the present, James asked, "Are you all right?"

"You're wasting your time, James." Her response was less sharp than she intended. "I told you before, I'm not the woman for you."

"That isn't want I asked."

Letty was momentarily silent. A truthful response to his question would be that she was not all right, that fear for her daughters' safety now governed her every thought—most especially fear for Meredith, who was currently defenseless in a wild country where it appeared she was being sought as a criminal, and where an experienced Pinkerton agent had been killed while trying to find her. Being truthful would mean telling him that she had only come to the soiree that night to squelch the rumors circulating about her absences with a dazzling appearance that would leave her admirers breathless.

Instead, Letty replied, "I'm pale, but I'm fine."

"That's not good enough." Studying her more closely, James said, "It's not a man that's troubling you. You wouldn't allow anything so insignificant to affect you so deeply. It's something else, something more personal." He asked her abruptly, "Does it have anything to do with your daughters?"

Letty responded harshly, "My daughters are my business!"

"So, that's it. What happened, and what are you doing about it?"

Stunned at the audacity of his questions, Letty said stiffly, "That's none of your business! Leave me alone, James. You have no place in my affairs." She attempted to brush past him when James gripped her arm.

Holding her fast, he said softly, "Let me help you, Letty. Don't you realize that it hurts me to see you suffer?"

Making sure that their tense exchange had had no effect on the frivolity progressing around them, Letty said through clenched teeth, "Let go of my arm." She waited until James' hand dropped back to his side. "I don't care what hurts you, do you understand? Nor do I want your help in any way. I want you to leave me alone." Looking up directly into his gaze, she said, "Do I make myself clear?"

James blinked at the severity of her reply. His brown eyes guarded, he replied, "Perhaps clearer than you realize."

Unwilling to examine his response more closely, Letty turned toward Arthur when he appeared opportunely at their side carrying two filled glasses. She smiled broadly as she replied to Arthur's unspoken question, "James is leaving, which will give us the opportunity to empty our glasses with a semblance of privacy, Arthur." Allowing her expression to slip for the briefest second, she said, "The din in this room is particularly intense tonight. I would prefer the peace and quiet of seclusion for a little while."

"I'm delighted to accompany you, Letty."

Aware that Arthur smiled triumphantly when she nodded toward James' tight-lipped farewell, Letty accepted her glass and started toward the small, private salon she maintained at that address.

Inwardly shaken at her exchange with James despite her pretense, Letty raised her chin and slipped her arm under Arthur's. She told herself that a few more hours would suffice, and she would then be free to separate herself from the horrendous noise and laughter that had formerly brought her so much pleasure. And she would return home *alone*, no matter how diligently Arthur pleaded. The reason was simple. She had no true interest in the young man, and she needed time to rest from the howlings that even now were growing louder.

Robert Pinkerton increased his pace as he entered the impressive building that housed the offices of

Wallace, Pittman, and O'Brien. He had returned to the city that morning after a tediously long journey back from Texas. He was exhausted from the hours of uncomfortable travel, but despite his fatigue, he knew he would not be able to rest before clarifying an important matter with Alexander Pittman.

Ushered into Alexander's office only minutes later, Robert shook the attorney's hand and asked stiffly, "Did you get my telegram?"

"Yes, I did." The young attorney frowned. "It puzzled me."

"What do you mean? I thought I made myself clear enough. I told you that Deputy Cobb made a mistake when he said my operative had been killed, and that he is alive and well, and still on the case."

"You didn't make yourself clear enough for me to take that news to Miss Wolf, because you didn't give me enough information about her daughter. I needed to know what the deputy meant by the word 'apprehended,' and what you were going to do about it."

"I didn't have anything definite to report about that then."

"Meaning?"

"Meaning," Robert said flatly, "the fellow who was killed was impersonating my agent for a reason that is still a mystery. That same fellow claimed that I had sent him after Meredith Moore because she was wanted for murder."

"Murder!"

"I cleared that up with the deputy. I told him I had never seen the dead man before, and that Meredith Moore was not a wanted criminal. I explained that my agency had been hired to find her because she had disappeared from New York City without letting her mother know where she was going. I felt he didn't need to know more."

"What was his response?"

"He was stunned. To be honest, the man is a fool who is intent on becoming a hero after the unexpected death of a well-beloved sheriff. Meredith Moore was his only viable scapegoat for the deaths that happened after she arrived in Winsome. He countered by saying that whether she was wanted in New York or not, she was wanted in Texas for bank robbery and murder."

"Bank robbery, too? That's impossible!"

"She supposedly helped a partner to rob the Winsome Bank. That fellow shot the sheriff as he was escaping with Miss Moore. He was later found dead under mysterious circumstances by my operative. A local fellow who the deputy assumes was on Miss Moore's trail was also killed shortly afterward, and the deputy was content to blame his death on Miss Moore and my operative."

"So they're both wanted by the law now." Taking a moment to wipe his handkerchief across his forehead, Alexander said, "We have to get Miss Wolf's daughter back to New York as soon as possible."

"She won't leave Texas."

"Why? Doesn't she realize how much trouble she's in?"

"Why she won't leave is a good question. I can't rightly answer it except to say that the young lady is adamant. She won't leave Texas until she accomplishes what she went there for."

"Which is?"

"She won't say."

"And the law be damned!"

Robert paused, then said, "Actually, she feels quite safe for the time being since my agent is protecting her."

"He wasn't hired to *protect* her. He was hired to bring her back to her mother."

"No, he wasn't. He was supposed to make sure she considered the consequences of her actions."

"Let's be honest, Robert. No reasonable young woman would take the chance of being cut from her wealthy mother's will just to prove a point."

"I suppose Meredith Moore isn't a reasonable woman, then."

Alexander did not reply.

"She won't come back, and Trace Stringer, my operative, is determined to stay with her until she's satisfied to leave."

Alexander's pale eyes narrowed. "I hear Meredith Moore is a beautiful young woman, almost as beautiful as her mother. Is he smitten with her?"

Robert replied noncommittally, "You'd have to ask Trace personally in order to get an answer to that question, but I wouldn't recommend it. That aside, I came here for another reason. I need to know who is aware of the stipulations Letty Wolf put into her new will, and who knows you hired my agency to find her daughters."

Alexander shrugged. "Miss Wolf did not request absolute secrecy, but then, she didn't need to. I'm not in the habit of revealing the personal requests of my clients. Since Miss Wolf's interests are solely my concern, I'm relatively certain no one knows except those involved in rewriting the will."

"Can you trust the people in your office?"

"The people in my office have worked for me for years."

"Do you know anything about their backgrounds?"

"Except when I checked their references when hiring them years ago, I've never felt it necessary to intrude on their privacy."

Robert noted Alexander's stiffening demeanor, but he persisted. "And the person who will benefit the most if Miss Wolf's daughters refuse to abide by her stipulations is?"

"Mason Little, Esquire, of course, but he is a very well respected member of the bar and above reproach. He is also her—" Alexander paused briefly before continuing. "Well, Miss Wolf considers Mr. Little her nephew although an actual familial tie doesn't exist. Miss Wolf has remained close to him since the death of her . . . her intimate friend, his uncle, Archibald Fitzsimmons."

"Mason Little is another attorney."

"An attorney who passed the bar with one of the highest marks ever achieved, I might add."

"Who told you that?"

"Miss Wolf. She said she practically had to pry that information out of Mr. Little. She's very proud of him."

"Too bad she wasn't as proud of her daughters."

Alexander's reply was rigid. "Mr. Pinkerton, Miss Wolf is a dear friend."

Robert stared at the darkening flush across Alexander's cheeks. It occurred to him that the fellow's feelings for the appealing Miss Wolf ran deeper than he was prepared to admit. Choosing to change the subject, he said, "Tell me more about Mason Little."

Taking a moment to rein his emotions under control, Alexander began speaking softly.

"Tell me more about Mason Little."

A fire burned brightly in the ramshackle cabin where Meredith and Trace had taken up residence that evening. Its warmth relieved the former mustiness and restored a semblance of coziness to the otherwise dank, abandoned structure that Trace was certain Meredith would have sneered at only weeks earlier. They had eaten a warm but spare meal cooked over the fire, after which Meredith sat next to him on the bedrolls he had spread beside the fireplace, and leaned casually against him.

Slipping his arm around her, Trace drew Meredith closer and brushed her temple with his lips. The moment was quiet and relaxed, a far cry from their increasingly tense attempts to elude Deputy Cobb's persistent posse. Trace knew that he would be content if the present moment lasted forever, but he was only too aware that Meredith was accustomed to more.

Turning toward him, Meredith smiled, appearing comfortable in his arms, and Trace wondered if she realized how her intrinsic scent set his pulses racing without any effort on her part at all, how her warm body heat raised a heat of another kind inside him, and how her small smile tore him up inside in ways she would never understand.

Trace also wondered with sudden sobriety if Meredith realized that they were running out of places to hide, while she grew more exhausted every day.

With that thought in mind, Trace had waited only until twilight began darkening the sky and he could be fairly certain that the posse had returned home until the next morning, before moving Meredith and their shrinking supplies into the abandoned structure that the posse had searched earlier. Yet despite her exhaustion, no manner of physical inconvenience appeared to weaken Meredith's determination to remain near Winsome until all was settled with the law.

It occurred to Trace that Meredith had inordinate faith in him. She believed he would keep her safe until they finally heard from Robert and found a way to prove that they were both innocent of all the charges against them. He hoped her faith was justified, because Deputy Cobb was becoming desperate. Accepting the imposter as a Pinkerton had made Cobb appear a fool, and Cobb's continued failure to find them was another heavy blow that he sensed the deputy was not ready to accept.

Meredith stirred against him as she appeared to consider his inquiry about Mason Little a few moments longer. Turning toward him at last, Meredith responded thoughtfully, "I don't really know very much about Mason Little. I do know that my mother was extremely pleased when he renewed his acquaintanceship with her a few years ago, and that she considers him family."

"But you don't."

"I only met him a few times, but"—she shook her head—"I didn't like him. Honestly, I don't know whether I had that reaction because of the condescension I sensed in his voice when he talked to my sisters and me, or because my mother seemed to regard him more highly than she did us."

"That can't be true."

"Yes, it can."

Silent for long moments, Trace replied, "Why do you suppose your mother made Mason Little the alternate beneficiary in her will?"

"She seemed to be flattered that he considered her his aunt although there was no formal relationship between them. Is that important?"

"Someone doesn't want you or your sisters to return to New York to be written back into your mother's will. Mason Little will benefit if that happens."

"Mr. Little is wealthy in his own right. He doesn't need Mother's money."

"Are you sure of that?"

"He has a well-established practice and he's respected by all his clients."

"Who told you that?"

Meredith considered that question before responding. "Actually, I don't know. That conclusion is generally accepted in my mother's social set. I can only suppose that also influences my mother's attitude toward him."

Their conversation was interrupted by a sudden, muffled sound outside the cabin. Trace went momentarily still. Picking his rifle up off the floor without a word, he moved stealthily toward the window. He peered out into the darkness for a few moments, then slid the lock on the door and slipped out into the yard.

Meredith held her breath. What was out there? What had he walked into? She remembered the vicious, yellow-eyed animal that she had glimpsed in the shadows the moment before it attacked the bank robber. It seemed to have appeared again, just as unexpectedly, when the imposter threatened her life.

The animal had left both men dead, their bodies savagely torn.

Her heart pounding, Melanie told herself that it was different this time. Trace didn't threaten her in any way. He was her lifeline, her consolation, her strength. His strong presence was the motivation for her to get up each morning and face the uncertainty of the day in a place that was totally foreign to her. Without him, she would be lost, but not because she depended on his Pinkerton expertise in order to make it through each day. She was a survivor. She had faced seemingly hopeless circumstances before and had emerged unscathed. She told herself she would have done the same again, somehow.

Yet with Trace, she had a sense of the future that went beyond the moment. She was able to look ahead for the first time in her life—a heady feeling, indeed. She had long since realized that she wanted to share that future with Trace—if the mysteries surrounding her could be solved, and if Trace felt the same way about her.

A few more moments passed before Trace reappeared in the doorway as silently as he had left. He shrugged casually as he said, "It was nothing. Just a possum rooting around."

Meredith took a deep breath at last.

Seated beside her again on the bedroll he had spread in front of the fire, Trace drew Meredith back against him. He felt her trembling and he drew her closer into the safety of his arms. Uncertain what he would find when he had slipped out into the shadowed yard a few moments previously, he'd had only one thought in mind—Meredith's safety. Relieved moments later to discover that there was no threat, he had been unprepared for her question when she said abruptly, "Why are you still frowning if it was nothing to be worried about, Trace? We're safe here, aren't we?"

Trace replied with a wry smile, "Sometimes I forget you're a city girl who thinks a lock on the door can keep out unwanted visitors, Meredith. That's not true in Texas. The country is too wide, and we've been tracked constantly since Robert left for the city. Deputy Cobb won't give up. We're sleeping with a roof over our heads tonight, but I can't guarantee that we will tomorrow. In other words, everything is uncertain here right now. In New York, it would be different."

"I won't go back."

"If you're worried about what I said about the Texas Rangers, Cobb refuses to call them in on this."

"I'm not worried about that. I . . . I just need to clear my name here."

"We can do that more safely if we leave the area."

"You don't understand, Trace." Her expression reflected a long-standing anguish. "It's important that I remain in Texas, more important to me than anything else. Unless I stay and find out who I am, I'm nobody. I'm haunted by a past that I don't know anything about. I have nothing to offer anybody, no past and no future."

Confused by her response, Trace shook his head. "I can tell you who you are. You're Meredith Moore, the daughter of Letty Wolf, a beautiful, successful, wealthy woman who wants her daughters home with her."

"No, I'm not." Adamant, Meredith continued tightly. "I'm Meredith Moore, daughter of a woman named Letty whose maiden name I don't even know. I think my mother was married to my father, but I'm not really sure. I've never met any members of my extended family. I'm not sure if I have any aunts, uncles, cousins, or any legitimate grandparents, either. All I know is that my father died before I was born. The only memory I have of my life before arriving in New York City is the image of my mother ignoring my sister's and my tears when she deposited us in a Texas orphanage and turned her back on us. For all intents and purposes, my sister and I were orphaned by her."

"Your mother was young. She wanted to escape her past."

"From a past she won't discuss, and from her daughters, too."

"She sent for you when she was able."

"She had another daughter—out of wedlock—which probably raised pangs of conscience."

"Meredith, you're not being very generous."

"She didn't love us, Trace! We were obligations that she tended to reluctantly. She had her own agenda, and we were in the way."

"I don't believe that. How could she not love you?"

Her eyes moist, amber pools, her lips only inches from his as they twitched with emotion, Meredith replied, "Too easily."

"Family history isn't as important as you make it seem, Meredith."

"Yes, it is. Trace, there are so many things I don't understand—especially the howlings that have warned me of every bad occurrence in my life and Grandfather's visits. You've found ways to explain them that seem logical in your mind, but I can't accept them." Somehow unwilling to mention the animal that had saved her life with vicious attacks on two occasions, she pressed, "I need to know *who* Grandfather is, and *why* he comes to me. He's trying to tell me something that I can't comprehend—I'm sure of it. I'll never find out what it is in the city. Grandfather is uncomfortable there. His visits are short. I can only accomplish what I need to do here, in Texas, where I was born."

His heart aching for her distress, Trace said softly, "But so many unexpected things have happened since you arrived in Texas. This might not be the right time."

"What is the right time, Trace? I've waited so long. I've planned so diligently. I need to know. I won't be free to go on with my life until I do."

"If you return to New York, you can ask your mother those questions outright."

"I've already done that. It's a waste of time. She said the past is dead. She won't talk about it."

"About your father . . ."

"He's a mystery man to me."

"You inherited your coloring from him."

Meredith gave a tight laugh. "That's all you know about him, too, is my guess."

"He was a good man. I know that much."

Suddenly hopeful, Meredith asked, "How do you know that?"

"Because his daughter is beautiful and smart, and because she is honest and determined to make her own way."

Meredith paused before responding, "Perhaps, although I've been almost totally dependent on you since I arrived in Texas."

"Because I was hired to find you, and I ended up

believing in you. I still do, Meredith, but I can't guarantee your safety here much longer. We've been lucky so far, but Deputy Cobb knows this area of the country better than I do. He's bound to find us sooner or later."

Becoming visibly agitated at his reply, Meredith said, "Robert Pinkerton will come up with something before Deputy Cobb catches up with us. We'll figure things out then and settle things with the law. Then we'll be able to go forward."

"We?" The simple, two-letter word tugged at Trace's heart. "My official involvement in this case ends when you sign the paper in my saddlebag that says you refused to abide by the stipulations in your mother's will."

"Oh, I thought—"

Unwilling to let the moment pass, Trace urged softly, "What did you think, Meredith?"

"I thought you would see this through to the end with me because . . . because this time we've spent together meant as much to you as it's meant to me."

"What has it meant to you, Meredith? I need to have you spell it out for me."

Meredith replied softly, "Don't you know? You changed my life, Trace. You showed me that I could believe in someone. You made me believe this uncertainty that has haunted me all my life really can end, because you're standing beside me. You made me understand the meaning of trust—something that Grandfather tried so diligently to impress upon me."

His heart pounding harder, Trace whispered, "Tell me what that means."

"It means . . . it means . . ."

Unwilling to allow another moment to elapse before he said the words, Trace whispered hoarsely into the breach, "Does it mean you love me the way I love you, Meredith?" Earnest, unable to hold back the flood of emotion he had restrained for so long, he whispered, "Does it mean you'd be willing to give up the luxurious life you led in New York City once you straightened out the mysteries of your past? Because I could never provide that for you."

"Provide it for me?"

He drew her closer. His voice deep with emotion, he said, "You're a rich woman's daughter. You're accustomed to more material things than I could ever give you."

"But you said love me."

"Is that so hard to believe?"

"Yes . . . no . . ." As she halted, Meredith's gaze assumed a vulnerability that nearly shredded his control as she continued. "I'm an unknown quantity, Trace. I'm a mystery that's yet unsolved. I don't really know who I am, exactly where I come from, or why my mother hid my family history from me and my sisters for all these years."

"I don't need to know any of those things about you."

"But *I* need to know them. Please try to understand, Trace."

Silence.

"Trace . . ."

"There's only one thing I need to know, Meredith—if you love me. I want you to tell me the truth. I need to be sure what you feel isn't gratitude, or a fear of being abandoned. You don't have to be afraid that I'll leave you, because whatever your answer is, I'll still love you." Taking a breath, Trace whispered, "This is your chance to say what you really mean, once and for all."

Incredulous, Meredith said, "Of course I love you! How could you doubt that for a minute? I'm only afraid that you might regret—"

Her response was cut short when Trace covered her mouth abruptly with his. He crushed her in his arms in a grip so perilously tight that she was momentarily breathless and she surrendered fully to Trace's kiss. Attempting to continue her aborted response when he drew back at last, she went silent when Trace placed his finger against her lips and said, "I don't need to know anything else. We'll get through this together."

"But—"

Drawing her closer, Trace whispered against her lips, "I'll talk to Doc Gibbs tomorrow. I heard Willard Dread at the mercantile store say that Doc visits Mrs. Lindstrom every Thursday to treat an ongoing physical condition. That's tomorrow. I'll wait for him on the trail and find out if Robert sent him any information yet."

"And we'll take it from there."

Silent for a long moment, Trace whispered, "I love you, Meredith."

He loved her.

Swallowing tightly, the joy inside her inhibiting her reply, Meredith responded in the only way she could.

"I suppose you're wondering why I called this meeting tonight." His limited stature seeming to swell as he addressed the assemblage in a town hall that was filled to brimming, Deputy Cobb felt a sense of power surge through him. It was evening. The streets outside were dark, lit only by flickering lampposts, yet everyone in town had shown up for the meeting he had called. Everyone was looking at him, listening, waiting for him to say what they wanted to hear. Well, he was ready.

Cobb continued. "I called all of you here tonight to make the report that I know you've been waiting for. You all know that we haven't found the two responsible for Sheriff Keller's and Sam Winston's deaths yet. It's been frustrating for my posse, but we're getting closer every day and those two are getting nervous. They ain't been hiding their tracks as well as they did before, maybe because we're so close behind them, but just a few more days and we'll get them. That's for sure. They have no place left to go."

"They can always leave the state, being's the woman's a city girl."

The voice from the back of the hall turned Cobb's head toward it with a frown as he replied, "But they don't want to, or they'd be gone already. Something's holding that woman here. Maybe she don't want to share with her boyfriend. Maybe she has the major portion of that bank money hidden somewhere and she wants it for herself. Maybe she's hoping her boyfriend will get tired of being chased and move on. Whatever her reason is, I'll find it out before her boyfriend and her do their final dance from the nearest tree."

Aware of the startled reaction his statement had on the crowd, Cobb said tightly, "Are some of you taking offense at what I just said? Are you people forgetting what a good man Sheriff Keller was, and how much he did for this community? No high-stepping city woman has the right to bring him to his end the way she did."

"That woman didn't shoot the sheriff!"

Looking back at the fellow who had shouted in reply, Cobb responded, "But her partner did, and then he got killed by some kind of animal, according to the fella who just happened to take his place the first chance he got. I know one thing for sure. Sam Winston wouldn't object to what I just said."

"Sam was a law-abiding man. He'd be the first to say you ain't got no proof against them."

His face reddening at the heckler's persistent replies, Deputy Cobb shouted, "I got all the proof me or any red-blooded man in this crowd needs! I don't know about you, but I'm going to get up at dawn tomorrow, and I'm going to ride out to find them two. I'm going to scour this country, and I ain't going to let up until they get tired of running and make a mistake. That's when I'll get them. I know I can depend on the men in my posse, but what I want to know now is how many of you fellas here tonight are in this for the long run like I am—how many will make a commitment to ride with me until I catch them, until I try them on the spot, and deal out the punishment they deserve!"

"Don't you think you're jumping the gun?"

Cobb shouted back, "No, I don't. I saw the sheriff's dead body. I also saw Sam's, and the bloody body of that fella Meredith Moore's boyfriend sent back into town. I ain't never going to forget it. Those two need to pay!"

Hearing the mumbles of agreement in the crowd, Cobb seized the opportunity and shouted, "So tell me! How many of you are with me? Let me see your hands."

Inwardly exalting when hands waved enthusiastically throughout the crowd, Cobb smiled. "All right, and I'll make you a promise right now. We'll get them two, and deal out what they deserve. You can depend on it!"

Cheers were still bouncing against the rafters of the hall when Rita turned toward Howard as he stood up beside her. She did not truly understand the reason why he had been reluctant to attend the meeting with her, but she had convinced him that it was important for him to go. She was almost sorry that she did. Her stomach had turned at his gasp of disapproval when Cobb mentioned the frontier justice he intended. He was weak, cowardly. Rita inwardly cringed. She wondered how he would react if he realized what his cowardice had forced her to do.

Well, she wouldn't take the chance of finding out. She was glad Deputy Cobb would make sure of that.

Hardly able to conceal her sneer, Rita said abruptly, "Let's go home, Howard. Deputy Cobb has said everything he's going to say."

"I'm going to stay, Rita."

"Why?" She pressed with a mocking smile, "You're not thinking of joining the posse, are you?"

"I told you once before, I'm a thief, Rita, but I'm not a murderer."

"Shhhh!" Glancing around her to make sure they were not overhead, Rita rasped, "What if someone overheard you? Are you crazy?"

"No, just honest."

Rita replied through clenched teeth with sudden heat, "If you were as honest as you claim, you wouldn't have taken that money in the first place."

Regretting her outburst, Rita glanced around her again to make certain that no one had heard her. "You've developed a way of pushing me beyond my control lately, Howard, and I don't like it. Let's go home."

"No. I'm going to stay to see if I can talk some sense into some of these men."

"It's too late to pretend to be a good Samaritan, Howard."

Howard's round face flushed hotly as he replied, "Maybe that's true, but I'm going to try, anyway."

His outright defiance irritating her, Rita snapped, "You always were a fool," before turning on her heel and heading for the door.

"You've spoken personally with Robert Pinkerton since he returned from Texas?" Seated across from Alexander Pittman in the solitude of her luxurious drawing room, Letty flushed with anticipation. The pale pink of her morning gown lent color to an otherwise pale complexion that revealed only too clearly the sleeplessness of the previous night.

Aching for her distress, Alexander said softly, "I did. Mr. Pinkerton explained that an imposter claiming to be his operative was the fellow who was killed—evidently by some kind of animal because his head was almost severed. The deputy was furious when the fellow was then tied to his horse by an unknown individual and sent back to town."

Letty paled further and Alexander said, "I'm not saying this to upset you, Letty. I just want to make sure you realize that this situation has turned out to be more complicated than expected. Robert has talked to your daughter and his operative personally, however, and they are both fine."

"Oh, I'm so glad." Relief registered in her voice. "It's all going to be straightened out soon, then. I'll have to tell Mason. He'll be happy to hear that news, too. He was almost as upset as I was when I told him that Meredith's Pinkerton had been killed and she was unprotected."

"Well . . ." Hesitating, Alexander hedged. "As I said, there is a complication. The deputy is inexperienced and he's confused. It appears it might take time to straighten out everything according to Texas law."

Letty shook her head. "Meaning?"

"Meredith and Trace Stringer, the Pinkerton assigned to her, are wanted by the law."

"Wanted? For what?"

Alexander paused to clear his throat.

"Alexander, please."

"They're wanted for bank robbery and murder."

"Murder!"

"It's all a mistake that was further confounded by the man professing to be Trace Stringer."

Breathless, Letty stood up unsteadily. "This can't be happening. My daughter is innocent."

"I know she is, but you needn't worry about her. The Pinkerton assigned to her is determined to straighten everything out and Robert Pinkerton himself is handling things on this end."

Letty sat down abruptly. "What does that mean?"

"Someone knew about the stipulations you laid out for your daughters in your new will. Someone knew you arranged to hire the Pinkerton Agency to find them. Someone doesn't want them to return—enough to send a man out to impersonate the Pinkerton so he could stop her."

"That's foolishness! The only person who would benefit from that possibility would be Mason, and he is totally unconcerned about my will."

"You're sure?"

"Alexander, I will try to forget you asked that question. If what you said is true and someone wants me to suffer at my daughters' separation from me, well—" Letty took a labored breath. "I've made some very important friends over the years, but I've also made some very important enemies. I admit that I never believed any of them were capable of such . . . such . . . malevolent vengeance, but it appears I was wrong."

"Letty, I wouldn't be doing my job if I didn't ask you to consider all possibilities."

"All possibilities but one. Mason is a dear friend, almost family. I depend on him."

"I know, but—"

Choosing to ignore his hesitation, Letty continued. "Please inform Mr. Pinkerton that I will gladly employ him and as many operatives as he deems necessary to bring this situation to a swift conclusion."

"Of course, Letty."

Apparently struck with a sudden thought that chilled her, Letty paled as she said, "If what you intimate is true, if someone is out for vengeance against me through my daughters, what about Justine and Johanna? Are they in danger, too?"

"I don't know."

Letty stood up again, her agitation rising. Barely holding herself in control, she demanded, "I want you to find out! I can't let my daughters suffer for the mistakes I made in the past. I couldn't bear it!"

"Letty, don't upset yourself."

Letty swayed unexpectedly. Alexander grasped her arm and called out, "Millie, come in here, please!" Sweeping Letty into his arms when she suddenly collapsed, he carried her toward her bedroom and ordered as the wide-eyed maid entered the room, "Call Dr. Bosworth, Millie. Call him now!"

Chapter Ten

Meredith woke slowly in the warmth of Trace's arms. Momentarily disoriented, she glanced around, noting that the night sky visible through the boarded windows was only touched with light. She heard the distinctive chirping of birds in the trees beyond, signaling the beginning of another day, and she moved instinctively closer to Trace.

She glanced up at his sleeping expression. Bare to the waist, the broad width of his shoulders partially visible above the portion of the bedroll covering them, he was totally relaxed. His lips were slightly parted, the strong planes of his face were still, and the light-eyed gaze that seemed to search hers with such intensity, demanding truths she did not always wish to declare, was not visible to her eye. Still, the sight of him sent a flush of emotion shooting up her spine.

Almost overwhelmed, Meredith fought back tears. She remembered the previous night when Trace finally said the words she had longed to hear. *I love you.* Through the long night past, he had proved those words to her with a passion that had shaken his powerful frame. Yet despite the supreme intensity of those emotions, he had proved instinctively with his gentleness the true meaning of love.

It occurred to her that she had never allowed herself to think past her uncertain present and future. With her mother as her only example, she had not trusted the affection of any man to be enduring. The only exception was Grandfather, the mystical individual who had never failed her. His visits had been brief and sometimes inscrutable, but she had never doubted his concern for her welfare and his desire to advise her wisely. It occurred to her that he had not visited her recently, and she missed him. She had become aware that whether Grandfather was a figment of her need as Trace believed, or he was . . . something else entirely . . . he seemed to have surrendered her to Trace's care. Even the howlings had lessened.

Turning toward her unexpectedly, Trace drew her close, his eyes opening into narrow slits as he said softly, "Now you can tell me what you were thinking when you were watching me so closely."

"You were awake all the time!"

"Most of the time, anyway."

Suddenly sober, Meredith said, "I woke up with such a sense of contentment, and then I realized that I had no right to feel that way, not with murder charges hanging over us both, and with my sisters in danger."

"Contented, huh?" An expression that was purely male flashed briefly across Trace's face. He brushed her mouth with his. His kiss lingered, and he drew back reluctantly. He frowned as he glanced outside and said, "It's getting light. It's almost dawn. We'd better get up. If Deputy Cobb follows his usual pattern, he'll be riding out with his posse soon. We don't want to be caught unawares."

Standing up, Trace pulled her to her feet. Slipping his arms around her unexpectedly, he held her close for long moments. She felt the tremor that moved through him the moment before he drew back and said soberly, "If it were up to me, we wouldn't move from this spot. But it isn't." Pausing, he said more softly, "Words don't come easily for me, Meredith, but just in case you don't remember what I said last night, I love you. That hasn't changed. It never will."

A touch of incredulity in her tone, Meredith responded in a suddenly choked voice, "I never dreamed I'd hear you say that to me when we first met. Neither did I ever think I'd hear myself say I love you, too, Trace. I just wish that we could . . . that things would—"

Meredith saw Trace's expression flicker before he pushed her away from him resolutely, halting her response as he said, "I know. I wish things were different, too, but they're not, and we have work to do. Doc will be starting out for Mrs. Lindstrom's cabin as soon as it's light. That should give the deputy and his posse time to get far enough away from Winsome so we won't run into them."

"Everything relies on what Doc has to tell us about whatever information Robert was able to find out, is that it?"

"No." Unable to resist touching her, Trace stroked a stray, fiery strand back from her cheek as he replied, "Whatever background information Robert is able to send us will help, but it'll be up to me to take it from there."

"Up to *us*." Trace did not reply and Meredith continued. "And if Deputy Cobb refuses to listen to reason?"

Trace's expression hardened. "He'll listen, or else."

"What do you mean?"

"I told you, I'll do my job, Meredith. That means I'll do it any way I think is necessary." The sparks in his eyes turning into shards of steel, he added, "I also promised you that I wouldn't let anyone or anything hurt you, and you know how I feel about promises."

"Yes, but—"

"Get dressed. We have to get out of here."

"Trace, promise me—"

"I've made all the promises I'm going to make right now." Waiting until his response registered in Meredith's gaze, Trace urged more softly, "Come on, it's getting late."

"I don't believe it."

The narrow alleyway beside the Night-Light Saloon smelled of stale beer and urine. The stench turned Mason's stomach, almost as much as the subtle rustling in garbage pails indicating the presence of slippery, four-footed creatures he despised. Yet he endured it all without comment. After a few hours that morning spent in his dear aunt Letty's company, he had passed the next few hours searching countless local bars in a dissolute part of town where he would have preferred not to be seen, and he was silently grateful to have finally located Humphrey Dobbs.

It almost amused Mason that his dear aunt Letty seemed to have a compulsory need to confide in him the very latest details related to her daughters' absence, but the news she had imparted early that morning wasn't humorous at all.

Mason's nose twitched. He had finally found Dobbs asleep with his head resting on a table still littered with the remains of a partially consumed meal from the night before, and more empty glasses than he cared to count. To his credit, Dobbs had awakened the moment he was approached, alert enough to motion him out the back door and into the alleyway so their exchange could not be overhead. Judging from Dobbs' appearance as he stood boldly in front of him in baggy, spotted, and wrinkled clothing, he had passed out at that table the previous night, and no one had had the nerve to wake him.

Mason could almost understand that fear, considering the look in Dobbs' eyes. Still, he felt no fear as he replied angrily to Dobbs' comment, "You may not want to believe it's true, but it is. The man you sent 'to take care of' Meredith Moore is dead. The real Trace Stringer is alive and well, and at present he is making certain that Meredith stays that way, too. My dear aunt Letty called me to her house the first thing this morning. She said Robert Pinkerton brought the news back personally from Texas. Pittman also told her that after much discussion, Pinkerton decided to begin investigating the situation on his own in New York." Mason's raspy voice dropped a menacing note lower. "And I tell you now, if Pinkerton ends up convincing my dear aunt Letty that I'm behind all this because of your man's failure—"

"He won't. I won't let it get that far." His eyes narrowing and his lean face twitching, Dobbs appeared even more rodentlike as he added flatly, "I accepted this job and I have a reputation to maintain."

"So it's your reputation you're concerned about!" Mason was irate. "My reputation and my entire life are at stake here!"

"Quit your caterwauling! I told you I'd take care of it, and I will!"

"You told me that your man would handle the situation with Meredith Moore quietly and efficiently, too, but it turned out that *he* was the one who was handled."

"How did he die?"

"I don't know. Supposedly some kind of wild animal got him when he was in the wilderness, but I find that explanation a little too convenient, especially since he was sent back to town tied to his horse with his head almost severed from his body."

Mason waited for a reaction from Dobbs that did not come. A chill ran down his spine at the realization that the horrendous manner of *his man's* demise had not affected him at all. He continued, "My dear aunt Letty told me that she believes someone is trying to exact a morbid kind of vengeance against her through her daughters. She's upset about that, but she hopes Robert Pinkerton will find out who that person is and prevent it from happening. Actually, it's my belief that Robert Pinkerton already mentioned my name to Aunt Letty as one of his suspects but that Aunt Letty wouldn't dignify that suspicion by repeating it to me."

"She likes you."

Dobbs' small smile was almost more than he

could bear. Mason snapped, "She'll only keep 'liking me' if you find some way to do your job."

"That Pinkerton probably realizes the best way to temporarily escape Texas law is to bring Meredith Moore here. He's probably on his way back with her right now, which will make it easy for me to handle the situation."

"They're not coming back. Evidently Meredith won't leave until she accomplishes what she went to Texas for."

"Which is?"

"She won't say."

Dobbs made an impolite, scoffing sound and then said, "Don't worry. I'll send another man down to take care of her."

"Oh no, you don't!" His reaction unhesitant, Mason went on. "From what Aunt Letty told me, the Texas deputy handling the situation has convinced himself that Meredith Moore and that Pinkerton are guilty of everything that's happened since Meredith arrived. He's tracking Meredith and the Pinkerton with a posse. He'll find them and do your work for you."

"I'll send another man anyway."

"I said no!" Mason was adamant. "I won't take the chance of having another stranger show up just before Meredith is 'taken care of.' We'll work out an alternative only if the deputy doesn't catch up with them."

"All right, that suits me fine for now." Raising his unshaven chin, Dobbs said flatly, "But I ain't letting it go at that. I need to make sure the right person pays for killing my man. It's a matter of principle."

Mason could not help but sneer. "Oh, you have principles, Mr. Dobbs?"

"Yeah, just like you do."

Mason went silent at Dobbs' gibe, allowing Dobbs to continue. "And you don't have to worry about me asking for any more money as far as Meredith Moore is concerned. Whatever I do about her from here on in won't cost you nothing."

"Really? How generous of you." Drawing his well-tended physique up to its full, meager height, Mason added warningly, "I don't like to think that the men you sent out after Aunt Letty's two other daughters will be as easily thwarted as this fellow was."

"You don't have to worry about that."

"But I am worrying."

"I'd stop worrying right now, if I was you."

Allowing his cutting gaze to impress that statement clearly, Dobbs turned abruptly and headed for the street. He said over his shoulder in way of farewell, "You'll hear from me."

Doc Gibbs' expression was taut. Drawing his buggy to a shuddering halt, he scrutinized the heavy woods trail around him before looking again at the two mounted riders who had ridden out unexpectedly onto the trail ahead of him.

Acknowledging Meredith with a nod, Doc addressed Trace with obvious discomfiture as he said, "Meeting me here like this isn't safe, Trace. Deputy Cobb left his cabin at the edge of town and met up with his posse at dawn, but those fellas were already mounted and waiting for him at his office when he got there. They rode off almost immediately. They're out there somewhere right now, trying to hunt you down. I'm telling you, that posse Cobb has with him is almost as determined as he is to end this thing once and for all."

"If they rode off at dawn, they should be far enough away from here by now not to be a problem."

Doc glanced uncomfortably around him again. "I suppose you're right, but I can't say I feel at ease right now."

Trace said tensely, "I need to know if Robert sent you any information that I can use, Doc."

"He sent me a couple of telegrams, but he didn't say much. All he said is that the terms of Miss Wolf's new will aren't a very well kept secret. Neither is the fact that she hired Pinkertons to find her daughters. Evidently, Miss Wolf doesn't believe that the alternate beneficiary in her will, Mason Little, could possibly have had anything to do with what happened here. She says she's made enough enemies over the years to make it possible that one of them is seeking vengeance."

Trace noted the revealing twitch of Meredith's lips when she interjected, "I wouldn't have expected my mother to say anything different. My mother likes Mr. Little. The fact that he seems to accept her as his aunt somehow legitimizes the relationship between 'Uncle Archie' and herself in her mind. I don't like him, but my mother never listened to the opinions of my sisters or me."

Trace remained quiet. He knew what Meredith thought of Mason Little. He turned back toward Doc and asked, "Did Robert have anything else to say?"

"He said he's going to look further into things in

New York. He said he'd send more information when he got it."

Meredith asked, "What about my sisters? Did he say anything about them?"

"Sorry, dear." Doc shook his head apologetically. "Mr. Pinkerton didn't mention either of them."

Trace saw the flush that colored Meredith's skin as Doc glanced nervously around him again and said, "There's something important I need to tell you, Trace. Deputy Cobb called a meeting in town last night. He said right out that he doesn't intend bringing either you or Meredith back for trial when he finally tracks you down. That's why he called a town meeting. He wanted to have a big enough representation from the town for him to conduct a trial on the spot, with the outcome—to quote him—a final dance from the nearest tree."

Trace glanced back at Meredith to see that she had gone pale. His own jaw tight, he said, "I can't believe he actually said that, Doc."

"Well, he did. Most of the surrounding ranchers were present, and he got enough support from them to ride out this morning feeling that they would back him in whatever he did."

"He's a deputy, sworn to uphold the law."

"That doesn't seem to make any difference to him." Doc emphasized, "I was there, Trace. I heard every word he said. A couple of other men present had the same reaction as I did. Howard Larson from the bank was one. We all tried talking some sense into the men, but the savage way that imposter was killed has the ranchers fearing for their families' safety. They believe it's all connected to the sheriff's and Sam's deaths somehow, and they're too worked up to think clearly. You have to remember that Sheriff Keller did a lot of favors for the people in this town, and everybody liked Sam. Deputy Cobb is counting on that."

"Why is Cobb so determined to wreak his own justice?"

"I don't know. Pride, I guess. Nobody figured he'd amount to much. Sheriff Keller took pity on him for his mother's sake and hired him as deputy after she died. Nobody gave him much respect then, neither. I figure all this attention he's been getting has gone to his head. I figure he doesn't care how he finishes this case off. He just wants to show everybody here that he can do the job without the sheriff looking over his shoulder."

"He's not thinking clearly, either."

"I don't mean to be sarcastic when I say this, Trace, but I don't think Deputy Cobb has the mental equipment to think much more clearly than he has already."

Silent at Doc's assessment, Trace said abruptly, "It looks like you're right when you say it's not safe for us to be here with you, Doc. You'd better be going. If you don't show up on the trail soon, Cobb might get suspicious."

"You heard what I said, didn't you, Trace?"

"I heard you, Doc. Thanks." Turning toward Meredith where she remained silently mounted, Trace said, "Let's go. We have a long day ahead of us if Cobb is that determined."

Ignoring the sound of the buggy snapping into motion, Trace led Meredith off into the cover of foliage. He stopped, and then turned toward Meredith when she rode up beside him. He said soberly, "You heard the Doc. Does anything he had to say change things for you?"

"Change things? How could it?" Uncertain exactly what he meant, Meredith scrutinized his expression. "I told you, I won't leave Texas until I accomplish what I came here for. We just need to find some way to convince the deputy that we're both innocent of any wrongdoing." Meredith halted her response abruptly, then added more slowly, "But if you feel it's becoming too dangerous here, if you'd rather go back to New York until things cool down, I'll understand."

Trace stared at her silently for an extended moment before sliding his arm around her waist and sweeping her from her saddle. Drawing her tight against him, he kissed her long and deep in an emotional response that left Meredith trembling. His own composure shaken, Trace separated himself from her with obvious reluctance and said hoarsely, "That's my answer to you. I just need to know one thing. Do you still trust me to keep you safe?"

"Yes, I do, Trace, but—"

"You don't have to say anything else."

Kissing her lightly, then kissing her again, Trace lifted her back onto her mount and then spurred his own horse into motion.

"What are you doing here?"

Seated uncomfortably breathless on her drawing room couch, Letty stared at James as he entered the room without waiting for Millie to announce him. She did not feel well. She was sure that James' strong, virile appearance contrasted sharply with her wan exterior, but the howlings continued to interrupt her sleep, and Grandfather's visits had become disturbing warnings of danger that she did not quite comprehend. The result had been the unfortunate scene when Alexander visited her, and her subsequent collapse in his arms. The medication that Dr. Bosworth had prescribed only seemed to worsen her confusion, besides leaving her weak. Her talk with Mason earlier, in which she confided the details of Robert Pinkerton's report and her deepening concerns for her two other daughters, had somehow drained her more.

Aware that James was silently scrutinizing her, she said as stiffly as she could manage, "I asked you what you're doing here, James."

"I heard you were ill. You were pale the last time I saw you and I wanted to make sure you were all right."

"I'm not ill."

"You collapsed in your attorney's arms."

"Who told you that?"

Refusing to answer her question, James covered the distance between them in a few steps. Crouching beside her, he said simply, "I need to know you're all right, Letty."

"Why?" Weary of the same conflict, she asked, "What possible difference could that make to you? Our relationship is over, James. I've tried to make that clear to you countless times."

"That doesn't mean that I've stopped caring about you, Letty."

Incredulous at his response, Letty said abruptly, "All right, then. I'm fine."

James moved closer and said, "You don't look fine, you know. You're pale, you have dark circles under your eyes, and you're too thin." He added, "Needless to say, you're still more beautiful than any woman I've ever known."

Letty heard herself say, "Is that what appeals to you so persistently, James, my beauty? I'm not responsible for that, you know. It's simply a matter of heredity. My daughters are beautiful, too, and they—"

Choking up, Letty was temporarily unable to go on. She swallowed tightly as James said, "Your daughters left the city and you don't know where they are. You're worried about them. Let me help you find them."

Adamant when James reached out to take her hand, Letty drew back and said, "You're wasting your time, James. I collapsed in my attorney's arms. He called the doctor, who said I was suffering from exhaustion, but I'm recuperating at a rapid rate. If I don't look particularly well at this moment, as you were kind enough to inform me, I will soon be my old self."

"And not much of what you just said to me is true." A smile touched James' lips as he said, "I could always tell when you were lying, you know. Your lips tighten and you squint, almost as if you're trying to convince yourself that you're telling the truth."

"I am telling the truth."

James' smile broadened. A dimple flashed in his cheek as he commented, "Another lie."

"Please leave, James."

His smile faded. "You know you can always count on me, don't you, Letty?"

"I don't need you."

"If you should."

"I never will."

"You're sure of that?"

Her eyes briefly closing, Letty whispered, "I'm so tired of this, James. I'm tired of trying to make you comprehend that there's nothing left between us as far as I'm concerned, and that nothing you can say will change that. But I'll say it one more way, and maybe you'll understand. If I did need someone, James, you'd be the last person I'd summon."

James went still at Letty's cutting statement. He said, "You don't really mean that."

"I mean that more than you seem prepared to accept."

Silent for a long moment, James drew himself slowly to his feet. He looked down at her soberly and said, "Strangely enough, I thought coming here today would make you see that I was different from all the other men in your life who somehow let you down when you needed them most. But I can see I was wrong. I'm sorry about that." His brow furrowing, he added more softly, "I hope you never regret what you just said, because I know I could have made you very happy."

"If there's one thing I've learned, it's that I don't need a man to make me happy, James, not any man in particular, that is. I've discovered the hard way that the best way to *remain* happy is to please oneself. That's my philosophy now, and it's working out just fine."

"That's why you look so content right now, I suppose."

His response struck a painful chord inside her, and Letty responded harshly, "Perhaps, but there's one thing I'm sure of. I'm happier right now than you could ever make me."

James took a few steps back at her cruel rejoinder. His robust color whitened as he replied, "I guess there's nothing more I can say, then—except, good-bye, Letty. I hope you believe me when I say I wish you happiness with the choices you've made."

Silent as James turned and walked out of the room, Letty listened for the click of the hall doorway closing behind him. At the finality of the sound, she brushed away the tears that coursed down her cheek.

Good-bye.

It was ultimately as simple as that.

Suddenly clamping her hands over her ears, Letty attempted to block out the sound of the persistent howling that returned to haunt her.

"Don't make a sound."

Trace's warning emerged in a whisper as the sun sank toward the horizon, signaling the conclusion of a difficult day. They remained mounted in a heavily foliated portion of the wilderness, watching as the posse that was too close for comfort drew to a halt in an almost blinding cloud of dust. A big man dismounted from his horse and bent down to study the trail for long moments. Meredith saw him stand up and face the other mounted men before he shook his head. She watched them confer for a few moments before deciding to ride back.

Hardly aware that she had been holding her breath, Meredith exhaled deeply when they disappeared from sight. She and Trace had been traveling hard throughout the day without a break. Doc had been correct in everything he had told them that morning. The men in the posse were even more relentless than the deputy seemed to be—and they were making frightening progress in tracking them.

Meredith looked up at Trace and said, "They're getting really close now."

Trace nodded. "Somebody evidently convinced the deputy to let that other fella do the tracking. He might not be the best tracker in the world, but he's making headway." Turning toward her, Trace said flatly, "We have to get out of this area, Meredith. This is a hard place to hide. The trails are narrow with steep terrain on either side, yet the open country beyond is too wide and without cover." He paused and then added, "It doesn't help that our horses are even more hungry and weary than we are."

Too tired to dispute Trace's statement at the moment, Meredith knew he was only being kind. She was exhausted, but Trace wasn't. He was accustomed to riding all day on rugged trails, with the sun a ceaseless burning heat that couldn't be avoided. His shirt was wet with sweat, but his back wasn't sagging wearily, and his face hadn't taken on an uncomfortable red hue that signified he was approaching the end of his rope.

As if reading her mind, Trace said, "I'm sorry, darlin'. I'd sit you on my horse with me for a while so you could rest if we didn't need to move fast right now."

"I'm fine, Trace." Meredith made a positive effort as she continued. "It's this redhead's complexion that I inherited from my father. It makes me look worse than I feel."

Taking only a moment to search her expression,

Trace said, "Let's get out of here before that posse turns itself around and comes back in this direction."

As if in response to Trace's concern, Meredith felt the ground vibrate under her horse's hooves and heard the distant thunder of hoofbeats approaching. Trace's expression needed no explanation. The posse had found their tracks and was traveling back toward them.

His response succinct, Trace ordered, "Follow me."

Dashing through the heavily foliated area, dodging low-lying branches that whipped out to dislodge her hat and leave it hanging against her back, Meredith breathed heavily. She ignored the curls that had spilled onto her shoulders, struggling to hold her seat in the saddle as her mare seemed to fly across the uneven ground in pursuit of Trace's swift gelding.

Her mind racing in time with her mount's flying hooves, Meredith reasoned that this could not truly be happening. She could not be believed to be a bank robber and a murderer, and by his presence beside her, she could not have implicated Trace in the confusing debacle. Yet the obvious could not be denied.

Trace looked back at her to make certain she was still behind him, and Meredith realized in a flash of insight that she was holding him back. She wasn't as good a rider as Trace. She wasn't accustomed to the hard Texas terrain that the others seemed to travel so effortlessly. She could not see the posse yet, but it was clear to her that it was gaining on them, and that in less time than she could bear to consider, it would soon be within view.

She needed to do something, and do it quickly.

Drawing her mount to a sudden halt, Meredith

said, "Go on, Trace! I'm going to let the posse catch up with me."

Meredith would never forget Trace's expression when he turned his mount and drew it to a shuddering halt. Breathing heavily as he looked back at her, he said, "Are you crazy?"

"Those men will listen to me if I'm alone, Trace." Her words sounding fanciful even to her own ears, Meredith continued in a rush. "I'm a woman. I'll appeal to them and they'll—"

"They'll hang you from the highest tree!"

"No, Trace, they won't!"

Apparently unwilling to argue as Meredith sat her mount determinedly, Trace rode up to her and swept her from the saddle. Placing her in front of him, he slapped her horse on the rump, sending it pounding into the wilderness foliage as he began ascending the steeply wooded rise nearby. They were still ascending, still following their difficult course, when the posse thundered past, apparently on the trail of her mount.

Meredith gasped. "They'll realize what happened when they catch up with my horse, Trace. You should have left me behind."

"Not a chance." Clutching her tighter, Trace said simply, "Hold on."

The terrain grew steeper. Meredith heard Trace's mount's wheezing in its struggle to maintain its feet as it stumbled, sending a shower of rocks down behind them as they climbed higher on the rocky slope.

Breathless, Meredith said, "Set me down here, Trace. It's the only way."

Trace did not respond.

Pushing his mount to a Herculean effort, Trace held the reins tightly as they rounded the top of the rise. He then rode a few feet before dismounting from his heavily lathered horse and pulling Meredith down beside him. Grasping his mount's reins, he drew the laboring gelding along with them behind a rocky outcrop where they were hidden from view.

"Trace, what are you—"

"Shhhh . . ."

Sounds of shouting from below echoed up toward them in the humid silence. Meredith held her breath as the mounted men began conversing heatedly.

"I've got her horse. Her boyfriend must have kept on riding when she fell. She's around here somewhere. She can't get far."

"She don't have to get far. It's going to be dark in a little while. We'll have to wait until morning if we don't find her before then."

"What about her boyfriend?"

"He won't get far, either."

"What if he turned back for her?"

"Hell, he wouldn't do that. He's not going to let that woman get him hanged."

The deputy's voice was distinctive when he interjected, "Either way, we'd better start looking. We need to find that Moore woman."

"What about her horse?"

"Hold on to it."

Meredith drew instinctively closer to Trace. She turned to see his expression was cold when the hoofbeats gradually disappeared from their hearing. He said, "They're going to start looking where they figure you first fell. They're confused. They have no idea what happened, and it'll be dark within the hour. Let's get out of here."

"But my horse—"

"If I don't miss my guess, they'll abandon the animal sooner or later so it won't slow them down. That mare will make its way back to town on its own."

"We can't make time riding double."

"If we can avoid the posse until it's dark, we'll be safe."

Mounting, Trace pulled Meredith up onto the saddle in front of him and dug his heels into his mount's sides.

Breathless, too tired to think, Meredith only knew that she believed him.

Trace looked down at Meredith's pale, sleeping countenance. He then looked around him at the derelict cabin he had managed to locate in the wilderness. It was one of many previously used by hunters or trappers when in the area, and then abandoned. It was small, hardly larger than a shed, and it was primitive and dark. It smelled of mold and decomposing debris, and it was littered with years of filth, but he remembered that Meredith had considered only that it was a roof over their heads, a broken window to look out of, and a door that could be locked behind them. She had followed him inside without a word of protest.

After the long day spent barely escaping Cobb's posse, she was exhausted and only a step from collapse. Barely touching the jerky or the water he had offered her, she had curled up on the bedroll he had spread in front of a small fireplace that he had not dared to light, and had fallen fast asleep. He knew that she would not awaken until he whispered to her the next morning that it was time to get up and begin a new day. A day that would be more of the same.

Trace assessed the situation emotionlessly. But it wouldn't be more of the same. Their circumstances were virtually hopeless now that both Meredith and he were forced to travel on his exhausted gelding. They could not outrun the posse under those circumstances, especially when he knew that the posse would be traveling on fresh mounts to begin their chase all over again. He had to do something decisive, and he had to do it before it was too late.

Trace crouched down by Meredith's bedroll and studied her more closely. She was still wearing his oversized shirt and pants, but she had long since shortened the sleeves of the shirt by slicing off the excess at her wrist. She had done the same with the bottom of the trousers, shortening the extended length so she might walk more freely. Tattered and torn, with the rope around her waist still holding up her pants and with her glowing hair filled with leaves from the chase, she appeared even more like an understuffed scarecrow than before—yet she was still the most beautiful woman he had ever seen.

That aside, he loved her. Prejudiced against the woman he had supposed Meredith to be when he first accepted the assignment, he had been surprised by the vulnerability he sensed beneath her hardened veneer. She had then gradually revealed the side of herself that had bound him to her with the strength of iron chains.

He had promised to protect her. He had promised that he would make the situation turn out right for her so that she could complete the quest that meant so much to her that she would risk her life to complete it.

She had confided in him about wolflike howlings that forecasted danger, and the appearances of a mysterious, shadowy figure that she called Grandfather. He didn't understand those unexplained happenings, but Meredith's insistence that they were real left no room for dispute.

Because he loved her.

Never more sure of anything in his life, Trace brushed a kiss across Meredith's parted lips. He heard her mumble softly, and he smiled. Barely restraining his inclination to lie down beside her and prove his love, he drew himself to his feet and then turned toward the saddlebags he had carried inside with him.

His expression sobering, Trace removed his spare revolver from his saddlebag and loaded it carefully. Placing it on the table where Meredith would easily find it, he scribbled a short note to her on the back of an official Pinkerton form that was also in his saddlebag. He then paused for a last look at the woman he loved before walking silently out of the dilapidated structure, before closing the door behind him, and mounting his weary gelding.

Trace did not look back again as he turned his mount toward the brightly moonlit trail.

Meredith stirred on the bedroll where she had fallen asleep after the long, strenuous day in the saddle. Exhausted, every bone in her body aching, she was not certain what had awakened her—until she heard it again.

The trailing howl of a wolf set her heart pounding,

and Meredith turned instinctively toward the bedroll beside her. Trace was not there. She glanced around the cabin's limited confines to see that he was nowhere in sight.

Where was he? Why was the wolf howling?

Drawing her emotions under control with sheer strength of will, Meredith stood up slowly. Trace's bedroll was empty, but that didn't mean he wasn't somewhere near. She had heard a wolf's howl, but that didn't mean it was *her* wolf. Meredith wandered toward the table in the meager moonlight filtering through the window. She halted abruptly at the sight of the revolver lying there. With a trembling hand, she picked it up, then grasped the sheet of paper beside it and stumbled toward the window where the moonlight filtering through made it easier for her to see.

She read:

> *Meredith,*
> *Deputy Cobb lives alone in a cabin on the outskirts of town. He and I should be able to talk privately when I approach him there. If he's reasonable, we'll settle everything with some straight talk.*
> *I'm leaving my extra gun for your protection while I'm gone. I expect to be back before daylight. I'll see you then.*
> *Remember that I love you.*
> *Trace*

Meredith's throat choked closed when the wolf's howl sounded again. It couldn't be *her* wolf. If it was, that meant—

Unwilling to finish that thought, Meredith opened

the cabin door slowly. Yellow eyes flashed briefly at her from within the foliage, and she gasped. She was unable to react before she heard a horse's shrieking whinny, and then saw her terrified mare emerge from the same shadows and begin racing toward the cabin. Behind it, the dark, furry form of a wolf leapt out of the darkness to pursue it.

Mesmerized, Meredith watched the scene unfolding as the wolf chased the still-saddled mare to within a few feet of the cabin—where the mare stopped, unable to run farther. Slavering, the furry beast lowered itself into a crouch a few feet from the screeching horse, its penetrating stare holding hers for a few seconds as her mount twitched, its eyes rolling with fear. She was still frozen to the spot when the menacing beast turned away unexpectedly, growling low in its throat as it ran off into the darkness.

Meredith grasped her mare's dangling reins and held the animal in place with all her strength. Trace had said that the posse would probably turn the mare loose again, rather than allow it to slow them down. She wondered how long the horse had been wandering before the wolf found it. She did not choose to consider why the wolf had chased it back to her.

A wolf's howl sounded from a distance. It resounded again, and Meredith started to tremble. The howls were still echoing when she picked up the revolver she had dropped and mounted her quaking mare. Shoving the revolver into a pouch on the saddle, she then spurred the horse into motion.

Rita twisted and turned in the bed she shared with her husband. She looked toward his half of the bed and discovered that it was empty, then looked at the clock and saw that dawn would not crease the morning sky for at least an hour. The overweight fool had already left for the bank, a habit common to him of late.

Her irritation heightened. The bank had become Howard's sanctuary—from her. He locked up the offices and came home when he could delay coming home no longer, and he left for its hallowed confines before dawn cracked through the night sky. She despised him for it, and she longed for the day when she would achieve her own sanctuary without him.

Deputy Cobb had left the previous dawn with his posse after a town meeting that had stirred the crowd, and she had waited with bated breath for the result of his foray. She had been certain that riding with a much larger group of men, Cobb would surely find the Moore woman and her boyfriend. She had known that he would not miss his opportunity to handle the matter then and there, with a rope and a tree, thereby freeing her to go on with the plans for the rest of her life. Yet the day had stretched on endlessly while she waited.

She had attempted to fill the hours with everyday chores so her activities couldn't possibly appear suspicious at some future point in time. She had visited Winsome's limited boutiques, but the offerings there were too common to suit her. She had gone shopping at the mercantile with the hope of engaging notorious rumormongers congregating there in conversation, but the results were too contradictory and undependable. She had even straightened up the house, a chore she had sworn not to assume when she dismissed her maids, but inactivity had almost driven her to distraction.

Her annoyance slipping up another notch, Rita recalled that she had actually found herself waiting avidly for Howard's return from the bank out of a simple desire to obtain an accurate report that she could not get elsewhere. After all, he was the banker. Everyone trusted him. People spoke to him confidentially, telling him things they would not dare tell others. She had always scoffed at their assumption that Howard actually cared, but she had valued the information Howard seemed so eager to share with her.

So she had waited.

And she had waited.

He had finally returned, still polite to a fault, but nevertheless barely communicative. So desperate was she to get him to talk to her that she had even attempted the same *intimate persuasion* that had never failed her before. To her embarrassment, her sexually deprived husband had turned down her efforts coldly.

Sitting quietly at the table where the meager supper she had prepared for him lay cold and congealed, he had only imparted the information that the posse had returned to town at nightfall. After much prompting, he had added that the deputy reported they came exceedingly close—perhaps within an hour of capturing the Moore woman and her boyfriend, and that they were expecting to pick up where they left off the following day.

Rita knew whose fault it was that the Moore woman and her boyfriend were still free. Despite his bravado, Deputy Cobb was useless. She knew his posse would be better off without him, but he was too puffed up with importance to turn over any portion of control to a more qualified individual.

Howard then added of his own accord that some men within the posse were beginning to rethink their emotional decisions to impose frontier justice on the spot when Meredith Moore and her boyfriend were apprehended. Howard had seemed relieved at that, but to her, the news was a disaster that she would not be able to abide.

An unladylike snort emerged angrily from Rita's lips at the thought. She wanted this ordeal over! Her plans for the future included a reasonable time to elapse before she went home a *grieving widow*, but she would not stay young forever. Now that her decision was made, she could not afford to waste another minute of her precious life as she had wasted it with Howard.

Throwing back the covers and setting her considerable bulk on her feet, Rita made her decision. She knew exactly how to make sure there was not a man in the posse who would change his mind about turning to the nearest tree once they found the two they sought. It would simply involve taking another step on a path that she had already trod. It would not be as difficult the second time, she was sure; and when she was done, there would be no further delay.

The darkness surrounding her was silent and grim as Rita stood outside Deputy Cobb's cabin with gun in hand. Fool that he was, Howard had given her the shiny new revolver for her protection a long time previously, never realizing what her protection might involve.

Rita scrutinized the foliage around her carefully. Cobb still lived in the meager dwelling where Matilda Cobb and her drunken husband had raised him. The cabin was just far enough from town to allow most of Hiram Cobb's drunken ravings to go unheard, allowing the poor, abused Matilda Cobb a semblance of the propriety that she had yearned for so desperately. She supposed the fact that the deputy had not made a single improvement in his life since his mother's death was telling. His only claim to success was the badge that Sheriff Keller had pinned on him out of pure pity.

Rita sniffed. Pity. That had been Sheriff Keller's mistake. She would not repeat it.

Holding her gun tightly, Rita listened at the door of the cabin. All was silent inside. A look through the window revealed that a fire burned low in the fireplace and a lamp flickered near the cot where Cobb slept with a half-empty bottle of red-eye beside him.

Like father, like son . . . totally worthless.

Rita pushed at the door. It slid open a crack and she sneered. Cobb had fallen asleep without bothering to slip the lock, exactly what she had expected from him.

Taking a breath, Rita pushed the door open wide and said in a voice calculated to raise Cobb from his alcohol-induced sleep, "Wake up, Deputy, and don't move, or you'll be sorry."

Startled awake, Deputy Cobb raised himself on his elbow to stare at the doorway of his cabin. He shook his head, disoriented and uncertain.

"You heard me, Deputy."

Rita saw Cobb glance toward the gun belt that lay

discarded on the table nearby. She growled menacingly, "Don't even think about it."

Rita entered the cabin and closed the door behind her. She glanced around the foul interior and grimaced.

"Get out of that cot slowly and walk toward the fireplace."

Still staring, Cobb threw back the covers and stood up fully dressed in the previous day's clothing. Rita was not surprised. He had probably intended to ride out with his posse in that condition, unwashed and smelling almost as foul as the cabin he inhabited. She watched as he took a few steps toward the fireplace, then turned toward her and said bewilderedly, "What do you want from me, Mrs. Larson?"

Rita could not help but respond, "You really are dense, aren't you?"

His face flaming, Cobb said tightly, "Maybe I am, but I can't see no reason for you to come here with a gun."

"That's because you're useless without Sheriff Keller to guide you. That's because you have no more place wearing that star on your chest than the man in the moon!"

"You think so, huh?"

"Fool! How many days has Trace Stringer and that woman of his been running you and your posse around in circles? How many more days do you think it'll take to find them?"

"Is that the problem?" His expression growing suddenly confident, Cobb said, "If it is, I'm telling you now that my posse and me finally got the best of them two yesterday. We were no more than an hour behind them. They're tired, they're down to traveling on one exhausted mount if they're still together, and they have no place to go that we can't follow. We're bound to catch them today."

"What then, Deputy?"

Cobb responded with a confused shrug, "What do you think? You were at the town meeting I held. You heard how everybody shouted their agreement with what I intend to do."

"I also heard that some of your men in your posse are having second thoughts about administering frontier justice."

"Yeah, well, maybe so, but that's only temporary. They'll feel different in the heat of the moment when we catch them two."

"I don't intend to take any chances."

"What do you mean by that?"

"What do you suppose the men in your posse will do when you don't show up to meet them this morning? They'll come here to get you, won't they?" When Cobb barely nodded in response, Rita continued. "What do you think they'll do if they find you lying here dead?"

"Wait a minute."

"They'll think that the Pinkerton slipped into town, tried to talk some sense into you, and then shot you dead in order to give him and his girlfriend more time to escape. They'll get angry, and after they tell the undertaker to take your body away, they'll ride out, find those two, and hang them from the highest tree without a second thought."

"Wait a minute! What's this all about? You can't be that angry about your husband's bank being robbed, and you were never friendly enough with Sheriff Keller and Sam to care too much about who killed them."

"You're correct there."

"So?"

"I want this whole matter to be over with quickly and decisively! I don't want the bank auditors that are due to arrive at the bank to end up discovering that my husband embezzled the funds that were missing in that vault when the bank was robbed, and then covered up his crime with *creative accounting*."

"What?"

"That's what I said." Rita's small laugh was void of mirth as she continued. "It never occurred to you or anyone else that my husband could be guilty of such a crime, did it? He's appears so trustworthy, so innocent—but he isn't. He set this whole fiasco up from the beginning, and when it looked like he might be found out, he came crying to me about the justice he deserved without giving a thought to how it would affect me."

"What are you talking about?"

"He left me to do his dirty work! He should've been the one to make sure that Sheriff Keller did not survive to discover his theft, not me!"

"You killed the sheriff?"

Rita shuddered as she replied, "And I'll never forgive Howard for it. I had expected the sheriff's death to be peaceful, but he struggled when I put the pillow over his face. The scene turned ugly and I was forced to use all my strength to hold him down until he stopped breathing." Cobb stared at her incredulously as she continued. "Howard should be the one here right now to make sure that this situation ends quickly and without reprisals, but he left that chore to me once again."

"You're a murderer."

"Hypocrite!"

The single word shouted in an enraged, feminine voice caught Trace's ear as he approached Cobb's cabin in the darkness beyond its closed door. He had traveled the trail back to town openly in the light of the full moon, desperate and certain that no one else would be as foolhardy as he to be traveling at night under uncertain circumstances. He had dismounted from his horse and had tied it up a distance from Cobb's cabin, preferring to approach on foot with less likelihood of being heard. His situation grave, he had hoped to be able to talk some sense into the deputy with a clear explanation of facts, but it appeared unexpectedly that someone else had had a similar idea and was not being well received.

Pausing outside the cabin, Trace peered inside. Startled to see that the feminine voice belonged to the very respectable Mrs. Rita Larson, he waited and listened more closely as the conversation continued.

He heard Cobb say, "That ain't no way to talk. I ain't no hypocrite."

"Considering that you probably don't know the full definition of the word, I would expect that response from you."

"Look, I ain't trying to get you mad." Cobb's smile, revealing yellowed, uneven teeth, was almost a grimace. "I was just trying to say that you and me both do what we have to do, that's all."

"Don't compare yourself with me."

"Why not? You killed Sheriff Keller. You probably killed Sam to shut him up, too. That don't make you any better than me any way you look at it."

"I didn't kill Sam—not that I wouldn't have done it if somebody else hadn't taken care of it for me. He was suspicious of me because of that pendant watch he found."

"What pendant watch?"

"The one I'm wearing!" Rita shook her head before continuing. "He pretended to have found it on the street, but I knew I couldn't have lost it there. The only time I could have lost it was on my way to Doc's back door to take care of the sheriff. It didn't take superior intelligence to know what he deduced from ascertaining that the watch was mine."

Still listening, Trace closed his eyes briefly at the pain Rita's admission had stirred. Sam had been killed—most likely by the man pretending to be him—but it was Trace who had sealed Sam's fate simply by asking him to determine positively whether the pendant watch belonged to Rita Larson.

Anger mixed with guilt raged inside Trace as the conversation within the cabin continued.

"Look, we ain't as different as you think." Inching toward Rita as he spoke, Cobb continued. "My mama was always keeping after me when she was alive. She got the cabin to look just like she wanted, but she didn't do too good with me. She said she didn't want me to turn out like my pa, but I knew the truth. She never believed I'd amount to anything. Neither did anybody else. She even talked Sheriff Keller into giving me a deputy's badge before she died, thinking that would make the people in town look at me differently, but it didn't. Everybody just thought I was the sheriff's dummy."

"Recounting your miserable past makes no impression on me," Rita said tightly. "Nor does it bear any resemblance to my situation."

"It does, whether you want to believe it or not. Everything changed in town after the sheriff died. All of a sudden, I was somebody, and I aim to prove that I *am* somebody by getting that Moore woman and that Pinkerton hanged."

"Whether they're guilty or not."

"It don't make no difference to me if they're guilty, and that's where you and me are the same. You see, everybody loved my mama, but she wasn't what she appeared to be. She hid the money she had saved from me, telling me that she would give it to me when I straightened my life out. I knew that day would never come, but I vowed I wasn't going to leave town a pauper like she wanted. She died before telling me where she hid the money, but she played right into my hands by begging the sheriff to make me a deputy before she died. She didn't know how friendly I was with Bart Willows."

"Bart Willows?"

"That's the name of the fella who used that Moore woman to help him rob the bank. He and I were in on the bank robbery together. I told him if he made sure to take care of the sheriff during the robbery, I'd make sure the posse lost his trail, and we could meet and share the money later. Bart liked the idea of that, but it looks like that Moore woman appealed to him even more, and he messed things up."

"So you knew all along that the Moore woman didn't have anything to do with the bank robbery."

"Sure I did, but she came in real useful after Bart ended up dead and she came back with most of the bank money missing."

Rita responded coldly, "So how does that make you and me similar?"

"I wanted to prove that everybody was wrong about me, that I could make something out of myself, and this was my chance." Cobb shrugged. "I figure everybody had to be expecting a lot from a woman like you, more than ending up married to a fat fella and living a miserable life in a dull town where you'd always be an outsider."

Rita's startled expression caused Cobb to snicker. "I ain't as dumb as everybody thinks, am I?" Taking advantage of Rita's silence, Cobb added, "That should tell you something else about us being the same too. Like you, I don't give up easy."

Outside the cabin, Trace became alert to the difference in Cobb's tone the moment before he made a flying leap for the gun belt on the table. Catching Rita unawares, he was able to snatch up his gun and roll away before Rita was able to aim and pull the trigger.

Instinctively diving into the cabin, Trace hit the floor amidst the burst of gunfire that followed. The room was clouded with gun smoke as Trace heard the thud of a body striking the floor. Rolling behind the protection of the table, he came up against Rita's still form where she lay sprawled there, her eyes wide and vacant as bloody circles widened on the robin's-egg blue of her bodice.

323

Trace shifted his position the moment before a bullet struck the floor where he had lain. Standing waveringly over him, Cobb fired again, and Trace felt the heat of the bullet that struck his chest. He shot back, and Cobb dropped on the spot.

Trace lifted his head weakly to survey the carnage of the violent scene. Rita and Cobb lay motionless on the floor a distance apart. They were both dead, and the mystery surrounding the bank robbery and everything that followed was clear.

Also clear to Trace as blood streamed from his chest wound and darkness began closing in rapidly around him was that he would soon be dead, too.

The funeral procession was silent and mournful. Riding behind the caskets in Doc's buggy as the entourage made its way up toward the cemetery on the hill, Meredith felt tears welling.

It was over. Rita's death in Cobb's cabin had brought Howard forward to confess with formidable grief the part his embezzlement and Rita's ambition had played in the sad affair. The pendant watch that Rita wore had filled in other portions of the tragedy.

Meredith looked up at Trace where he sat beside her, and she forced back tears. She remembered that echoes of howlings had plagued every mile that she had traveled toward Winsome that fateful night. She also recalled that when entering Winsome at last, she was uncertain exactly where Cobb's cabin was located. Aware that she had no time to waste, she had gone directly to Doc for help.

Meredith remembered belatedly that the howling had stopped abruptly when she and Doc arrived at

Cobb's cabin and discovered the gory scene. With his blood pooling beneath him, Trace had been unconscious and near death, and she recalled the fear that had shaken her as she had held him in her arms and whispered loving endearments to him. She had waited a lifetime to find Trace and discover what love could truly mean, and it suddenly seemed she might lose him.

She had remained beside Doc as he had worked over Trace's still form. She knew she would never forget the moment when Trace opened his eyes briefly and whispered words that might have been unintelligible to others, but that had been instantly clear to her.

He had said he loved her, and she had known in that moment that all would be well.

With Howard's confession, and with Trace filling in the rest from the conversation between Rita and Cobb that he had overhead at the cabin, so many questions were answered.

Trace was still weak and suffering the effects of his wound, but he had insisted on being present for the final interment about to commence. It was important to him to be present when the entourage rode past Sam's and Sheriff Keller's well-marked graves for final review. She knew that seeing Cobb buried a distance away from that hallowed spot, beside the unmarked grave of the imposter and others of his ilk, was equally important to Trace. She believed that observing Rita Larson's interment in a grave bearing the simple headstone that she would have abhorred had somehow given him a sense of closure.

Meredith sensed that Rita would also have abhorred Howard's sincere grieving at her graveside, as well as the fact that no charges had been pressed against her husband for his crime. Somehow, that satisfied Meredith even more.

Meredith's gaze locked with Trace's, and a warmth spread through her that he alone could elicit. Yet some questions lingered.

Meredith said softly, "You never told me, Trace. You never explained what you would have done if Rita hadn't been at the cabin when you arrived, and if the deputy had still refused to cooperate after you talked to him."

His eyes searching hers as he reviewed the question silently, Trace finally responded, "I'd have done what I needed to do, Meredith."

"Which means?"

"Which means exactly that." Silent for a few more moments, Trace continued. "I don't break promises."

Promises . . . the word that had taken on a new meaning for her, just like the word *trust*.

Her eyes intent on his, Meredith lifted her mouth to Trace. She felt the light touch of his lips. She whispered simply when he drew back, "I love you, Trace."

She felt the sincerity that radiated deep within him when Trace replied hoarsely, "Never more than I love you."

Those words touched her heart, as did the words that went unspoken, that Trace accepted the mission she had yet before her—a mission that could only make their love stronger as they accomplished it together.

Together. It was a beautiful word.

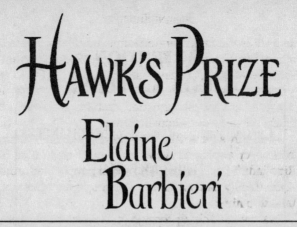

HAWK'S PRIZE
Elaine Barbieri

Drew is the last of the four siblings to return to Galveston, the first to admit he is in over his head. Stranded in a high-priced bordello because of a wounded leg, Drew finds himself being nursed by a woman of mystery. Sensual lady of the night or innocent angel of mercy, she keeps her identity secret. But as he is reunited with his brother and sisters, and the wrongs of the past are righted, one thing becomes clear: Tricia Lee Shepherd is the other half of his soul, the only person who can make his future shine bright.

ATTENTION
BOOK LOVERS!

Can't get enough of your favorite **ROMANCE**?

Call **1-800-481-9191** to:

* order books,

* receive a **FREE** catalog,

* join our book clubs to **SAVE 30%!**

Open Mon.-Fri. 10 AM-9 PM EST

Visit **www.dorchesterpub.com**
for special offers and inside
information on the authors you love.

We accept Visa, MasterCard or Discover®.
LEISURE BOOKS ♥ LOVE SPELL